Glad One: Crazy is a Relative Term

A Val Fremden Midlife Mystery, Volume 1

Margaret Lashley

Published by Zazzy Ideas, Inc., 2017.

1

What Readers are Saying about the Val Fremden Midlife Mystery Series

"Hooked like a fish. OMG Margaret Lashley is the best! Val could be Stephanie Plum's double!! Phenomenal writing."
"A hug for the soul[1]."
"Margaret writes with a "smirk" of a Cheshire cat. Fantastic read."
"I loved every line of this book!"
"I have no idea how the author is able to write (about) trauma in a way that is also hopeful and uplifting. Whatever it is, it is beautiful."
"A funny, frenetic, fantastic read! Every bit as entertaining and maybe more so than Stephanie Plum at her best."
"Her characters are real and full, her situations believable, and her dialogue marvelous."
"There's a mystery at the heart of this book—a few of them—that will hook fans of Janet Evanovich and other comic mystery writers."
"More twists and turns than NASCAR. Beach bums, sane and insane, abound in this high-paced accidental thriller. Sit down, buckle up, hang on for bunches of enjoyment."

---

1. https://www.amazon.com/gp/customer-reviews/R2H445TU8JBEPV/
ref=cm_cr_othr_d_rvw_ttl?ie=UTF8&ASIN=B06XTKBMWT

Chapter One

S ome people lead lives under a dark cloud. Others, under a lucky star. As far as I could tell, *my* life was under the control of a sadist brandishing a cattle prod and a whoopee cushion.

THE PLANE FROM FRANKFURT, Germany wobbled erratically as it hit heavy turbulence just north of Orlando. My drooping head lurched forward, and I startled myself awake with a piggish snort. I shot an apologetic smile at the man wedged in the seat next to me.

"Sorry. I must have dozed off for a second."

"Right. Lady, that snore of yours could put a jackhammer to shame."

I shrunk back in my seat and groaned. My feet hadn't even touched the ground back in the US, and already I'd had my first rude awakening. What else should I have expected? My whole life to date had been akin to one long, never-ending, rude awakening.

But all that was about to change.

After all, it was New Year's Eve.

I glanced around at the other bleary-eyed passengers around me. They probably had their minds on fresh beginnings, too. As for me, I had no other choice. The past I'd just fled was still too raw and painful to touch. I studied the pale strip of flesh encircling my now-naked ring finger. The ghostly reminder of yet another failed attempt at love sent a hot jolt of desperation racing through my gut.

A puff of jaded air forced its way between my pursed lips, like steam from a relief valve. I needed a good cry. But this was not the time or place for it. To distract myself, I decided to count my blessings.

One decimated pocketbook. Two cottage-cheese thighs. Three maladjusted ex-husbands.... Crap!

Whoever was running the show up there had a wicked sense of humor—and I was getting darn tired of being the punchline. I scrounged around for my powder compact and opened it, intent on repairing my makeup after the nine-hour flight. One glance in the mirror at my worn-out face made me snap it shut.

Why bother?

In forty-five years, I'd accumulated a good portion of wrinkles, a fair amount of belly fat, and, apparently, precious little wisdom. These questionable assets, along with $5,726 and a suitcase full of inappropriate clothes, were all I had left to launch my latest life makeover. I slumped back into my seat. I was bone-dragging tired. Even so, a wry grin snuck across my lips, like a stolen kiss from a stranger.

I was not defeated. Not yet, anyway.

The way I saw it, I still had two viable options. One, I could finally learn to laugh at myself. Or two, I could drink myself into oblivion.

I fished around the bottom of my purse for a coin to determine my fate. I flipped a tarnished nickel into the air. It did a triple gainer, plunged into my coffee cup, and splashed a nasty brown stain onto the crotch of my white stretch pants.

Awesome. Let the festivities begin.

MY LAST LIFE MAKEOVER had begun a little over seven years ago, and had turned out to be a spectacular, downward spiral akin to diving off a cliff with a bowling ball in my pants. Drowning in dullness and fueled by movie-inspired stupidity, I'd ditched a tiresome marriage and lucrative writing career, sold all my belongings, and took off for Europe.

In Italy, I'd met a German and fell in love with the idea of life with a stranger in a strange land. Things had been great for a while. But then the shiny wore off and the cracks showed up...like they always did.

On my arrival back in St. Petersburg, Florida, I'd quickly discovered that seven *wasn't* such a lucky number. In fact, seven years abroad had been just *exactly* long enough for my entire credit history to be erased—just like most of my money. I'd gotten off the plane in Tampa with no driver's license. No place to live. No credit card. No phone. No job. And, worst of all, no friends.

Incredibly, I'd somehow managed to become *a foreigner in my own homeland.*

As a lifelong lover of irony, I'd had to shake my head in wonder at my own warped ingenuity.

How many other people on the planet could claim such a monumental screw-up?

Over the next few weeks, my solo climb back aboard the American dream had required counting pennies and swallowing more than just pride. After that, I'd had to scrounge around for a tire jack and lower my expectations to half a notch above gutter level. That's how I ended up in a "no credit check" hovel of an apartment, living a "no foreseeable future" scrabble of a life.

A few months into what I'd sarcastically dubbed "my adjustment period," I'd been contemplating a *Smith & Wesson* retirement plan when something unforeseeable happened.

I met an old woman named Glad.

I'd been in desperate need of a life coach. Glad had fit the bill perfectly. The fact that she was a crazy, homeless woman had been the icing on the cake.

I could afford her fees.

Chapter Two

S t. Petersburg only had two seasons—summer and not-summer-yet. It was not-summer-yet, but just barely. I first met Glad in the first half of May. I remember because I was trying to make the most of "the end of days." I called the first two weeks of May that because anybody with any sense (translation, not a tourist or a transplant), didn't venture out in the Florida sun between 10 a.m. and 5 p.m. from the middle of May to the end of October. Not if they could help it, that is. And with no job at the time, I could help it.

As usual, I was determined to get to Sunset Beach early that Sunday. Not just to beat the heat, but the five-dollar parking fee as well. If I got there before the lot attendant, I could sneak into the lot at Caddy's, my favorite beach bar.

Sunset Beach was attractive to me for three reasons. One, it was gorgeous—with sugar-white sand and water the color of a fresh robin's egg. Two, the tourists hadn't discovered it yet. And three, it was the only local strip of beach that allowed open containers (aka BYOB alcohol). Caddy's bar sat right on gorgeous Sunset Beach, sandwiched between a patch of virgin sand dunes and a recently erected, three-story McMansion the color of pumpkin puke.

In stunning contrast to the prissy new house, Caddy's was pure, relaxed, old-school Florida. To be honest, it wasn't much more than an old beach shack with a front porch and a rooftop deck scabbed onto it with bent nails and duct tape. The bottom floor facing the

Gulf didn't even have an exterior wall. If it rained hard or the temperature dropped below sixty-five degrees, the easy-going folks at Caddy's would unfurl plastic flaps like tent windows against the inclement weather.

But on good days, which were most days, there'd be nothing between Caddy's tipsy patrons and the turquoise Gulf of Mexico but a hundred feet of squeaky, blindingly white sand. Caddy's fit right in with its laid-back vibe, good food, live music, and full liquor bar. Being a native Floridian, I appreciated that it wasn't a *tiki* bar. After all, this was *not* freaking Hawaii.

When I got to the beach that Sunday morning, I'd planned on getting in a stroll before the humidity turned the air to soup and the sun heated that soup to steam. I even thought about splurging for breakfast at one of Caddy's picnic tables on the beach afterward. But, being a loner and on a budget as tight as last year's jeans, I decided against it.

I got lucky and pulled into the lot in time to avoid the attendant. I slipped off my flip-flops and shorts and put them on the floorboard of Shabby Maggie, my 1963 Ford Falcon Sprint convertible.

Maggie was the perfect car for me. Modern vehicles all looked the same. I couldn't have told a Prius from a Pontiac to save my life. But older cars like Maggie had style. With her curvy, Batmobile rear-end, cherry-red upholstery and Wimbledon-white exterior, Maggie was a classic beauty. All the nicks and dents and faded spots reminded her she'd seen better days. Boy, could I relate.

As I reached into the backseat for my beach bag and chair, a loud wolf whistle rang out over the rumble of a diesel engine. I didn't waste the energy to look up. Instead, my head shook in sympathy for the desperate soul who'd found the sight of my flabby butt in a bathing suit worth that much effort. I snorted a laugh, hoisted my beach chair under one arm, hooked my bag over the other, and picked my way across the crushed-shell parking lot.

It was Mother's Day. Not being a mother myself, *or* having one I was keen to celebrate, I planned to let the day go by as unnoticed as possible.

As I reached the white picket fence leading out to the beach, I spied an old woman lying on a lounger a good fifty feet from the shoreline. I'd seen her there countless times over the last few months. She was a wiry, leather-skinned old bat who, had I met on the street, I'd have labeled a bag lady. But there at the beach she fit right in.

Maybe stripping down to a bathing suit somehow leveled the playing field.

From outward appearances, the old woman reminded me a lot of my friend Berta, a crusty old psychologist from New York. We'd shared some laughs together in Italy, and she'd helped me get through some tough times in Germany. Before she'd died, Berta had warned me about making friends with strangers. I hadn't heeded her advice then, but I was trying to now. Heaven knew I couldn't afford another disastrous mistake.

The old woman always set up camp near the same wispy clump of sea oats, so it had been easy to avoid her so far. That Sunday, however, my luck finally ran out. The wind blew sand in my eye, and as I fumbled along trying to get it out, I wandered blindly within earshot of her.

"Nice toe rings," she croaked in a scarred, toady voice that perfectly matched her appearance.

Sprawled out on a pink, plastic beach lounger, she reminded me of one of those dried-up frogs you can still find now and then in politically incorrect souvenir shops.

I was running on just one cup of coffee that morning, so it took a moment to realize she was talking to me. I sighed and wiped my eye again.

"Thanks."

I turned to take a step toward the water, but the old woman wasn't having it.

"Wanna beer?"

She grinned at me from under a pink Gilligan hat. Her oversized dentures looked clownish, wedged between two wide smears of bright-red lipstick.

"It's Sunday, you know. They ain't servin' booze 'til 'leven today."

Her salty-sweet Southern accent had a familiar ring. I'd spent three decades trying to rid myself of one just like it. She tilted her head and motioned toward a small cooler nestled in the sand beside her. I shook my head.

"No thanks. I'm good."

I forced a smile and gave her a quick once-over. The old lady was one shade up from mahogany and as wrinkled as a linen pantsuit after a high-stakes game of Twister. Her arms and legs looked like four Slim Jims sticking out of a neon green bathing suit. It was the kind of simple, one-piece suit women over forty wore. One that supported the boobs and hid the belly.

I was grateful for her modesty.

Freckles and white spots covered the old woman's dark-brown arms and legs. The Florida sun hadn't been kind. She could have been fifty-five or ninety-five. With hard-core beach bums, it was impossible to tell. But given the full-on dentures, I placed her in her late sixties—at the youngest.

"Okie dokie then, have it your way," Slim Jim said.

She watched me carefully from behind black, bug-eyed sunglasses. Her gaze never shifted as she reached instinctively into the cooler, pulled out a can, then cracked the tab on a family-size Fosters. I seized the opportunity and turned to take another step toward the water. That's when I thought I heard her say, "Screw you, kiddo."

I whirled around to face her.

"What?" I asked, thinking I must have heard her wrong.

"Screw you, kiddo!" she repeated, flashing her denture-cream smile.

She hoisted up the pint-sized beer between her boney fingers, causing half a pound of costume jewelry to cascade toward her elbows and twinkle in the glaring sunlight.

Uncertain if the woman was a witch or a comedian, I tilted my head and cautiously mirrored her ear-to-ear grin. "That's what I thought you said," I replied. "Well, screw *you*, too."

"Love it!" she shot back. "Where you from?"

I let go of my grip on my fake grin. "Someplace you've never heard of." I turned and took a getaway step toward the shore.

"Try me."

I sighed and turned back to face her. "Greenville, Florida, okay?"

"No kiddin'! I know *exactly* where that is."

My mouth fell open. "You and three other people. How on earth do you know about Greenville?"

"Well, kiddo, that's a long story. Used to travel around a lot. I think I've been to every two-bit town east of the Mississippi. Sit down and I'll tell you about it. You don't look like you're in no hurry, now. Are you?"

I thought about taking off running, but the heat had zapped my will to flee. Besides, it would have been rude, even for me. So I plopped my bag onto the powdered-sugar sand, unfolded my chair and sat my flabby butt down.

So much for a walk. Maybe tomorrow.

SHE TOLD ME HER NAME was Gladys, a dirt-poor Kentucky girl who'd escaped a life of farm labor by marrying a traveling revival preacher named Bobby.

"I used Bobby the way he used the Lord—as a ticket out of Nowheresville," she said with a cackle. "After the weddin' I spent the better part of a decade traveling the country with Bobby, pitching re-vival tents and per-tendin' to be the perfect wife. *Pious Patty,* I called myself."

"Why?" I asked, more out of Southern hospitality than curiosity.

Gladys shrugged and fortified herself with a slug of beer.

"I had to do *somethin'* to cope with those dang church people and their mindless jabber over endless, Sunday-go-to-eatin' buffets of tu-na casserole, squash casserole, green-bean casserole and some kind of godawful dessert casserole they called a trifle."

The old woman explained that back then, staying overnight in random parishioners' homes was part and parcel to the life of a trav-eling preacher and his wife.

"Even over the dad-burn tedium of pot 'piss out of luck' dinners, I dreaded havin' to stay in other people's houses," she said. "After a while, I just stashed myself away and per-tended to be what others expected. It was just easier that a way."

"I know what you mean," I said absently.

Gladys eyed me dubiously from behind her sunglasses.

"*Do* you, now? Well, I took it to a *whole new level*, kiddo. Even started watchin' soap operas for acting tips, you know? But after a few years starrin' in *The Pious Patty Show*, I was bored outta my gourd. That all ended one night in Hoboken when I got up to sneak a late-night smoke. Ran right into the husband of the house. One look at me in my nightgown caused that man to 'revive' somethin' of his own, if you know what I mean."

I was pretty sure I didn't want to hear what came next. But I was powerless to stop the old lady. Gladys was barreling down memory lane in a Mack truck with no brakes.

"I tell you what!" she cackled with glee. "When that dirty old man tried to hit on me, I flat-out told him 'No sir!' Then I hit *him* up *for fifty bucks!*" She laughed. "Quick as a flash, I went from Pious Patty to Blackmail Betty."

"You don't say," I offered.

"A guilty conscience can be an expensive liability—if you hit the right target," she said proudly, without a hint of embarrassment. I had to hand it to her, Gladys was a good storyteller. Crude, but entertaining. I relaxed back into my chair, and my desire to flee slowly dissipated in the late-morning heat.

"What'n long before I had my *own* revival business goin'," she continued with unabashed entrepreneurial pride. "I started savin' ev'ry dollar Blackmail Betty earned me. Tucked the cash away in my J.C. Penney jewelry box. Hid the money in the secret compartment under that dancing ballerina, don't you know. When I'd cashed up to nearly a grand, I was gettin' ready to cash out and leave Bobby's old butt behind."

Gladys took another swig from her Fosters and looked out at the Gulf. Her face was devoid of emotion. I watched her carefully, glued to my cheap beach chair by a fast-holding mixture of curiosity, disgust and morbid fascination. That, and I had absolutely nothing else to do with my life.

"What happened then?" I asked.

"That's when Bobby told me he'd landed a revival gig at a church in St. Petersburg, Florida. We were in butt-crack Alabama at the time. I remember thinking, 'What the hell.' I tell you, kiddo, when me and Bobby got to St. Pete, it only took me one look to know I'd been right to hang on for one more of his stupid gigs."

Gladys sat up, slapped her knee and laughed.

"Woo hoo! I was hooked like a snook, kiddo! Blue sky. No chance of snow! There was even a place that gave away free ice cream if the sun didn't shine on any given day. I liked that. St. Pete had—what 'cha call it—an an *optimistic vibe* about it."

I shook my head in admiration. Over the years, I'd heard countless tourists tell how, after taking a gander at the sugar-white sands and turquoise waters of St. Pete Beach, they'd decided to ditch their old lives like losing lottery tickets. But nobody had ever matched Gladys for grit and gusto.

The old woman stood up.

"Honey, I grabbed onto the Sunshine State's butt with both hands." Gladys' hands latched onto her own scrawny butt cheeks in a way-too-literal visual accompaniment. She grinned, shook her boney hips for good measure, then lowered her arms and sat back down.

"Nope. It didn't take me long to hatch my escape plan, kiddo. Last day of Bobby's dang revival, I snuck out the back of that church tent and into the driver's seat of a 1966 Minnie Winnie RV."

She winked at me salaciously. "I'd done got it real cheap off the guilty husband me and Bobby been staying with."

I watched sparks dance in Gladys's eyes as she recalled that day.

"Kiddo, I climbed into that Minnie Winnie and shifted gears in more ways than one, you know? Drove to Sunset Beach and never looked back. It was 1974, by golly. Back then a body could do that. Just up and disappear."

Gladys drained her Fosters and shook her head wistfully. "Nowadays, they ain't no good place to be a vagabond. Some uptight jerk with *property rights* always shows up to chase you away."

I thought back to all the quaint little beach houses I'd seen bulldozed over the years in the name of so-called *progress.*

"Yeah, you're right about that, Gladys."

The old woman flipped back her sunglasses and locked her beady eyes with mine.

"Name's *Glad*, kiddo. Not Gladys. I ain't that scared young woman no more. No more Pious Patty. No more Blackmail Betty. No more Gladys. I'm just *Glad* now. Plain and simple."

I studied her a moment. A smile crept across my lips.

"The name suits you."

Glad beamed at the compliment. "That's mighty nice a you. What's *your* name, sugar?"

"Name's Val. It's nice to meet you, Glad," I said, surprised to find I actually meant it.

Since my disastrous return to my hometown of St. Pete Beach, friends had been hard to come by. Glad didn't fit the usual profile of who I would have considered for a new pal, but as the saying went, beggars couldn't be choosers.

I reached over and shook Glad's boney brown hand. She grinned from ear to ear.

"Sure you won't have a beer?" she asked. She let go of my hand and tempted me with a wink and a frosty silver can.

I bit my lip as I weighed the consequences.

Since that fateful coin toss in the plane on New Year's Eve, I'd tried to retain some kind of standards as to how low I'd allow myself sink in this latest incarnation of my tattered life. I'd broken them all except one; No drinking before 8 a.m.

I checked the time on my cellphone. It was 8:03.

I smiled at the old woman and took the pint of Fosters she offered. I cracked the tab, tilted my head back, and took a long, deep draught.

Author's Note: If you'd like to know the whole story about how Val went from top-of-the-world business woman to down-and-out amateur sleuth, check out the Val Fremden prequel novel, Absolute Zero: Misadventures from a Broad.

https://www.amazon.com/dp/B06ZXYK776
Sign up for my newsletter and I'll send you a copy of Absolute Zero as a welcome gift! You can find the newsletter signup link by going to the table of contents and clicking Epilogue. The link is at the end of my special note to readers. Enjoy!

Chapter Three

May melted into June and I fell into a comfortable routine of sharing a brew and a blab on the beach with Glad four or five times a week. No matter when I showed up, she never failed to be there, sprawled out on her pink beach lounger like a pile of spilled beef jerky.

"Screw you, kiddo!" she said every time I set my stuff down next to hers. Then she'd shoo me off with a flick of her sun-spotted hand, encouraging me to take my usual morning walk on the beach.

The walks didn't help much. I usually wasted the time wondering what was wrong with me.

A little over a year ago, I'd known precisely who I was—the "exotic" American wife of a handsome but moody German vintner. I'd lived in a fabulous, ancient winemaker's house made of stone in a quaint country village nestled in a picturesque fairytale land dotted with vineyards and apple orchards and castles on hilltops. Now that I was back in St. Pete, I was living in a wooden hovel above somebody's garage—and I couldn't even land a job as a waitress.

Even worse, the long years abroad had slowly turned me into a stranger to everyone I used to call a friend. During the long years away, punctuated only by sporadic phone calls and rushed holiday visits, the cozy familiarity I'd once enjoyed with them had eroded into the kind of arms-length, shallow kindness afforded to the lost and the elderly.

I'd become nothing more than a random tourist wandering the outskirts of my former life.

Worse still, too many of the people I used to know, I'd morphed into a *curiosity*—an odd puzzle they couldn't comprehend. Perhaps my all-or-nothing, sink-or-swim life choices had made them fearful of wading out into their own deep waters. Maybe they didn't *have* any deep waters. But whatever the reason, since my return from Germany, the majority of my estranged family and former friends had labeled me as *reckless* at best—*pathetic* at worst.

And I'd begun to fear they were right.

"MY LIFE SEEMS TO BE one screw-up after the next," I said to Glad at the beach one morning. "Career down the drain. Three bad marriages." I blew out a breath of frustration. "I wonder what my next mistake will be."

"Maybe it's that bathing suit," the old lady quipped and stuck out her lizard tongue.

Her sharp humor made me wince.

"Screw you," I shot back, only half joking.

The withered prune of a woman studied me from under her Gilligan hat. Finally, she spoke.

"Girl, don't you know by now? Mistakes are just thangs you hat'n figured out the reason for yet. Once you do, their worth shows up. You either learn somethin' or get somethin' from ever'thing that happens to you."

I stared at the wrinkly sage in a fluorescent-yellow bathing suit and matching turban. "Yeah, sure. Everything's a lesson or a gift. I've heard that before."

"Then maybe it's time you started listenin'."

A surge of restless energy jerked my body to standing. I looked down at my stomach. It spilled over the bottom of my two-piece bathing suit like a fallen soufflé. Suddenly, I became as self-conscious as the runner-up at a Ms. Middle-Aged Muffin-Top Pageant.

Maybe Glad was right. This bathing suit was a mistake.

I shifted my gaze from my belly over to the old woman.

"Glad, have you ever made any mistakes you've never found the reason for?"

Glad twisted her beer can slowly into the white sand and looked out toward the Gulf.

"Just one, kiddo. Lost my true love once. My only real regret in this lifetime."

"Who was it?"

Glad didn't answer. She just kept staring out at the sparkling water as a single tear snaked its way down a ravine in her wrinkled, raisin of a cheek.

SUNSET BEACH WAS ON the back burner this morning. I had plans to meet an old acquaintance, Tamella Fitz-Franklin, at a coffee shop in downtown St. Petersburg.

While I was in Europe, Tammy had married a bigwig banker and moved into his mansion on Snell Isle (aka Snob Isle) off Coffee Pot Bayou, adjacent to the swanky Old Northeast neighborhood. In anticipation of seeing her for the first time in ages, I'd applied full makeup, blow-dried my hair, and donned a dress and heels. No big deal for most. But for me, it was an effort I usually reserved for first dates and funerals, which, given my track record, had often proved difficult to distinguish one from the other.

I was heading out the door to meet her when my cellphone pinged. It was a last-minute text from Tammy, cancelling for the third time in a row.

It read, "Something's come up. Maybe next dweeb."

I was contemplating whether I was a victim of auto correct or a Freudian slip when I realized that maybe I was *neither!*

Maybe she really thought I was a dweeb! A dweeb who no longer fit in her social circle, obviously. Crap!

The only thing "circling" me these days was the credit vultures—my FICA score stunk to high heaven.

"OK," I texted back, then kicked off my heels and unzipped my dress.

I hated that crap like that still bothered me, but it did. I flung the dress onto my old couch. Was Tammy ashamed to be seen with me? Maybe I'd sunk too low to be worth her time anymore. It wouldn't have hurt so badly if she had been the only one to reject me like this. But like life itself, Tammy had moved on, just like almost everyone else I used to know.

Painful memories stung my heart and caused my eyes to water. I'd let go of so much lately. Tammy was just one more drop in a huge barrel. So why did it hurt so much? Then I studied my face in the mirror and realized that even *I* was embarrassed by me.

Oh, crap on a cracker!

My thoughts turned to the old lady I'd met on the beach, and what she must have had to give up, too. Glad was *homeless,* as far as I could tell. She'd lost *everything.* Yet she'd found a way to be happy despite it all. I hoped I could, too. I just needed time—*nd a new set of skills.*

Specifically, I wanted to be immune to the stinging hurt of other people's judgement. I wanted to be free to live my life my way, with no regrets. But what I wanted most of all was to *not give a crap anymore* about what anyone else thought of me.

Period.

From what I'd witnessed over the past few weeks, Glad was the Jedi Master of Don't-Give-A-Crap University. Her carefree attitude and genuine, everyday happiness did more than intrigue me. It made me envious. More envious than I was of Tammy Fitz-Franklin, to be sure.

Who needed a witch like that for a friend, anyway?

I pushed up my chin, pulled on my best bathing suit, grabbed my purse, and headed to Sunset Beach, still sporting my full-on war paint.

"HOW DO YOU DO IT, JEDI Master?" I called out as I picked my way across the sand in Glad's direction.

The summer sky and lazy gulf were the same gorgeous shade of azure blue. As I crossed the thirty feet of beach that separated us, the late-morning sun set about frying the back of my neck like eggs in a skillet.

Thank heaven for the slight breeze, I thought as I stood over Glad. She was sprawled out in her lounge chair, and my body was casting a sliver of shade across her face.

Taking advantage of the respite from the sun, Glad flipped her bug-eyed sunglasses up on her forehead and stared at me with eyes as blue and piercing as a glacier shard.

"What you mean, kiddo? How do I do *what*, exactly?"

I crinkled my nose. "Stay so upbeat. I mean, it's like *nothing* gets you down."

"Oh!" She laughed. "There ain't no magic hocus pocus to it, kiddo. You just gotta remember that *you* decide how you feel about whatever's happenin' around you. You're in complete control a your feelin's. Don't let nobody take your power, child."

"But what about...."

"No buts!" she said, cutting me off. "You wanna be sad, Val, be sad. You wanna be happy, be happy. It's always a hunnert percent your choice. *Own it*, girl."

I grabbed a beer and plopped down in my chair. I didn't say anything for a while. Actually, I was kind of pissed.

*So that was Glad's secret to a happy life? It was so freaking simple.
So utterly profound. So undeniably true. How had I never figured this
out before? And why was I so pissed about it?*

I was on round three of beating myself up inside when Glad sat
up in her lounge chair and studied me.

"Why the makeup today, kiddo? You don't need it."

"I was going to meet a friend...or should I say, *ex-friend* for coffee
this morning. She ditched me. I guess I'm no longer up to her standards."

Glad leaned across her beach lounger and took my hand in
hers—something she'd never done before. "Let me tell you something, girlie. Who gives a crap what that cow-brained heifer thinks a
you? All that matters is what *you* think a you. And if you don't mind
me sayin' so, I think you're kind a wonderful, Val."

I couldn't remember the last time anyone had complimented me.
Hot tears sprang up and spilled from my eyes. My throat tightened
so that I couldn't speak.

Glad smiled, let go of my hand and sank back into her lounger.
After a while, I wiped my eyes on my beach towel, picked up my beer
and took a big gulp.

Jedi Master Glad chose that precise moment to lift a scrawny
butt cheek and trumpet out a magnificent, flappy-assed fart.

Two foamy furrows of Fosters shot straight out my nostrils.

As I half-suffocated between gasps and giggles. Glad shrugged
her shoulders nonchalantly and smiled at me with a grin Jimmy
Carter couldn't match.

"See how easy you can change your own mood?" she said.

I was too stunned to reply.

A few short weeks ago, I would've been aghast at Glad's behavior.
But as I sat there beside her on the beach, I felt nothing remotely

on par with horror or disgust or shame. Glad's flatulent act was no longer an embarrassing faux pas to me. Instead, it was...it was—a *wake-up call*—a noisy refusal to be defined by social mores. It was...*total freedom!*

Wait a second, Val. Have you lost your mind? Farting *equals* freedom?

I scowled.

Why the hell not?

Looking back on my life thus far, it made as much sense as anything *else* ever had. Besides, Glad's words weren't just some bull-crap theory from an old gasbag. She had mastered total, who-gives-a-crap self-acceptance. I wanted that, too!

An empty beer can hit me on the elbow, startling me out of my inner machinations. I looked over and saw Glad grinning at me playfully.

"We create our *own* dad-gum prisons, Val," she said. "But I'm here to tell you, we always got a-hold of the keys. We got the power to set ourselves free anytime. *Anytime*, I tell you. All you got to do is choose to feel good, no matter what kind a crap rolls your way."

I nodded at the wise old guru disguised as dried beef sticks.

She's right.

I sniffed back a drop of inhaled beer still tickling my nose and looked out at the ocean. A single thought whirled around in my head like a water sprite.

I have the keys. I have the keys. I have the keys.

So why was I still loitering around in an orange jumpsuit, waiting for someone else's permission to go free?

Chapter Four

Over the next few weeks, a new feeling began to take hold in my heart. I wasn't sure what to call it, but I think it might have been *hope.*

In a surge of renewed optimism, I dusted off my old resume and writing portfolio and began to look up some old contacts in the advertising industry. I also applied for waitress positions at a couple of restaurants on the beach and downtown, just in case my old copywriting career was as dead on arrival as I'd felt on that plane home from Frankfurt.

Yes. Glad's crazy-but-effective, no-bull-crap tutelage had started to take root. I felt freer, *looser* somehow, like a crab that had sloughed off an old carapace that no longer fit. With new room to breathe, a tightly bound knot of rubber bands had begun to unravel in my chest. The unexpected snaps pinched and hurt, but the relief always outweighed the pain. With Glad's help, I'd even managed a good laugh or two at my situation.

Glad was good medicine, even though her remedial words were often hard to swallow.

ONE MORNING AS I PULLED Shabby Maggie into Caddy's parking lot, my cellphone pinged. It was a text from Cannon & Tate

Advertising, thanking me for my interest in a position there. Unfortunately, the feeling was *not* reciprocal.

Another rejection. Argh!

I grabbed my beach chair out of the backseat and picked my way across the parking lot. Halfway across, I tripped on a broken whelk shell and blew out my left flip-flop.

Really?

I scowled and limped my way toward the picket fence, my cheeks hotter than the morning sun. When I reached the beach, I took off the other flip-flop and tossed both cheap shoes into a garbage bin. Glad was waving at me from her spot by the clump of sea oats. I forced my pursed lips into a smile. My phone pinged with another text message. Beachshore Grille didn't think I had what it took to be waitress, either.

"Crap, crap and double crap!" I grumbled as I marched across the sand.

"What's up, kiddo?" Glad asked from beneath her floppy hat and sunglasses.

I held my phone out for her to see.

"Look. Two job rejections in five minutes. With my luck, I couldn't land a job cleaning shoes in a crap factory."

Glad took off her hat and glasses and glanced at my phone.

"Don't sweat it, kiddo. You'll get a job when you set your mind to it."

She smiled and wagged her McDonald's-arches-for-eyebrows at me. The perfect crescents of black eyebrow pencil scrawled on Glad's sun-spotted forehead gave her a permanent look of astonishment that had, at first, made me secretly embarrassed for her. Now, seeing the double arches in action caused a smile of endearment to curl my lips, despite my frustration over my unemployment situation.

"When I *set my mind to it?* I really need a job *now*," I said as I set up my beach chair. I fumbled through my bag for a copy of *The St. Petersburg Times* I'd folded to the job classifieds.

Glad sat back in her lounger. Her pink Gilligan hat returned to its perch atop her short shock of silver hair. She reached a long, Slim Jim arm toward the cooler for another beer and said, "I think you should hold out for the job you really want." She punctuated the end of her sentence with the click and vacuum-whoosh of a fresh can of beer opening.

As I watched her take a slug of beer, what was left of my tentative good mood evaporated.

"You don't get it," I argued. "I lost my *career*, Glad! I need to get back in the workforce. Otherwise, how am I going to be a worthwhile citizen?"

Glad shot me a sideways glance, then burst into a laugh that shook her entire boney body. Beer sloshed onto her purple swimsuit as she slapped her knee and said, "Worthwhile citizen! What kind a horse crap is *that?*"

My mind raced around for the right answer. Somehow it wasn't as easy to pluck black-and-white from my grey matter anymore. Glad watched my struggle with the kind of patient amusement usually reserved for kindergarteners and idiots. I finally fumbled out something that sounded familiar.

"To be *productive*, Glad! To keep the *economy* going. To make a *difference* in the world. It's what we were taught to believe is right!"

Glad sat up in her pink lounger, dug her brown toes in the white sand, and beamed at me like a mother who'd just taught her daughter to go potty all by herself.

"Bingo, kiddo! You hit the dang nail on the head!"

Glad's blue, laser-beam eyes stared intently into my own dark-brown ones for what seemed like a minute. She appeared to be searching for something inside me, but ultimately failed to find it. Finally, she explained, "It's what we were *taught* to believe, all right. But whose beliefs are they *really*, Val?"

"I don't know, Glad!" I shrieked, then shriveled into a growing grey cloud of uncertainty. "*Everyone's*, I guess."

"Not mine!" Glad slapped her thin brown thigh and cackled out a laugh. It wasn't a cynical laugh. It was a genuine, hearty chuckle laced with a good Southern dollop of joy.

I stared at her blankly.

"I ain't done much else but sit my butt in this chair and drink beer for the last twenty years," she said. "Do you think I'm a worthwhile citizen, kiddo? Tell the truth now. You know it's all the same to me."

I turned the ignition on my old belief system, but the judgmental engine just sputtered and failed. I got out of the old jalopy and slammed the door defiantly.

"Before I got to know you, I might have said 'no,' Glad, you weren't a worthwhile citizen. But now...now I'd say 'yes.'"

Glad's expression never wavered. "So, Val, what changed your mind?"

I pursed my lips. "*You* did."

"Little ol' me?"

Glad grinned and planted a hand on her hip, then jabbed an index finger into her dimpled cheek and twisted it provocatively, like a pinup girl from back in her day.

I wanted to laugh, but my throat was swollen tight with the pressure of unshed tears.

"You're the most worthwhile person I know, Glad," I finally choked out.

Glad's arms dropped to her sides and her eyes grew as liquid as mine.

"But I haven't changed a peep since we met, Val."

"I know," I whispered. "What does that mean?"

Glad sat back in her lounger and grinned at me proudly. "It means *you* have."

Chapter Five

Glad was right. I'd not only changed. I'd been turned upside-down and inside-out.

Before I met Glad, I'd read about six million self-help books trying to fix my broken life. But nothing ever cut through the crap like a single hour with her. I'd never laughed so hard or felt so totally accepted in my entire life.

Over weeks of "drinkin' and discussin'" as she called it, Glad had become my friend, my confidant, my surrogate mom, even. I could tell her anything and she'd find the bright side. I could be so down I didn't know up and she'd get me laughing until I nearly peed my bathing-suit bottom.

"There ain't *no* subject off limits to a good laugh," she liked to say.

After six weeks of "Glad Therapy," I'd begun to see her point.

So I was surprised one Monday at the end of June when I dropped my beach bag by Glad's lounger and she didn't say a word. The orange glare of the rising sun reflected off her dark sunglasses, obscuring her eyes.

I grinned. She was asleep.

Feeling lighter and more playful than I had in years, I decided to have some fun. I snuck through the sea oats behind Glad and tried to catch her off guard.

"Screw you, kiddo!" I yelled, and jumped flat-footed in front of her, my arms posed Karate-chop style like in a bad ninja movie.

Glad didn't respond.

I touched her arm. Even in the summer heat she felt cold. I nudged her. Nothing. The hair on the back of my neck bristled. I squatted down beside her and shook Glad by her boney brown shoulders. Her sunglasses fell off. Her once bright-blue eyes were dull. The heat had already wicked them dry.

Glad was dead.

A knife blade stabbed my heart, making my knees buckle. My mentor, my touchstone, my only friend was...*gone!*

Stunned, I stared at Glad's peaceful, smiling face for a moment, then folded her arms gently across her chest and covered her with my beach towel. I tried to stand, but my legs wouldn't work, and I collapsed down on top of Glad and cried. Pain ripped through me, hot and heavy and draining. I lay across her chest and cried for Glad, for myself, and for all the other people I'd lost along the way.

"Thanks for being my friend," I whispered into her cold, brown ear. "I know wherever you are now, they're lucky to have you."

In my grieving mind, I heard her whisper back, "You better *believe* it, kiddo."

A laugh escaped my lips, and I hugged Glad's body tight one last time.

As if offering me one final goodbye, Glad let out a long, flappy fart.

I laughed out loud, then ripped into another crying jag. How could the world ever realize what a treasure it had just lost?

After a while, I pulled myself together and wiped the dripping snot from my nose with the beach towel. I whispered goodbye to Glad one more time, then got up and stumbled blindly toward Caddy's beach bar.

I bumbled out the sad news to the first waitress I ran across.

"Not Glad!" she screamed. Her voice sounded strange, as if it were underwater.

Two other waitresses came running over to find out what was wrong. Before long, a knot of people had gathered up in a circle around me, hanging on each other's shoulders and sobbing. Even the old guy who picked up trash on the beach broke down when he heard the news.

I soon found out that all the employees and half the customers at Caddy's had known Glad. Why wouldn't they have? Unlike me, Glad had been an open book worth reading. Making friends had come easy for her.

Paralyzed with grief, I watched through a yellow-grey haze as the usual stuff that happened next swirled around me. An ambulance arrived. An EMT pronounced Glad dead. Strangers loaded her onto a stretcher. A grey bag zipped up around her until her face disappeared. They shoved her into the back of an ambulance.

Its lights were off. There was no hurry.

As I stood in a semi-stupor, one of the paramedics came up and asked the crowd who was going to identify and claim the body. Glad had no identification on her.

It was quiet for a moment, then several people all at once said, "I will."

I was one of those voices. The sad chorus that accompanied me belonged to three grungy guys I'd seen loitering around Caddy's. I didn't know their names, so I felt obliged to introduce myself.

"I'm Val," I said, squeezing the required breath out of my tight, empty lungs. My words wafted softly in the steamy air. My eyes wandered, unseeing, nowhere in particular.

"We knows who you are," one of the men answered.

The thick, Southern twang in his voice coaxed me back to attention. The first thing my watery eyes focused on was a herniated navel protruding from a swollen beer belly as tight as a satiated tick's. The belly was attached to a short, thick man in a baggy, knee-length bathing suit.

"I'm Wally," he said, and held out a pudgy, freckled hand for me to shake. "But Glad liked to call me Winky."

"*Wee Willie* Winky. *Get it?*" Glad's familiar voice whispered in my ear.

Instantly, the stabbing pain in my heart was forgotten. I struggled to stifle an unwelcome giggle rising up my throat like soda bubbles, pinging against my tonsils. I had the unfortunate habit of giggling when I was nervous, but this was something different. This was a real, honest-to-goodness laugh trying to get heard.

I bit down hard and shook Wee Willie's hand.

Dang it, Glad! Won't you let me be sad even at your passing?

"How do you know me? Have we met?" I asked Wee Willie...Wally...*whatever!*

"We seen you sittin' with Glad all them times," said Winky, scratching his bare belly with a dirty index finger. "But she told us not to bother you two. Said you had important thangs to discuss that didn't need no man messin' it up."

"Oh. Well...thanks for that, I guess." The words felt strange and sticky in my throat.

"I'm Stu," said another man, sidelining Winky for my attention. He was taller. A good six feet at least. Thin build. Thick moustache. His head was as bald and brown as a roasted peanut.

"But Glad called me Goober."

I nearly choked.

Another freaking inside joke!

I made a pathetic attempt to pass my unwanted laughter off as crying. Failing that and not wanting to appear insane, I excused myself and bolted to the ladies room to compose myself.

"Dang it, Glad!" I said under my breath as I closed the stall door behind me. "This isn't *funny!*" I collapsed onto the toilet and buried my face in my hands, laughing and crying and laughing and crying until I couldn't tell one from the other anymore.

God I'm going to miss that woman!

"You all right in there, honey?" a woman's voice sounded from the other side of the stall.

"Yes, thanks," I answered, then blew my nose on some toilet roll.

"Okie dokie then. I'm here if you need me, you know."

"Thanks Glad," I said without thinking.

I sat there another second before it hit me.

Glad!

I jumped up off the toilet and slung open the stall door. No one was there.

I know I heard Glad's voice—first outside and now in the restroom.

I wondered if I might be going crazy. Then I caught a glimpse of myself in the mirror and removed all doubt. Suffice it to say, Alice Cooper was not a good look for me.

I stared at my pathetic, mascara-meltdown reflection for a moment, then yanked a paper towel from the dispenser on the wall. As I reached over to turn on the tap, my hand jerked back involuntarily. A huge, greenish-blue dragonfly was perched on the faucet handle. Its iridescent wings spanned a good four or five inches.

It rested on the tap patiently as I cleaned an inch of smeary black grunge from under each of my eyes. As I smoothed my afro-wannabe hair with my hands, I realized the insect's presence hadn't freaked me out like it normally would have. Instead, I'd felt a strange calm wash over me.

With the mascara erased and my hair tamed, I reached out my right index finger toward it. The dragonfly crawled onboard. I studied it for a moment, then carried it out of the bathroom. As soon as we hit the open air, it flew off with a bee-like buzz of its rainbow wings.

"There she is!" I heard someone yell.

I looked around, half expecting, as if by dragonfly magic, to see Glad appear out of a mist. Instead, I saw the three beach bums heading my way.

"There you are!" Goober, formerly known as Stu, said. He hitched up his baggy cargo shorts. "We were worried about you."

"You *were?*" I asked incredulously. "You don't even *know* me."

"We don't stand on no gaul-dang formalities here, Miss Val," said Winky. He folded his hands over his naked beer belly in a way that made me feel it was a display of redneck respect.

"Any friend of Glad's is our friend, too," said the third man in a shy, half-whisper. He was of medium height and build, with blue-black hair and café-con-leche skin. Nice looking in an Antonio-Banderas-hits-the-skids kind of way.

"I'm Jorge," he said, then looked at my sandals.

"I told the paramedics to take her to Grabb's Funeral Home on Central Avenue," Goober interrupted before I could say anything. He absently smoothed his huge moustache with a swipe of his right thumb and index finger. His eyes shifted left and right as if searching for something. "But without ID, they'll only take her to the county morgue," he continued. "We'll have to figure something out. Meantime, we need to take up a collection for the cremation, pronto. Death doesn't come cheap nowadays. Once we get Glad's remains back, we can have a little ceremony out at the beach. Scatter her ashes out in the Gulf and stuff."

"I want to help," I said. "What can I do?"

"Thanks, Val," Goober said. "That's really nice of you. Well, first off we're going to need a big coffee can. Anybody here got one?"

The short, redheaded redneck blew a gasket.

"We ain't puttin' her in no gaul-dang Folgers can like they did in *The Big Lebowski!*" Winky yelled. The pudgy little guy's lips were white. The rest of his face was the color of a Bloody Mary. "I won't stand for it, I'm tellin' ya right now, it will not stand!"

I studied Winky for a moment. Having come from a family that made *The Jerry Springer Show* look like *The Sound of Music*, I knew the difference between a bat-crap crazy redneck and a Southern man who just happened to have a red neck. (Neither one should be crossed, mind you. But while both would sleep with your sister to get back at you, only one would kill your dog to even the score.) When in doubt, I always looked for a ponytail. It was never a good sign. Winky had a buzz cut, no tail.

I quietly breathed a sigh of relief.

"Cool your jets, Winky," said Goober, putting a hand on his friend's shoulder. "I thought we could use the can to collect the donations in. Decorate it up nice. Put it by the cash register. Maybe glue a picture of Glad on it. We've gotta do something quick, you know. We've gotta to pay the piper, sore to speak."

Sore to speak. Ugh.

As a professional writer, I'd come to realize that being highly literate was definitely overrated. When applied too liberally, it could be the ruination of your life.

"I'll take care of it," I heard myself say.

From the looks of it, I was probably the only one among us with more than twenty bucks to my name. Relatively speaking, I wasn't *that* short of cash at the moment. But I *had* been short on friendship. Glad had filled that hole for me for an amazing six weeks. I was grateful. And if she really *was* still hanging around, I wanted to let her know it.

"I'll have a nice donation container here in an hour. You can count on me."

"That would be really great," said Jorge. He batted back tears from his big, blackish-brown eyes, and stared at my feet again.

"Okie dokie, then," I said, involuntarily mimicking Glad, like people tend to do when they've spent a lot of time together.

I flushed with embarrassment at my faux pas and hesitantly scanned the three guys' faces. They all registered nothing but sad, wistful smiles. Relieved, I nodded and turned toward the parking lot. Back at my car, I slipped my shorts on over my bathing suit and inched my feet back into my flip-flops. To save time, I left Maggie's convertible top down and headed to the nearest Target store.

THE COMFORTING NEARNESS of Glad and her whispered inside jokes dissipated in the steamy heat during the drive to Target. In their wake my heart grew numb and hollow with shock.

Walking into the harsh, fluorescent-lit retail extravaganza was an assault on my overwrought senses. Everything screamed with hideous brightness, garishness and pointlessness. I rummaged half-heartedly, then angrily through the ludicrously large selection of storage containers and kitchen canisters. Nothing seemed right.

Who makes all this crap, anyway?

I was about to panic when an idea struck me. I padded over to the children's section in search of a piggybank. I found a white ceramic one about a foot tall, complete with pink wings and a halo. The chubby cherub's huge, hound-dog eyes looked up sweetly at the inscription, "For My Little Angel."

It was perfect.

Perfectly awful.

I wanted to smash the idiotic thing to bits with a freaking pink hammer. But it was either that insipid angel or a Dalmatian-spotted cow that mooed and wagged its tail every time someone shoved a coin down its throat.

I was carrying the blasted angel bank up to the register when I caught sight of something sitting at the register endcap. I grinned like Jack Nicholson in *The Shining*. I shoved the sappy angel back onto a shelf between bags of charcoal briquettes and tubes of sunscreen. I grabbed my prize and was back at Caddy's in under an hour, as promised.

"What on Earth ever made you pick *that* thing?" Goober asked.

He frowned at me as I sat the foot-and-a-half tall Mr. Peanut piggybank down by the cash register next to a picture of Glad.

I stepped back and compared Mr. Peanut with Goober. They were twins if I ever saw a set—except for the winking holographic monocle on the *plastic* peanut head. The fact that Goober didn't make the connection raised the irony factor to darn near orgasmic for me.

I could have sworn I heard Glad snickering in my ear.

Chapter Six

Glad had lived in a universe where last names didn't matter. Come to think of it, neither had first ones. In her world, everyone had been free to make themselves up as they went along. It seemed to me that the practice had worked pretty well for her in life. Death, however, had proved to be another story.

The trouble was, no one knew Glad's last name or where she'd lived. As weatherworn as she'd appeared, she could have called that pink beach lounger home, for all I knew. She'd had no ID on her when she died. A Jane Doe. That meant there was no known next of kin to notify of her death. Legally, I didn't have any right to her remains. But there was just no way I was going to let Glad's body go unclaimed and forgotten.

A corpse for the medical university or a body farm? No! Not for my precious friend Glad.

At a loss as to what to do next, I'd arranged to meet Goober, Winky and Jorge to discuss our options for springing Glad out of the morgue. I was supposed to meet them at a restaurant called Water Loo's in St. Pete Beach. When I walked in the dive I knew instantly that the universe was having another laugh on me. And, truth be told, I hoped it pissed its own pants.

Even in its heyday, Water Loo's couldn't have hoped to be as respectable as, say, an inner-city Waffle House. The cockroach-hued, fake-wood paneling that covered every wall came in handy as camouflage for both filth and free-ranging arthropods. The dirty linoleum floor bore a sad, worn-out trail to a row of dark-brown vinyl booths teetering on the edge of dilapidation.

I would have fled if I'd had any place better to go.

"Hey Val!" shouted a voice from the corner booth.

I recognized the Marlboro-inspired baritone. It belonged to Goober. I shot a glance in that direction. The sight of the three men from Caddy's sitting together in a booth caused me to suck in a short breath. I took a fumbling step in their direction like a tattered moth flittering headlong into a bug zapper.

Goober and his pals looked as if they'd just washed ashore from some catastrophic and idiotic sea voyage. Sunburned faces. Stubble beards. Tattered clothes pungent with the smell of booze and sweat. They were the kind of guys whose mere presence caused eyes to shift and minds to narrow. I had to admit, the first time I'd met them I'd been no exception. But their redeeming desire to help Glad had softened my feelings toward them to something undefinable...somewhere between *unease* and *resignation*.

I plopped down next to Goober feeling numb with shock. Glad's unexpected departure had shoved me into my own personal episode of *The Twilight Zone*—one where I'd been spun around and around until I couldn't catch my bearings, because *any bearings I'd ever known no longer existed*.

"Off in Lady Lala Land?" Goober asked.

He poked me to attention with a coffee spoon, then returned the dull silver utensil to his mouth. He sucked on it like a lollipop, clicking it against his teeth as he grinned at me from under a bushy, brown moustache he'd probably lifted from an unsuspecting walrus. It didn't suit his bald, peanut-shaped head. Every time I looked at him I couldn't help but think of that Mr. Peanut piggybank.

"What? Oh. Umm...just thinking," I fumbled, giving myself a second to come up with a lie. "I was just thinking...about how we all met."

I flicked my wavy brown hair off my shoulder and glanced at the spot on my arm where his spoon had made contact. I contained my disgust to discreet tightening of my jaw and looked back up at Goober.

"Yeah, that was one hell of a day," he said, nodding slowly. He flung a sideways glance across the booth in the direction of his buddies.

"One hell of a day," Wally and Jorge echoed in unison, then sighed like lovelorn losers.

Though the two acted as a pair, physically they were as opposite as bookends. Wally was a fat, loud-mouthed, short-tempered, über-freckled redneck. Jorge was a deep, dark mystery of quiet contemplation inhabiting the form of a lean, caramel-skinned Hispanic.

The idea of associating with these remnants of men caused a marble-sized knot of panic to lodge just below my larynx. Light years from familiar territory, I imagined myself a kind of urban Jane Goodall studying a tragic subspecies of homo erectus.

Homo rejectus, perhaps?

But like a good anthropologist, I swallowed hard and got the marble down. After all, as I said before, I really didn't have any place else to go or anything better to do.

"We need a gaul-dang toast!" bellowed pig-bellied Wally, jerking up from his slump like he'd been stuck with a pin.

I had to commend him. Wally was actually wearing a shirt today. No sleeves and a hole where his left nipple peeked out, but a bona fide shirt nonetheless.

"Jes. A toast," echoed thin, sad-faced Jorge, his eyes brightening at the prospect of a drink. Judging from the bulge in the pocket of his faded Hawaiian shirt, Jorge had brought along an amigo from the liquor store.

A pocket rocket. Oh boy.

The men raised their scuffed brown coffee mugs in their right hands, then placed their left hands over their hearts in what appeared to be a well-worn ritual. Like a victim of Stockholm Syndrome, I followed their lead. When everyone was in position, Jorge made two sharp clicks out of the side of his mouth. Apparently, that was the signal for us to raise our mugs toward the center of the table until they all clunked together.

"Screw you, kiddo!" the men belted out over the dull clinking of plastic on plastic.

I blinked back a bittersweet blush of memories and watched the men take solemn, misty-eyed glances at each other like soldiers of some distant, yet never-to-be-forgotten war.

I was familiar with the skirmish.

Survival of the fittest.

I was becoming a veteran of it myself.

The sudden realization of my close camaraderie with the three social pariahs curdled my stomach and made me glance around the diner self-consciously. The dump was empty except for us, so I knew the dirty looks from the waitress in her ugly brown uniform were for our benefit alone.

Mornings spent gulping down complementary Water Loo's coffee refills looked to be the high point of the day for these guys. I hoped I wouldn't suffer the same fate. With the toast to dearly departed Glad over, all three men collapsed back into the booth like sacks of unwashed potatoes. The blank looks on their faces made me wonder about the thoughts that plagued people with too much time on their hands.

Booze. Sex. Regrets....

As for me, I let my unemployed writer's mind sink to a new low, just like my butt in that dilapidated booth. I amused myself by giving the guys a secret pet name—the Three Stooges. After all, they really *were* stooges. And there really were *three* of them. Hell, one of them was even named *Stu*.

I knew it was an easy joke. But hell. Sometimes fish in a barrel *needed* shooting.

"So what are we going to do about Glad?" I tossed the question out to no one in particular.

Goober looked up from his coffee cup.

"Oh. We already held that meeting."

"Really?" I asked. "So what's the plan?"

"We all voted that you should take care of it," Goober replied, then smashed a cockroach on the table with his bare hand.

Chapter Seven

In Florida, people died in droves from the heat, old age, exhaustion and suicide. Bodies stacked up like cordwood in summer, and cold storage was prime real estate. I was hoping to put these facts to my advantage when I called the county morgue. At our Water Loo's summit, the stooges and I had agreed it would seem less creepy if a woman tried to claim Glad's body. So, I thought up a cover story and made the call.

"Hello, I'm calling about the woman brought in yesterday," I said, not knowing where to begin a conversation involving a dead body.

"Which one?" asked a man's deep, raspy voice.

"An older lady. Silver-white, short hair?"

"Lady, you just described half of Pinellas County."

"Oh. Ummm..."

"You got a *name*, by chance?" he asked impatiently.

"Yes. Glad...uhh...Gladys."

The line was silent for five seconds. "You really gonna make me ask for the last name?"

"Oh! Look, I'm sorry, but I don't know her la...I mean...she came in as a Jane Doe. I'm her...*niece*."

Geez! I almost blew it!

"Okay, that narrows it down to six, maybe ten I got at the moment. Any identifying marks? Scars? Tattoos?" he asked wearily.

"I don't think so. Oh. Wait. She's wearing a green bathing suit. Does that help?"

"Aww, yeah. Tanned like a leather wallet? I know the one," Mr. Sensitivity said.

"What do I have to do to claim her body?"

"Come in and fill out a form."

"I'll be right over."

I JUMPED IN MAGGIE and hit the gas. I was at the county morgue before the phone got cold.

"Can I help you, ma'am?" a man asked when I walked in the door.

I recognized the voice. The guy on the phone was the clerk on duty. It made sense.

"Hi. I think I was just talking to you about Gladys?"

"Hmmm?" he asked and scratched his right ear.

He was younger than he'd sounded on the phone. Slimly built, his eyes were the same piercing, ice-water blue that Glad's had been.

"Green bathing suit?" I prompted.

"Oh yeah. Old crocodile hide."

The man's goatee and grin made him look devilish, but in all the right ways. I nodded and did my best to smile.

"I just got off the phone with you, right?" he asked.

"Right. I'm Gladys's niece. I'm here to make arrangements for her...uh...*remains*."

"You got a picture ID for her? Driver's license?"

Crap!

I looked down and faked going through the motions of searching my purse for them.

"Oh no," I said, and shot him my best pathetic, pleading look. "I must have left them at home!"

The clerk eyed me, his face emotionless except for a slight uptick of one eyebrow.

"Is this going to be delivery or to go?"

My gut flopped. "What?"

"What do you plan to do with the body?" he asked, his finger tapping on the counter.

"Oh. I want her sent to Grabb's Funeral Home. For cremation."

My reply seemed to satisfy something in him. The clerk gave a quick nod, grabbed a form from a pile and handed it to me. "I'm going to need to see your driver's license."

I handed it over.

"Okay," he said. "Look, I'll do you a favor, since you're sending her to Grabb's. Just fill out the form with her vitals as best as you can remember 'em. Just make sure your contact information is accurate. That way, if anybody comes asking questions, we'll have you on file. I'm gonna need to make a copy of your license."

I nodded. He photocopied my license along with the form.

"Sorry about your loss," he said as he slid my license back across the counter.

"Thanks."

"No, really. Sorry about the morbid humor. It's just that this job is...incredibly *desensitizing*. You wouldn't believe how many people never get picked up. I'm glad your aunt isn't going off to unclaimed freight." He winced at me and slapped himself on the forehead. "Ugh! Sorry again."

"Don't worry about it," I said. "My Aunt Glad always told me there is no situation you can't find the humor in if you look hard enough. I think she would have found your comments a real hoot."

The thought of Glad cackling out a laugh made me feel better. I picked up my driver's license and my copy of the form. I had substituted my own last name for Glad's unknown one.

Gladys Fremden, born the day after she died.

That was one irony I didn't stop to savor.

THE MORTICIAN AT GRABB'S was more than happy to take Glad and the money required for her cremation. I was grateful and relieved he did. I gave him Glad's case number assigned by the morgue and he said he would take care of everything. He tried to guilt me into buying a fancy coffin, but I told him basically he couldn't get caviar from a can of pinto beans. He sniffed and informed me she'd be ready for pick-up at the end of the week. I gave him my cell number and made an appointment for Friday morning.

I drove back to my apartment and crept inside. Even though Glad had never visited me there, the hovel I called home seemed emptier somehow. I cracked open a Fosters I'd picked up on the way and toasted my dearly departed friend.

"Screw you, kiddo," I said, then stared at the cellphone image of Glad in her lounger, shooting me her unabashed, red-lipstick, clown-faced smile. It was the only picture I had of her.

When this picture is gone, will there be anything left of Glad at all?

"Screw me," I whispered.

I was tired of trying to be brave and strong. I let go, and let the pain wash over me, warm and wet and aching to my bones.

WITHOUT MY DRINKING buddy and confidant, I tried to return to my original solo act. But in the deafening silence left in the wake of Glad's cackling laughter, quiet contemplation had lost a great deal of its appeal.

Left to my own devices, the next four days drifted along as empty and aimlessly as a paper bag on a windy street. Once or twice, I thought about going to Sunset Beach. But I just couldn't muster up the courage.

One eternity and half a gallon of gin later, I woke up on the couch to discover it was Friday.

Finally.

I got myself presentable and drove to Caddy's to get the donations from the Mr. Peanut container. The breakfast crowd was thin, so I took the opportunity to pull the rubber bottom stopper out of Mr. Peanut and shake his innards out on the counter by the cash register. Norma, the tough, mannish lead waitress, helped me count out the dollar bills and change. I was shocked. Since Monday, the good people of Caddy's had stuffed $547.36 into Mr. Peanut for Glad's cremation/memorial fund.

"Let me make that right for you," Norma barked. Her voice sounded as if it would break down if she tried to say more.

She opened the register and counted out $550.00 in twenties and a ten. She handed them to me and said, "Thanks. You're a good egg." She slammed the register, shot me a quick, tight-lipped smile, and walked determinedly to the ladies' room.

I tucked the money in my purse and walked back to my car feeling as used up and useless as an empty booze bottle. I needed to keep my mind off Glad, so I did mortician math. The bill for cremation in a cardboard container had come to $635.00. I steeled myself. I'd have to pony up the rest.

Eighty-five bucks. Ouch!

Still, the sting felt more like an honor than a burden, even though my bank account was shriveling faster than a spider on a hot stove. I pulled out of Caddy's and drove through thick clouds of memories all the way to Grabb's Funeral Home.

I NEVER UNDERSTOOD why beige and chocolate brown seemed to be the favorite color palate of funeral homes. Grabb's was no exception. I walked inside the unremarkable building and into an even less remarkable lobby to be greeted by beige walls, a fake potted palm and a woman at a dark brown desk wearing a cream-colored dress. Maybe funerary proprietors believed that any use of color in their décor would set grieving people off.

I guess nobody ever went ballistic over beige.

"I'm here to pick up Gladys Fremden's cremains," I explained to the lady.

"Cash or credit?" she asked, glancing up from her computer screen.

The answer "cash" made her smile. Once the bills had traded hands, she disappeared behind a darker beige door. A minute later, the mortician, a thin, bald man dressed in a dark brown suit, crept from behind the door and shook my hand with the dead, five-fingered fish at the end of his arm.

"Into what would you like to put the cremains?" he asked. "We have a biodegradable Ocean Scatter Tube for the value price of just $135.00."

A hundred and thirty five bucks for a cardboard toilet-roll tube? Unbelievable!

I didn't have the time or energy to argue.

"No worries. I've got my own container." I made a quick run back to my car.

Mr. Peanut to the rescue once again.

I handed the piggybank to the mortician guy. To his credit, he didn't even blink. He took Mr. Peanut through the dark-beige door and returned a few minutes later. He handed me a noticeably heavier Mr. Peanut and dismissed me with a simple, "Good day to you."

A weird giddiness enveloped me when I stepped outside the funeral home with Glad in my arms. It was as if she and I'd just pulled off a robbery—and we were making a clean getaway together. I looked down at Mr. Peanut and grinned. I knew Glad wouldn't mind taking her final ride in a goofy plastic piggy bank. But then again, maybe Winky, Goober and Jorge would.

I bit my lip as I put Mr. Peanut and his stomach full of Glad on the seat next to me. An idea struck me, and I turned the ignition. I'd find a drugstore to buy a nice, gold-foiled gift box. After all, I could say Glad was like a gift. As good as gold.

I knew it was corny. But lots of simple folks *liked* corny. And, ironically, most rednecks didn't even *get* corny.

I spotted a drugstore on the corner of Gulf Boulevard and 107th and was in and out with the box in my hand in under five minutes. Even so, with the top down, I'd given the July sun plenty of time to turn Maggie's red vinyl seats into molten lava. As I slid into the bucket seat, I felt my naked thighs start to sizzle where they jutted out below my sundress.

"Yow!"

I jumped up from the driver's seat and was engrossed in a curse-pocked commentary with an inanimate object when a sudden realization stopped me mid-syllable.

The seat next to me was empty.

Mr. Peanut was gone!

I searched the floorboards. Nothing. I scrambled over the backseat for a look. Empty. My mind flooded with panic.

No! No! No! Glad's memorial was in less than an hour and some jerk has gone and stolen Glad's final freaking remains!

"Arrgh!" I screamed into the parking lot.

A fat woman stuffed into a pink polyester shirt and shorts waddled by, looking like a bipedal pig in a cheap blonde wig. She stared at me as if she'd just smelled a rat turd.

"Maybe she did. Maybe she likes rat turds."

That voice inside my head was back. Was it Glad...or was it my crazed mind saying what I thought she would say?

As I debated with myself, pig-woman hoisted her fat butt into a white minivan. She backed out of her parking space and shot me that look again.

"Maybe she's got a van full of rat turds. Sells 'em on eBay."

I wanted to snicker, but I was in a bit of a jam.

Okay, whoever you are, shut up! I don't have time for this. I've lost Glad's remains! Think of something, Val!

I was making plans to leave the state when another idea hit me like a squirt of warm bird crap. I peeled out of the parking lot and made a beeline for the public lot at St. Pete Beach.

Maggie lurched into a parking space. I cut the ignition, grabbed the gold box, snatched a colander I used for sorting shells, and sprinted toward the barbeque grills. I knew the park had five grills in total. Each was about the size of a briefcase and soldered onto thick metal pipes about three feet tall. They were ugly and indestructible, and did their best to mar the beauty of public parks throughout Florida.

After sieving through the ashes from four grills, I'd scraped together about two cups of whitish-grey powder. I had no idea how much cremains I should have, but the amount seemed kind of skimpy to me. The fifth grill was in use. A guy dressed in nothing but a blue banana hammock and ball cap was grilling chicken wings on it.

What the hell. I decided to give it a try.

"Hey, you got any ashes I can have? I use them to grow tomatoes."

"Nope, sorry," he answered, flipping over some wings that looked as if they were on the verge of becoming cremains themselves.

"Thanks anyway." I turned and walked back to the car. I was about to crank the ignition when wing dude came running toward me. Not a pretty sight.

"Hey lady, wait! I forgot!" he said, out of breath from a twenty-yard sprint. "I still have the bag of ashes I dumped when I cleaned the grill before I used it."

He tossed me a beige plastic grocery bag with what looked to be about another two cups of ashes inside.

Score!

"Thanks a bunch!"

"No problem. Hope your tomatoes do good."

"Yeah. Thanks again. Enjoy your wings!"

I dumped the ashes in the gold box and clapped on the lid. I glanced at my cellphone.

Crap on a cracker!!

The service was supposed to start in fifteen minutes. I peeled out of the parking lot, dual glass packs rumbling, and headed south on Gulf Boulevard toward Sunset Beach.

THE PARKING LOT AT Caddy's was crammed, but the attendant knew I was coming and had left a space open for me. I was surprised at how many people were there for Glad's memorial. Probably a good hundred. I handed the gold box off to Goober, who looked mighty relieved to see me.

"That was cutting it close, Val," he said.

He nervously smoothed his moustache down with his thumb and index finger. Goober had dressed for the occasion in the uniform of a burnout—a wife-beater t-shirt and impossibly baggy grey shorts that hung low on his waist and covered his knobby knees.

"You have no idea," I said.

"I was beginin' to thank you run off with the money, Val," Winky said sarcastically. He shoved me on the shoulder and shot me a dirty look.

"Sorry to shake your confidence in me, Winky. I ran into some...uh...technical difficulties." I was contemplating getting peeved at the thankless jerk when Jorge interrupted.

"Val! Good to see you!"

The poor guy looked even more relieved to see me than Goober. "I was getting worried," he said. "I don't want to lose another...you know."

Jorge smiled shyly and offered me his arm.

Besides handshakes and haircuts, I hadn't been touched by a male human being in the better part of a year. Taking Jorge's arm felt weird, but a good kind of weird. It made me feel lighter, somehow.

We walked arm-in-arm down to the beach and joined the crowd milling about. It was a few minutes before 5 p.m. and at least half the people there already had a good buzz going. Jorge offered me a slug from his pocket flask, but it was whiskey. I didn't do whiskey. After all, I had my standards.

The air cracked with the sound of someone tapping on a microphone. In the silence that followed, a familiar voice said, "Okay, everybody, listen up."

Winky.

He was going to lead the eulogy. I settled in.

This ought to be good.

"I wrote a pome 'bout Miss Glad," Winky continued. He cleared his throat, then spoke slowly, with a scholarly hillbilly affectation. "I call it, *I Miss Glad*. It goes like this:

Glad was my friend. A friend to the end.

She loved us all. And she was purty tall.

I ain't that tall but she never complained.

She never complained 'bout a gaul-dang thang.

A lady to the end, Glad made us all feel dear.

Always there to lend an ear—and a good, cold beer!

They's a word for Glad. And that word *is* Glad.

I was glad to know her. Y'all can yell now, if you wanner."

And with that, Winky yelled the most countrified, "Woo hoo!" I'd ever heard, and I'd heard plenty.

The crowd did its best to follow Winky's lead, and we bayed pathetically in the hot breeze like a pack of wormy hound dogs.

"Please now turn your attention to the water," Winky's voice cracked over the mic again like a carnival barker. The crowd grew silent. "Goober's gonna put Miss Glad to rest in the sea."

I turned toward the Gulf and saw Goober, six feet of skinny arms and stork legs, cussing and trying to balance himself on a stand-up paddleboard. I snorted back a laugh. From thirty feet offshore, Goober looked like a praying mantis afflicted with both Parkinson's and Turret's.

A shirtless teenage boy paddled the board at the back while Goober did his best to stay upright, holding onto the gold box containing our girl Glad. Goober gave the crowd a stunted wave with his left hand, lost his balance and nearly fell face forward. Somehow, he managed to pull off a spectacular recovery by wind-milling his left arm and right leg like a pair of yard whirligigs in a cat-five hurricane.

The crowd gasped in horror as Goober teetered between sea and air. They sighed in relief as his feet settled back onto the board.

I held my breath as Goober took the lid off the glittering gold box. A light breeze blew a swirl of ashes from the container right into Goober's face as he swung the box first behind him, then forward and up, as if he were pitching a softball.

As Glad's ashes flew up and out over the Gulf, I saw what appeared to be a chicken thigh bone fly out of the box and arc against the late afternoon sun. A huge, white seagull cried out and grabbed the bone midair.

I shriveled for a microsecond in horror and shame.

But there was no time for self-loathing.

With all eyes still on Goober's lanky frame, he lost his balance again. After tossing the cremains, Goober lurched backward on the paddleboard like a deranged zombie, overcompensated forward, then leap-frogged face-first into the gulf with a stupendous bellyflop. In a flash, he surfaced for air, only to be beaned on the noggin by Glad's gold box. The box bounced once, flipped over, and found purchase on the right side of Goober's shiny, bald head. It perched there at a rakish angle, like a square beret on a sunburned walrus. The crowd went wild with laughter. Catcalls pierced my ears.

Without missing a hitch, Goober stood up in the thigh-high water, grabbed the box from his head, and bowed as if he were an orchestra maestro in top hat and tails. The crowd erupted again into a riot of catcalls, cheers and applause.

I laughed so hard I peed my pants a little.

I think Glad would have not only approved—she would have done the same.

Chapter Eight

After another lonely weekend made blurry by potent cocktails of Tanqueray and tears, on Monday I decided it was time to start getting my life back on track. I ponied up some courage, drove Maggie out to Sunset Beach, and walked through the picket fence toward the crystal blue gulf.

I hesitated at the vacant spot in the sand where Glad used to sit. Her absence felt personal and mortifying and raw, like the empty socket of a freshly missing tooth. But like everything in life, it would just take some getting used to. It was a beautiful, sunny day, and the pelicans and seagulls were already getting on with *their* lives, fishing and flying and preening their feathers as they had before Glad or I or mankind itself had ever walked the Earth.

The insignificance of life itself pressed down hard upon my head, making me stare at my feet.

"You're as significant as you wanna be, Val," I heard my old friend say.

I smiled sadly and unfolded my chair. I propped it up where her lounger used to be, tossed my beach bag on it, and headed toward the shoreline.

If life truly does *go on, I might as well get to it.*

AFTER AN HOUR OF BEACHCOMBING, I was a little bit perkier and a lot more parched. I slipped a beach cover-up over my suit and ducked into Caddy's for a drink. Three days had passed since Glad's memorial service, but it appeared that the good folks at Caddy's were still in mourning. The waitresses were gathered around in a circle, sobbing.

"I still can't believe he's gone. It's just too much," said Cindy, an impossibly blonde, impossibly tanned waitress who reminded me of Malibu Barbie.

"He? Don't you mean *she*?" I coughed through my bone-dry throat.

"No...not Glad. *Tony*. Tony's dead!" snuffled Cindy between sobs, her face a smear of soggy Cover Girl. "Two in a row. Norma, I can't take it!"

Cindy collapsed into Norma's manly arms.

"Tony was broke up real bad over Glad," said Norma, her own rugged face stained with tears. Even though she sported a man's short-cropped hair and a face to match, the hard disguise couldn't mask Norma's soft interior. "He hadn't showed up for work since Glad died a week ago Sunday. Her passin's probably what did him in."

Norma patted Cindy's back like a mother hen and shot a glance at me over her shoulder. "Read it for yourself." She jabbed a meaty thumb toward a newspaper laying on a nearby table. "Cindy was checking the obits when she saw a familiar face."

I knew Tony as the old guy who raked sand and picked up garbage on the beach around Caddy's. The headline in the *St. Petersburg Times* article read, "Hoarder Dies Under Ton of Garbage." Apparently, Tony had been really *really* into garbage. So much so, that he'd brought his work home with him. My warped sense of humor made it impossible for me to ignore the delectable irony that Tony had been killed by the very thing that had given his life meaning.

Ambushed by a lifetime subscription to National Geographic, I presume.

I didn't really know Tony, and I wasn't going to cry for him. I'd just learned the hard way that tears didn't bring anyone back from the dead.

I leaned over the table and studied the article. A picture of Anthony B. Goldrich, Esq., looking decades younger and clean shaven, was, nevertheless, still recognizable as good-old, garbage-man Tony.

The paper had had a field day with his nasty habit. Below his mugshot was an 8x6, color picture of his living room. Stacks upon stacks of newspapers, garbage bags and beer cans stood heaped in huge piles, like an anti-consumerism display at some hip, modern-art gallery.

Tony's "art" had filled every corner of his home, leaving only narrow trails to squeeze through. As morbidly captivating as that picture was, the third shot was the one that really caught my eye. The backyard. Tucked in amongst hills of discarded chairs and doors and god knows what else, sat a vintage Minnie Winnie nearly concealed by junk. My heart pinged.

Could this be the same RV Glad had used to make her getaway from Bobby all those years ago?

I grabbed the paper off the table and read the article word for word. A line break in the news column reported with a comical pun not wasted on me that Tony had been dis-covered by a neighbor, dead of an apparent heart attack after being buried under an avalanche of periodicals.

The article went on to report that Mr. A. B. Goldrich, Esq. had been a lawyer of some repute in Hawesville, Kentucky. He'd moved to St. Petersburg in 1985 and had worked "in maintenance" at Caddy's since 1988. A will had been found taped to a bathroom mirror at his residence. According to his lawyer, J.D. Fellows, Anthony Goldrich, "Tony" to his friends, had left all his worldly possessions to someone named Thelma G. Goldrich. The will also stipulated he was to be cremated and buried at sea.

My heart skipped a beat.

Thelma G. Goldrich. Could the "G" stand for Gladys?

I needed to find out. And thanks to my new friends in low places, I knew somebody who might be able to help.

Chapter Nine

Most people living on the fringe didn't start out that way. They'd given the world a try and got their spirits crushed. For some, the heartless rat race killed their compassion for anything—including themselves. For others, mindless materialism hollowed them out, making everything seem pointless. But if I had to bet on the number-one reason people gave up and dropped out of normal society, I'd put my money on lost or betrayed love. It's blown apart more people's will to keep trying than all other things combined.

I fell into that last category. So did Jorge.

After Glad's memorial service, I'd learned that Jorge pulled his chips off the table after his wife and children were killed in an automobile accident on I-275. I was shocked to find out he'd been a traffic cop back then. He'd also been the first to arrive on the scene. That was all he'd said to me about it. That had been enough. Eight years had passed since that day, but post-traumatic stress disorder, whiskey, and a general lack of will to live had kept him from holding down a steady job ever since.

Unlike Jorge, whose demise via lost love had come suddenly, mine had crept in so gradually as to be almost imperceptible. Due to inattentiveness, or, I could finally admit, not *wanting* to see, I'd allowed the tapestry of my love life to unravel. Like a rug slowly stripped bare by a moth, thread by thread, until the pattern was compromised and the beauty threadbare, I'd let both my love *and* my life erode away until their value was irretrievably lost. When each had become something no longer worth holding on to, I threw them away, along with a good portion of myself.

Jorge had spoken his few words about his family between lubricating slugs of Mr. Dude 20/20—hands down the worst rotgut I'd ever tasted. Even though he was no longer either sober *or* a cop, I was hoping Jorge still had a couple of friends on the force who were.

I wanted to get a look inside the Minnie Winnie behind Tony's house. Maybe it was Glad's old escape vehicle from Bobby. Maybe she'd still been living in it when she died. If it *was* her RV, maybe there was something inside it that could put an end to the mystery of Glad's identity. I needed to do it soon, too. I figured it wouldn't be long before Pinellas County code enforcement came in and hauled away the RV, along with the other mountains of junk that stood as a final testament to Tony's lifetime obsession with trash.

I FOUND JORGE IN HIS usual spot. He was drinking in his parked car on a side street north of Water Loo's. Too gun-shy to go into the dump of a restaurant alone, Goober told me Jorge always waited for backup (namely himself or Winky) to arrive before making his move.

Apparently, no amount of whiskey could help Jorge muster up enough courage to brave a solo run inside—not even to use the toilet. The guys told me Jorge had gotten busted for peeing in the parking lot three or four times already. So far, he'd gotten off with reprimands from sympathetic cops. But nowadays, he parked his Buick stakeout-style down a side street, away from Water Loo's greasy windows and the waitresses' prying eyes.

As I pulled up behind Jorge, a thought dawned on me that I wished hadn't.

This is the guy you're turning to for help, Val? Who's more pathetic, him or you?

I blew out a breath and cut the ignition.

Jorge was busy taking a slug from his pocket rocket when I tapped on the window of his grey-and-Bondo colored Buick.

"Hola, Jorge, como estas?" I asked through the glass, pretty much using up all the Spanish I knew.

Jorge came to life like a puppy in a petting zoo.

"Bien! Y tu?" He jumped out of the ratty Buick and gave me a hug. He smelled of Old Spice and whiskey, but he was steady on his feet. I took it as a good sign.

We walked into the depressingly dingy, greasy-spoon diner and slid into the usual corner booth. The waitress wiped her hands on her dirty apron and rolled her eyes at us from behind red-framed glasses.

What's with the 'tude? We're paying customers.

I shot her a look and turned back to Jorge.

"Jorge, we've got to do something about Glad."

"What?"

I wiped sticky coffee rings off the table with a mysteriously damp paper napkin. "I think I found her Minnie Winnie. The one she said she lived in when she first came to St. Pete."

"Yeah? So what? She's dead."

I watched the fledgling spark of interest falter in Jorge's eyes.

"I know," I said quickly, hoping to rekindle it. "So is *Tony*, the garbage guy at Caddy's. It said in the paper that Tony left everything to Glad in his will."

I knew I was taking a leap on my "G" theory, but I didn't want to complicate things too much for Jorge's sloshed brain cells. My strategy seemed to work.

"No chit!"

Jorge sat up. His mouth formed a smile, then a frown, then a smile, then a frown again. I guess he was trying to decide whether to be sad about Tony or happy about Glad. Then his mouth went slack and he spoke woodenly. "Like I said before, Val. So what? Glad's dead."

Jorge sunk back into the dilapidated booth. His dull eyes followed the plump waitress as she slammed two worn, brown, plastic mugs of coffee down on the table. She rolled her eyes again, plastered on the fakest smile I'd ever seen, and asked the obligatory question, "Will there be anything else?"

"Not at the moment," I answered.

Again with the attitude. WTH?

I don't like attitude. I waited tables to pay my way through college, and knew what a pain in the behind customers could be. We weren't that type. We were nice enough. We just stayed for hours. No big deal most days. Who went to Water Loo's anyway? Nobody but drunks and dirtbags. We were mostly the former, so I didn't get why the waitress found us so annoying.

"All-righty, then," she said dismissively, then padded off behind the serving station to get busy ignoring us.

I tried to do as Glad had taught me and shrug off her negative vibe. I turned my attention back to the guy next to me, who was busy spiking his coffee from a pocket flask.

"Jorge, I know Glad's dead. But she might have a family somewhere who could use the inheritance, whatever it might be."

I watched Jorge's expression go from "so what" to "complete shutdown."

Crap! I'd gone and used the "f" word—family. A big no-no with Jorge.

Based on his reaction, I might as well have slapped Jorge in the chops.

"Sorry! It just slipped out," I whined, trying to backpedal.

Jorge turned away from me. He lowered his head and started nodding at some unseen object in the seat beside him. The moment felt surreal, and I felt like a human turd.

Then I remembered that I'd brought the ex-cop a bribe.

"Look what I got you!" I squealed with fake delight.

I held up a green-and-silver can. Jorge stopped nodding at his invisible demons and cocked his ear in my direction.

"Your favorite!" I teased.

He ventured a glance my way.

"Coco Rico!" I said in my best Spanish accent, and wiggled my torso in a mock cha-cha.

Jorge turned around and smiled tentatively. I handed him the can of coconut-flavored soda and beamed a smile big enough to be seen from an orbiting satellite.

He took the can, nodded and cracked the tab.

"Salute," he said solemnly, then slung his head back and took a deep draught.

As he did, I could see three small crosses tattooed like a necklace into the crease where Jorge's neck met his chest. One cross for his dead wife, two for his kids, I presumed.

Jorge was a broken man, but as far as I could tell, he still enjoyed a few simple pleasures. Coco Rico and whiskey appeared to be the main two. As I studied Jorge, his blue-black wavy hair reminded me of a dark, tempestuous sea. A reflection of his tormented soul, perhaps. Winky's sudden arrival saved me from diving in too deep.

"Thar's my peeps!" the stubby redneck crooned, swaggering shirtless over to the booth like a bulldog pimp. Winky's chest was almost hairless, but he made up for it in freckles. In fact, the rusty orange spots looked as if they might overtake his skin completely one day.

As I studied the constellation of freckles that held Winky together, the plump waitress with a black bob and a bad attitude came running over with a spare shirt. Winky puffed up like a movie star.

"This here fine establishment keeps a few extra shirts on hand for us lackadaisical beach fellers."

"When you gonna learn?" chided the chubby little hash slinger. She held up a huge yellow tee shirt that probably belonged to Big Bird from *Sesame Street* before he lost it in a drunken brawl. The arms of the young waitress were as tight as sausage casings and as white as alabaster. The contrast was striking against her black hair and red glasses.

"No shirt, no service, Winky," she cooed. "You know the rules."

"Yes ma'am," Winky said almost shyly. He winked salaciously at the waitress and took the wilted shirt with a dainty pinch of fingers.

Redneck etiquette? Rednetiquette!

The waitress upped the ante on his wink with a slightly naughty, deeply dimpled smile.

Interesting.

"You got somethin' against clothes?" Jorge asked as he grudgingly slid over to make room for Winky's pudgy and, most likely, freckled butt.

"At least I can still park in the parkin' lot, Peemeister," Winky shot back.

Jorge opened his mouth to say something, but I wanted to nip this dogfight in the bud.

"Did you hear about Tony?" I blurted at Winky.

"Yep. Pummeled by a pile a pornos, I bet. All in all not a bad way for a feller to go."

"Since when do you read the paper, Winky?" I asked, incredulous.

"Thay's a lot you don't know about me, Val. Still waters run deep, don't cha know."

"I got chore still waters right here," Jorge said, grabbing his crotch.

"I bet you do...," Winky shot back. He tried to stand up, but was thwarted by the lack of maneuvering space between the booth, the table and his impressive beer belly.

"Knock it off, guys!" I said, exasperated. I tried again to shift their focus. "Winky, did you see the picture of the backyard? There's a Minnie Winnie in all that junk. I think it may be Glad's. We might have a chance to find out more about her. Who she really was. If she had a fa.... If she had *friends*. Aren't you guys curious at all?"

"Sure. Tell us more."

The baritone voice from overhead belonged to Goober. He'd snuck up on us during our enthralling intellectual exchange.

"I want to get inside that Minnie Winnie," I began.

"Me too!" Winky hollered, cutting me off mid-sentence. He laughed like a deranged woodpecker while Jorge and Goober snickered and exchanged high-fives.

"What? I don't get it," I said, not bothering to hide my annoyance.

What am I doing here? When did I sign up to be the butt-end of a joke for a booth full of bums?

Goober edged into the booth beside me, absorbing me into his mushroom cloud of body odor. He picked up a spoon and used it as a pointer. He seemed to have a thing for spoons.

"See that waitress over there? Chubby one with the red specs?"

I scowled and took a glance. "Yes."

"Name's Winnie."

Goober laughed and elbowed me in the ribs.

"Ah. Good one," I said, and nodded at Winky. "You'd like to be inside...ha ha. I get it. Very funny."

Winky scrunched up his freckled face like a naughty kid and grinned.

I faked a smile and tried for a third time to herd the hapless hobos toward my own topic of interest.

"Like I said, I want to get into that RV, maybe even inside the house."

"Why?" Goober asked.

"Tony left all his stuff to a woman named Thelma G. Goldrich. I think that could be Glad."

"It's a long shot," Jorge said, straightening up in his seat. "Why would he leave everything to a dead woman?"

Interest and something approaching coherency appeared on Jorge's face. Impressive, considering how pickled his brain must have been.

"He probably made the will before Glad died and didn't have time to change it," I offered.

"Maybe," Jorge said. "I dunno. But if you think it's worth looking into, Val, I'm pretty sure I can get my friend Tommy to get us the address. Maybe let us in the house, too. We're still tight. His brother married my cousin Mercedes. Tommy's a lieutenant now, so he can pretty much do what he wants without a lot of other guys breathing down his neck."

"Great! Call him," I said.

"I don't have a phone."

"Use mine."

I fished around in my purse and handed Jorge my cellphone. He punched in Tommy's number from memory. His friend on the force didn't need any arm twisting. A minute or so later Jorge clicked off the phone and smiled.

"He's checking on the address. Then he's on his way."

We had just enough time to pay the bill and offer up a "Screw you, kiddo" toast to Glad before Jorge's friend Lieutenant Tom Foreman pulled into the parking lot. I piled into his squad car along with the stooges and headed off to commit my first official crime—breaking and entering.

Chapter Ten

On the ride over to Tony's place, I found myself wedged between Jorge and Goober in the backseat of a cop car. Winky'd called shotgun, so he got to ride upfront with Lieutenant Foreman. Apparently those were stooge rules. I made a mental note of it for next time.

We headed south on Gulf Boulevard past a line of 1950s era, pastel-colored hotels and motels situated just yards from the road since it had been widened to four lanes. Crammed together cheek to jowl, the small, two-and-three story mom-and-pop establishments obscured any trace of the stunning beach that lay just on the other side. In fact, the only hint we were near the gulf at all came from the carnival parade of sunburned, hungover tourists stumbling along the sidewalk in too-tight bathing suits and too-late sun hats.

As we passed the bumblebee-striped Bilmar hotel, Jorge and Goober began discussing whether or not Winky could be trusted inside Tony's house. Sandwiched between the two, I had no alternative but to eavesdrop like a nosy ping-pong ball.

"He'll mess things up for sure," Jorge whispered to Goober. "You remember what he did at Kat's New Year's party."

Jorge put his mouth to my ear. I got the heebie-jeebies as he whispered, "He went through that poor lady's drawers and came out wearing her leopard print bra like a pair of earmuffs."

"Point taken," Goober said under his breath. "I'll never forget the scene at Sea Hag's. Who knew so many toilet rolls could fit down somebody's pants?"

"Or at Hal's funeral when he..."

"Oh god. Don't even say it," Goober said, cutting Jorge off. "Nothing's sacred to Winky. Not even the dead. Better leave his butt in the car."

"How we gonna do that?" asked Jorge. "The boy's got a fuse as short as his Johnson."

"Leave that to me," Goober said. He closed one eye and tapped his bald noggin with his right index finger. "Hey Winky!" Goober yelled across to the front seat.

Winky's head popped around to face us, tongue out like an eager, ginger-haired pug.

"We need you to keep an eye out for Tony's nosy neighbor while we search the place," Goober explained like a military strategist. "Tony told me she looks spot-on-a-match like Pamela Anderson. Likes to prance around half-naked in front of her windows. Even sunbathes topless sometimes in the front yard. We don't want her poking around, messing up our plans."

"I'm on it, chief!" Winky shot back. He made a thumbs-up next to his right ear. "You can count on me!"

I took a sideways glance at the peanut-headed commander in chief.

Maybe Goober wasn't such a dummy after all.

The squad car turned east off Gulf Boulevard into the low-key, red-brick entry to Bahia Shores, one of the first subdivisions built on the strip island in the 1950s. Officer Foreman drove slowly along the curvy streets with kitsch names like Bikini Way and Bali Hi Court before finding Bimini Circle.

At the end of the cul-de-sac, he backed his car expertly into the driveway of a flat-roofed, ranch-style house painted tired shades of taupe to match the desolate, gravel-strewn yard. The only specks of green around the place were one straggly pygmy date palm and a few knots of hardcore weeds that had managed to scratch a living amongst the graveyard of dusty stones. The nondescript house was a dump, probably no bigger than a thousand square feet. But the backyard butted up against the Intracoastal Waterway, making the shack worth half a million, easy. Welcome to Florida.

"We'll be back in fifteen, tops," said Jorge to his cop friend.

The blond lieutenant gave one quick nod. Then, without a word, he got out, opened the backdoor to let us out, and returned to his place in the driver's seat. He pulled out some paperwork and tried to ignore Winky, who was wiggling in the passenger seat beside him like a love-starved puppy.

The rest of us tumbled out of the squad car and made our way toward the backyard. Dusty gravel crunched under the soles of our shoes. I glanced back at the squad car just before we rounded the corner of the house. Winky had his greasy nose and pudgy hands pressed against the glass of the passenger window, giving him the appearance of a fat kid trapped underwater.

I shook my head. The other two stooges had been right.

Good call to leave him behind.

Jorge and I watched as Goober picked his way through the backyard and squeezed his tall, lanky frame between a jumble of abandoned stoves and discarded jalousie windows. He climbed over a rusty refrigerator carcass with his grasshopper legs and tried the door on the RV.

"Locked!" he called out. "Let's check out the house. Maybe there's a key somewhere."

Jorge stepped around a jumble of dead bicycles and picked the backdoor lock in a matter of seconds. I wondered how many times he'd done *that* before.

The door cracked open and a smell like fruit-flavored death came pouring out. The back door was right off the kitchen. On the counter, a black pile of slime wriggled. Houseflies buzzed around us like kamikazes. Against my will I took a closer look at the writhing lump on the counter next to the sink. Hundreds of maggots were making the heap of rotten bananas squirm like a nerd on a first date.

I gagged involuntarily. Jorge just looked at the pile and grunted. He disappeared between the two-meter-high columns of magazines, his eyes darting around as if taking in every bit of the scene around him.

"Holy mother of god, would you just look at all this crap!" Goober shouted, causing me to jump. He'd trailed in behind me, and was the only one tall enough to view the chaos in its entirety.

"Cripes, Goober!" I said, annoyed at myself for being frightened. "Can you see Jorge?"

He peeked around and shook his mustachioed head. "Negatory."

The small, galley-shaped kitchen was surprisingly clean, except for the banana corpses. Besides the backdoor, the only way out of the kitchen was through the narrow gauntlet formed by stacks of yellowing *St. Petersburg Times*.

"He went that way," I said, pointing at the foot-wide slit between newspapers.

"Oh goody. Onward and upward," Goober said dryly. He wiped the sweat from his bald head with a handkerchief. "You're the teeny-tiny lady. You get to go first."

I wished I had on a hazmat suit instead of a sundress and sandals. I took a deep breath and squeezed myself between stacks of dusty magazines and newspapers and sacks of god knows what else. Goober followed behind me, punctuating the journey with curse-laden comments. Finally, we reached an opening that led to a bathroom. I flipped on the light switch.

Like the kitchen, it, too, appeared perfectly normal. The vintage, flamingo-pink tiles gleamed in the light provided by three round bulbs above the vanity. The matching pink tub and toilet were immaculate.

I could make out telltale tape marks on the mirror where something—most likely Tony's will—had been affixed for someone to find. Two lonely toothbrushes hung in a black ceramic holder built into the wall by the sink. In the center of the holder stood a tube of denture cream. My heart flinched.

Could it be Glad's?

But lots of people have dentures. Especially in St. Petersburg, the city known affectionately as "God's waiting room."

I opened the medicine cabinet. Unlike most people's bathrooms, there was no huge collection of caramel-colored prescription bottles.

Who needs Prozac when you've got pilsner?

No drugs. Just mouthwash and deodorant...and nail polish and lipsticks! My heart raced.

A woman had lived here, for sure!

I picked up one of the lipsticks. The color was called Certainly Red.

Glad's color if there ever was one!

I opened a drawer and discovered I had spoken too soon about the prescription meds. I picked up the lone brown plastic bottle and read the label. It was a fake prescription for "Screwitol." Against my will I burst out laughing.

"You all right in there?" Goober poked his peanut head around the doorframe.

"Yes. Hey, Goober, Tony wanted you to have this." I tossed him the bottle. He caught it midair with his long, basketball-player fingers.

"Hmmm. Screwitol," Goober read as he held the bottle close to his face with one hand and smoothed down his moustache with the other. "Recommended by six out of five doctors. I like the odds. But honestly, I prefer JD myself. That's Jack Daniels, in case you didn't know."

"I get it. I'm a TNT gal, myself."

"Ah, Tanqueray and tonic," Goober said, raising his eyebrows a good inch. "Classy, yet unsophisticated."

"High praise indeed," I sneered. I was about to close the bathroom drawer when I heard a muffled voice.

"Guys, come look in here!" Jorge called from somewhere in the house.

"Where are you?" Goober called back. "Say something. We'll follow your voice."

Jorge did one better. He began to sing. In Spanish. Goober and I smiled at each other. It had to be a good sign.

"Ladies first," he said, waving a hand down the hall in the direction of Jorge's tenor.

"Always the gentleman," I replied. I frowned and eyed the newspapers and garbage bags stacked along both walls. There was barely enough room for a rat to get through.

"Winky's fat butt would have never fit," I muttered. I sucked in my stomach and inched sideways down the hall.

It took a full minute to squeeze down twelve feet of hallway. At the end, the garbage subsided, revealing a bedroom as orderly as the kitchen and bath. On the edge of a queen-sized bed covered in a white chenille spread, Jorge sat crooning like the leader of a teen boy band. He stopped singing as we entered.

Jorge shook his head softly. "It was a love story, man. *Amor.* Take a look."

He handed me a framed picture of Tony and Glad. They were arm in arm, smiling at each other like contented lovebirds.

"What?" I gasped. Glad had mentioned nothing to me about Tony. My heart pinched from feeling left out of the loop. I started to sulk, then caught myself. "This looks like it was taken a good twenty years ago."

"Secret lovers. The best kind," Jorge said dreamily.

"Secret lovers my butt," said Goober. "Find anything else, lover boy?"

"Jes, Señor Suave. I found t'ree chooboxes of letters and photos and stuff. They must have been together for years. There's a Polaroid of them in Hawaii from 1998, with hotel receipts and those little drink umbrellas. They kept everything."

"No surprise there," Goober said sarcastically. "This guy didn't even toss his cookies."

"Come on, Goober. Where's your sense of romance?" I teased.

"Romance? What the hell's that?" Goober threw his hands in the air. "It'll take us hours to sort through all this crap, and this place smells like a monkey's butthole. I say let's take the boxes and get the hell out of here. This place is getting on my nerves."

"Okay," I said. "I'll take the three boxes home tonight. It was my idea, so I'll do the dirty work of sorting through them."

"Suits me," said Goober. Jorge nodded.

I'd lied to the guys about my motive for wanting the boxes. But it was a white lie—the so-called polite kind of lie we women in the South were weaned on. I was practically dying of curiosity to find out more about Glad. But beyond that truth was another, bigger one: I couldn't fathom trusting these guys with Glad and Tony's personal belongings.

The thought of Goober or Winky or Jorge pawing thoughtlessly through the remains of their life together gave me heartburn. I knew these guys had been Glad's friends too, but that didn't make the thought feel any better. It still seemed wrong. Really, really wrong. Plus, I was hurt that Glad hadn't mentioned her relationship with Tony to me. Unless...*he* was the true love she'd lost. At any rate, I didn't want to be the last to know what else she might have kept a secret.

"Guys," I said, "Glad and Tony kept their relationship quiet for some reason. Let's not blow it for them now. Not yet. At least not until we find out more about it."

"No problemo," said Jorge.

"Okay," agreed Goober. "Fine. Whatever it takes to get us out of here!"

"I guess we've got what we need for now," I said. "We can try the RV later if this doesn't pan out."

We put the three shoeboxes in a garbage bag and Goober balanced them on top of his bald head like one of those jug-carrying desert wanderers. We inched our way back to the kitchen, then exited the house. Jorge locked the door behind us.

Relief swept over me as I took in a deep breath of hot, humid outside air—as fresh as it got in St. Pete in July. "Remember, we tell no one," I said as we crunched through the dry gravel along the side yard.

Both men nodded a silent oath as we rounded the corner and walked toward the squad car. As soon as we came into view, Winky jumped out of the vehicle and ran toward us, waving his arms wildly.

"Coast is clear!" he yelled at the top of his lungs. "Nobody seen us!"

I cringed and turned to Goober and Jorge. "That means not a word to Winky, either."

"That really goes without saying, Val," Goober said drolly, and rolled his eyes.

Chapter Eleven

Since Glad's death, I'd let the stooges creep into my world, little by little...like a stray cat you give a meal to, then a name, then wake up one day to find pawing at you in bed, wanting something you weren't sure you wanted to give. Unlike that hypothetical cat, however, I hadn't allowed any of these strays into my bed. Not yet, anyway. I took comfort in that. I still had some kind of standards.

Maybe I should call these guys the Schrodinger's cats. Until I am actually observed screwing one of them, my dignity can remain undetermined, both dubious and intact....

The irony that I was growing increasingly reliant on three of the world's most unreliable men was par for the pothole-laden course that was my life to date. In fact, bizarre events and situations like this had, over the past forty-five years, shaped me into one of irony's biggest admirers. One couldn't be faulted for saying my life had been founded on the pillars of irony. Even so, the most ironic twist of all had to be my experience with Glad. The woman had taught me to enjoy life again, then died and left me in agony. Her passing reminded me that irony had a dark side. Maybe even a mean streak.

Actually, I was beginning to think irony could be a downright dirtbag.

I LEFT MY PARTNERS in crime at Caddy's and drove home with the three boxes of booty lifted from Tony's place. I parked Maggie in the assigned spot behind my apartment and hit the switch to close the convertible top. I'd found my girlie hotrod four months ago. Landing in the States with no credit and not a dime to spare, I'd tried to live without a car for three months. But the summer heat kicked in and fried my will to walk. So I'd scoured the FSBO ads and found Maggie. After seeing the price and the owner financing option, it was love at first sight.

Lots of small imperfections had taken her worth down bigtime, but she still retained her classic beauty. Besides, what was a little rust and a couple of dents among friends? Lately I'd had plenty of hard lessons on the topic of beauty running deeper than shiny surface veneer. Truth be told, a few weeks ago I didn't think I had any veneer left. But Glad's advice had changed me. I once thought of perfection as a goal. Now I saw it for what it really was—an overrated illusion designed to keep us anxious and dissatisfied.

Being fifty-six years old, it took Maggie a couple of minutes to drag her ragtop out of its compartment behind the backseat and shimmy it slowly over her chassis like a tired old hooker giving it one last go. She squealed the whole time, too, whining like an overwrought can opener. I used to fidget impatiently as I waited for her to finally flop the canvas top onto the chrome windshield frame. Now I kind of liked that she took her time. Just like Glad, Maggie reminded me to relax...and breathe...and live and let live.

Chill. You've got time, kiddo.

I cut the ignition and snapped the heavy chrome clips down that clamped the ragtop in place. Then I cranked the windows shut and grabbed the garbage bag on the seat next to me.

A garbage bag containing the life of Glad's garbage-loving man.

Another taste of bittersweet irony.

I slung the bag over my shoulder and climbed the rickety wooden stairs to my home-sweet-home. No larger than the double garage it sat above, my apartment wasn't a bad place, all in all. Built in the 1920s, it had wooden floors, built-in cabinets and lots of windows. Having said that, the floors slanted like a funhouse, the painted-shut drawers required dynamite to open, and the original, single-pane windows provided absolutely *no* insulation or soundproofing whatsoever. I could actually hear the neighbor two doors down raking his leaves—among other things.

But the location was cool. Weather permitting, it was an easy walk to the bars and restaurants downtown. From the top of my stairs I could see the eccentric, pink-and-white spire of the Vinoy Hotel. It jutted into the sky like a whitewashed Greek temple encircling a pink, amputated stump, capped with an improbable terracotta tile roof. In the last twenty years, this fallen sister of the famous St. Pete Beach Don Cesar Hotel had transformed itself from a twenty-dollar-a-pop flop house for degenerates into a fancy destination resort commanding three hundred bucks a night. The surrounding neighborhood and downtown area were being dragged along for the gentrification ride in fits and starts of redevelopment.

At the moment, restored turn-of-the-century mansions sat next to run-down concrete duplexes from the 1960s. New, million-dollar condo towers butted up to dubious liquor stores and weed–infested vacant lots. St. Petersburg's schizophrenic state left it harboring places where people of all economic strata could feel both at home *and* ill at ease. Given my questionable standing in the social hierarchy, the confusion was a perfect fit.

Like most of Florida's beautiful places, I knew St. Pete was doomed to be pounded and pulverized into a sanitized Disneyland for the rich. I figured she still had a few good years left before she gave up the struggle and became a generic, chain-store ghost of her former self. I saw it happening before my eyes. The certainty made me determined to enjoy St. Pete's final funky days while they lasted, and while I could still afford the rent. After that, well, I guess I'd just have to wait and see what life sent my way.

I held back the rickety screen door to my apartment with my right foot. I balanced the garbage bag on my left shoulder while I fiddled with the key in the front door. When it finally cracked open, the air-conditioned breeze emanating from inside felt like an arctic blast against the sweltering heat and humidity of outside. I pushed my way in, set the garbage bag down on the couch and kicked off my sandals.

Thirsty, I opened the rusty door on the fridge. A lonely jar of olives stared back at me through bloodshot, pimiento corneas. Their only companions were a pint of half-and-half, a bottle of tonic water and a banana on the verge of imitating the ones I'd seen earlier today at Tony's house. I fished around in the vegetable drawer and found a plastic bag amongst the dried-up potatoes with their spindly white shoots. Inside the bag was a tiny key lime not much bigger than a grape.

My lucky day!

I opened the freezer and pulled out the half-gallon jug of Tanqueray. My green goddess of goodness. The one real splurge I still allowed myself. I poured a generous portion in a glass, added two ice cubes, a squeeze of lime and some tonic. Presto! Instant TNT.

Life is not *that bad.*

Libation in hand, I turned my attention to the shoeboxes. I pulled them out of the garbage bag one by one. They weren't labeled. I figured Tony just kept throwing stuff into a box until it was full, then sealed it with duct tape and started a new one. With that theory in mind, I was surprised when I peeled the tape off the first box and found it neatly arranged inside. Everything was sorted by year with index cards, like a homemade filing cabinet. The index cards in the first box spanned from 1945 to 1974.

I took a long drink of my TNT and pulled out the papers for 1945. A yellowed newspaper clipping from April 24th 1945 edition of the *Hancock Clarion* announced the birth of daughter Gladys Kinsey, firstborn child to Mr. & Mrs. Roy G. Kinsey.

Hmmm. This must be Glad's stuff, not Tony's.

A faded, black-and-white picture was paper-clipped to the article. It showed a surprisingly old couple for the time, probably in their early forties, proudly holding a bundled baby. I presumed they were Glad's parents.

The next index card skipped to 1950. It housed a small collection of grade-school mementos. A photo of a girl about age five, standing in front of her parents in a fancy petticoat dress, tiny white gloves, ankle socks and patent-leather shoes. The hat on her mom's head and the basket of eggs hanging on her father's arm made the occasion obvious. The back of the photo simply read, "Easter 1951." A faded, red, construction-paper valentine from a boy named Timmy nearly fell apart when I unfolded it. Scrawled in a child's hand was the inscription, "I love you, sis." Another picture showed a gangly, blonde girl around age ten holding a kitten in her arms. Even at that young age anyone could tell that Glad was destined to become a tall, classic beauty.

I put the pictures back in their tidy filing space and pulled out the contents labeled 1964. There was just a single letter addressed to Miss Gladys Kinsey, postmarked December 12, 1964. I unfolded the letter and a black-and-white photo fell onto my lap. It showed an exhausted-looking girl lying in bed holding a tiny baby. The sad, desperate look in the girl's eyes didn't jive with it being a happy occasion. Her tired, drawn face reminded me of Glad's—the day I'd found her dead on her beach lounger.

The letter itself was written on the official stationery of a boy's academy in Huntsville, Alabama. It read:

My Dearest Gladys,

I wish I could be there with you now. My parents have seen to it that I can't. I am virtually a prisoner here. I have no money and no phone privileges. My father's influence over the faculty here has me under tight surveillance. I'm even escorted between classes. I hope this letter reaches you. If it does, it will be because my roommate Jacob was able to smuggle it off campus and post it.

But my worries are nothing compared to yours. I don't know what to say, Gladys. I love you doesn't seem to be worth much. I'm sorrier than you can know about the situation I've left you in. I hope you know that I would marry you today if I could. I vow one day to make up for what I've put you through.

I'm hoping against hope that I will be able to get your letters, if you choose to write me. I'll leave that up to you, Gladys. Just know that you have my love no matter what you decide. I only ask, if you do write to me, that you let me know if it's a boy or a girl.

Forever in my heart,
Anthony

HOLY MACKEREL! GLAD and Tony had a child together?

I flipped the envelope over to check for a mailing address. It was sent to Miss Gladys Kinsey in care of Mrs. H. E. Wannabaker, Coolidge Street, Hawesville, KY. I took out a notepad and wrote down the address, along with Glad's full name and date of birth from the newspaper announcement. I also noted a general date of birth for her baby. Sometime in the fall of 1964, most likely. The math told me

Glad was no more than nineteen at the time. Back then a single girl rarely got to keep a so-called illegitimate baby. It usually became a shameful secret, shipped off to a faraway family member or an adoption agency. I hoped Mrs. Wannabaker was still alive to tell the tale. But probably not. After all, this had happened nearly a half century ago.

Chapter Twelve

I woke the next morning to the sound of my cellphone buzzing. It was Jamie. I already knew what she wanted, and I had been dreading the call. Still, I owed it to her to pick up. I practiced saying her name out loud a few times to kill the hangover frog in my throat.

"Jamie, Jamie, Jamie," I croaked, then punched the green button on my cellphone.

"Hey Jamie," I said.

"Hey Val."

I bit my lip through about ten seconds of silence, then cracked. "You just calling to see if I'm still alive? Nice of you."

"Come on, Val. You know why I'm calling. You've gotta deliver a synopsis for your story by Monday if you want a chance at being awarded a book contract."

Dang. I truly was *a master of self-sabotage.*

During the last few months with Glad, I'd let idleness creep into my soul and eat away most of what had remained of my tattered ambition. Uninspired and unemployed were two situations a washed-up writer like me could ill afford. Yet there I was, staring both in the face like the evil twins they were.

I needed a lie, and I needed one quick. "You're in luck, then. I'm working on a new idea based in Kentucky," I said, winging it as I went along. "About a girl who had a baby back in the 1960s and had to give it away."

"What's the plot line?" Jamie asked.

"Fast forward to modern day. The illegitimate kid has grown up and is set to inherit a fortune, but first he has to be found."

"How did he get lost?"

"I'm still working on that."

"Is that it, Val?"

"That's what I've got so far."

"Then you'd better get your butt in gear!" Jamie coughed out a sharp, cynical laugh. "Remember, synopsis by Monday." She hung up.

I padded over to the kitchen and made myself a double espresso with the help of Mr. Coffee, the only truly reliable man in my life. I took a sip and thought about Jamie Diesel. She really did deserve better from me. She'd pulled some strings to get me a shot with her publisher nearly three months ago. I'd had all that time to get a storyline together and I hadn't come up with squat. I guess Tanqueray wasn't as inspirational as I'd thought.

Jamie was the sole person who still acknowledged my professional existence when I returned from Europe seven months ago. She'd been the only one to throw me a lifeline and a chance to climb back aboard my floundering writing career. She was a writer, too, and had a desk job with a small, independent publisher in New York. She kept me up-to-date on publishers looking for novels in my genre—mysteries with a strong female lead.

I should've been more grateful. I'd been pillaged by a German pirate, but I wasn't sunk yet. With any luck, maybe I could turn Glad's story of Blackmail Betty into a novel, and help her heir and myself at the same time.

Double Booty. Hmmm. Not a bad working title.

I looked over at Glad's boxes, then back at the blank screen of my computer.

Dear gods of irony, please let there be some way to make this work....

When I'd crash landed back in the States, my eight-year-old laptop might as well have been a dinosaur turd. I'd crawled out on an optimistic limb and forked out six-hundred bucks on an all-in-one touch screen computer with a full-sized, *real* keyboard. I was an old-school, ten-finger typist. On-screen keyboards and tiny laptops were for two-finger peckers, aka, *amateurs*. I had everything I needed to get cooking. The call from Jamie had just turned up the heat.

I hoped digging into Glad's history would provide some interesting plot points. That way I could kill two tough-old birds with one last-ditch stone.

I drained my coffee cup and flopped onto the worn-out old couch sagging against the wall in my tiny living room like a punch-drunk sailor. The unfortunate sofa had been abandoned where it stood by the woman who'd lived here before me. Looking at it now, I could hardly blame her. It was truly hideous—coffee-stain beige with poop-brown cushions that slumped over the back like lumpy, misshapen bags of garbage. Good thing my broke butt didn't care. Actually, I was grateful. It sure beat sitting on the floor.

The prior tenant had also left a microwave, some mismatched dishes, a worn-out, full-sized bed and a lawn table with four mismatched chairs. Arriving with nothing, I'd felt like I'd hit the jackpot. The only things I'd had to buy were a towel, a set of sheets, Mr. Coffee and a computer. Truth be told, the simple life had its charms.

I owned next to nothing, so I had next to nothing to lose.

I reached over and grabbed the shoebox of memories I'd been sorting through last night. The first thing I pulled out of the box was a marriage certificate dated January 3, 1965, legally joining Gladys Kinsey to Robert C. Munch in holy matrimony.

That marriage date wasn't more than a few weeks—a month or so tops—after poor Glad had given birth. Her parents must have wanted her gone, big time.

The yellowed news clipping I picked up next erased that thought. Dated December 26, 1964, it was the obituary of Mr. Roy G. Kinsey and Mrs. Roy G. Kinsey. They, along with their son, Timmy L. Kinsey, had been killed December 24 in a car crash while away visiting relatives in Florida. They were survived by their only daughter, Gladys Kinsey, and Mrs. Kinsey's cousin, Mrs. D. B. Meyers of Tallahassee.

Poor Glad! Tragedy heaped on tragedy! A lost love. An illegitimate baby. Parents and brother dead. Left to cope alone with some woman named Mrs. Wannabaker, who probably wasn't even a relative!

I wracked my brain. In all our beachside talks, Glad had never mentioned a baby to me. She must have had to give it up. Or it died.

Could it have been this baby—and not Tony—who was Glad's lost love?

Life must have been pretty bleak for Glad to run off with a man she barely knew, and so soon after giving birth. But as harsh as it was, Glad was probably lucky Bobby would have her. Back then, women with a past like Glad's didn't have a lot of options. Neither did women in general. Looking through those old letters and clippings made me realize that until a few decades ago, no part of a married woman's name was used in official correspondence. Instead, her identity was overwritten by her husband's, leaving only the tiny letter "s" in Mrs. John Doe to distinguish her from him. That wasn't going to make tracking down Glad's relatives any easier, and it was starting to annoy me. I decided it was time for a break.

I PULLED INTO THE PARKING lot at Water Loo's at 10:15 a.m. Through the glass I could see the shiny melon heads of the three stooges bobbing around in the brown corner booth. It was already over ninety degrees and as humid as a sauna in Botswana. Sweat trickled down my back as I trudged across the parking lot and up to the greasy entrance door. As I reached for the handle, something in my mind clicked awake as if from a dream.

How did I get here?

I'd driven Maggie as if I'd been on autopilot...maybe even against my own will. I kicked at the pile of cigarette butts loitering around the front door.

What am I doing here at this horrible place full of lost souls and derelicts?

I took a deep breath and wondered how my life had sunk to this moment. Worse still, I worried if I might look back at some point in the future and call *this* the good old days. A thread of panic stitched my throat tight.

God, if that's true, kill me now.

I swallowed hard, opened the door and stepped inside.

"Val Pal!" shouted freckle-face Winky. His face beamed at the sight of me coming through the door.

I grimaced something I hoped resembled a grin.

Welcome aboard the SS Sphincterville. Bend over and crack a smile....

"Hey guys," I said with all the fake enthusiasm I could muster. I slunk into the booth next to Winky. I tried to maintain a bit of space between us, but he reached over and gave me a one-armed bear hug. Suddenly my face was an inch from a curly muff of ginger armpit hair. It stuck out of the armhole of his sleeveless tank top like Bozo the peeping Tom.

I held my breath and struggled in vain to get free.

"Always glad to see the Val Pal!" he chortled, squeezing me tighter. I was beginning to worry I might asphyxiate when he finally eased up on his grip.

"Yeah, always a pleasure," I said as I recoiled from his headlock. I was anxious to report my findings to Goober and Jorge, but as we were keeping things secret from Winky, I needed him out of the way.

I spotted my chance sulking over by the register. "Hey Winky, could you go ask the waitress to get me a cup of coffee?"

Winky jumped at the chance to speak with Winnie. I got up and let him out of the booth, then slid over next to Jorge. We waited for Winky to get out of earshot.

"So what'd you find out?" asked Goober, a spoon clicking away in his mouth.

"You're not going to believe it, but I think Tony and Glad had a baby together."

Jorge, who had been sitting silent as a stone, suddenly burst to life. "A little muchacha! Or is it a muchacho?"

"I don't know yet," I said. "And that baby would have to be in its mid-forties now."

Goober stopped clicking his lollipop spoon and straightened his back. "Wow. That means there may actually be somebody to claim Tony's will."

"Exactly," I said. "So Glad and Tony had a baby. But that's not all I found out. I'm not sure she kept it. Long story short, Tony got sent off to some boy's military school or something. Glad's parents died in a car crash not long afterward. A couple of weeks, maybe a month after the crash Glad married a preacher named Bobby Munch and left town."

"What happened to the kid?" Goober asked.

"I don't know. She could have given it up for adoption. Her family may have taken it to live with relatives. It could have died for all I know. But I hope not."

"Via con Dios!" exhaled Jorge. "Poor, poor Glad. We have to find that kid. *Her* kid."

"I was hoping you'd say that," I confessed. "I've got Glad's birth date and a few names of people that could be friends or relatives. I was thinking you could get your friend Lieutenant Foreman to run some stuff for us through the police computers. What do you say?"

"Jes, of course!"

"Great!" I pushed my notes across the table toward him. I glanced around for Winky and saw a fly buzz around Goober's bald head. He swatted at it absentmindedly, nearly backhanding Winnie the waitress as she came up from behind, trailed by lovesick Winky. She slammed a cup of coffee on the table in front of me, shot me a witchy look and left. Winky snorted out a laugh and climbed back into the booth, sandwiching me between him and Jorge.

"What's up with her?" I asked Winky.

"She's yell us," said Jorge, cocking his head toward Winky.

"Yell us? What the blazes you talkin' about?" demanded Winky.

"Jealous, you idiot," said Goober. "You just gave our lady friend here a hug. Winnie didn't like that. Better watch out you don't get any special sauce in your coffee, Val."

I looked down at my coffee. A line of fine bubbles swam around the edge of the cup. Maybe it was always like that. Maybe not. I didn't feel like taking the chance. I shoved the cup away, causing the guys to roar with laughter.

"You and Winnie have been flirting around for months. When you gonna seal the deal?" joked Jorge, reaching around me and jabbing Winky with an index finger.

Winky waved a chubby fist at Jorge, his fat fingers an inch from my face. "I'm gonna seal *your* deal right now!" Winky's face was bright red, but his anger seemed feigned.

Poor little Winky was actually embarrassed! Redneck puppy love.

"All right already," I crabbed. Keeping these guys on track was harder than getting a bucket of bait worms to form a straight line and do the conga. I was about to ask Winky to get me another cup of coffee when he spotted the note I'd given Jorge. He grabbed it out of his hands like a grade-school bully.

"Ha ha! Gotcha," Winky sneered as he studied the paper. He inhaled, then blew out a whistle. "Hawesville, Kentucky, huh? I got a cousin up in them there parts."

"I didn't know you could read, Winky," I said. The comment garnered a snicker from Goober and Jorge.

"Like I said before, Val. Still waters." Winky tapped an index finger on his fat, buzz-cut noggin, never looking up from the note. "Woo hoo. Born in 1945. Glad what'n no spring chicken, that's for sure."

"None of us are," interjected Goober. "Have some respect for a lady."

"What lady?" Winky said, craning his head like a tortoise in an exaggerated search of the vicinity.

"I'm talking about *Glad*, you twit," said Goober. He shook his bald head at me as he pointed a thumb at Winky. Then he remembered *I* was a woman, and hastily said, "And Val here, too."

"My deepest apologies to ladies both present and passed," Winky said melodramatically, bowing his head in mock respect.

"I thing it's time for a toast," said Jorge, snatching the paper back from Winky.

"A toast!" echoed Goober and Winky.

I knew what came next. And despite all the crap going on in my life, I let the thought of Glad make me smile.

Chapter Thirteen

When I peeled out of the Water Loo's parking lot, the sky looked as if the gods had gotten drunk and spilled merlot all over the place. Dark reddish-purple smears surfed their way across the horizon eastward from the gulf. I could already smell that familiar hint of metal and muck in the thickening air. I knew what that meant. I had about fifteen minutes to get home before the weather hit—and hard. I mashed the gas pedal. Maggie's V8 engine roared deep and steady, like Barry White imitating a lion's roar. I swung wide and turned off Gulf Boulevard onto First Avenue South, hoping the synchronized lights would give me a straight shot to Third Street, then home.

Summer storms in Florida always started out with a smattering of big, fat raindrops. They ended with torrential sheets of water being blown to bits by schizoid winds whipping first one way then the other. Our tropical storms rarely lasted more than half an hour, so they didn't have any time to waste. In a matter of minutes you could count on at least a half-dozen lightning strikes cracking the ground, each one always just a bit too close for comfort.

I was on Third Street and almost to the alley when the first tablespoon-sized drops battered the windshield. By the time I parked a minute later, I had the choice of waiting it out in the Sprint or getting soaked to the bone. A solid torrent of water turned the visibility to zero. I was reaching for the door handle when lightning struck nearby, filling the liquid air with a crackling blue-white light reminiscent of an old-time flash bulb. A kinetic boom of thunder came two seconds later, and echoed a long, trailing rumble that rattled Maggie's windows and my back molars.

As I sat waiting out the rain, I recalled reading somewhere that a car was the safest place to be in a thunderstorm. There was something about the rubber wheels grounding the car against electrical charge....

Well, screw that!

Upstairs in my apartment, my new computer was still plugged in. If it got toasted by lightning I may as well be dead, too.

I jumped out of the car and slammed the door behind me. Instantly, I was soaked to the skin in the deluge. I scrambled up the rickety stairs, fighting a vertical, monsoon-strength current. As I reached the top of the landing, I slipped and nearly did a split. Like a scene from a Charlie Chaplin movie, I grabbed ahold of a pole, pulled my legs back together and skittered to the small porch sheltering the front door.

Wiping rivulets of rain from my eyes, I fumbled the key into the lock, tumbled inside, did a swan dive across the floor and yanked the computer's plug out of the socket. About a half-second later, another bolt of lightning filled the apartment with angry, blue noise. The light over the kitchen stove went out. The microwave blurted a long, high-pitched, farewell bleep.

Great.

Still, it could have been worse. Much worse.

I got in the tub and peeled off my sopping clothes. After hanging them on the rod, I towel-dried my hair and slipped into what I'd dubbed my "house dress." It was a loose-fitting, blue shift I'd found at a thrift store for three bucks. I'd convinced myself it wasn't a moo-moo. I might've been middle aged, but I wasn't ready to give up yet.

My house dress was the feminine equivalent of a guy's t-shirt and sweats.

Fair was fair.

I stumbled to the kitchen, pulled a beer out of the dark fridge, and spent the next ten minutes playing hide-and-seek with my reading glasses. I finally caught them under a pile of unpaid bills on the tiny kitchen table. Fortified with beer and bifocals, I plopped on the living room rug, snuggled my back against the ugly old sofa, and dug further into the shoebox labeled 1945 to 1974.

By the storm-grey daylight filtering in through the window, I could just make out the pictures of Glad and Bobby Munch together. There was no fancy wedding photo. But given the era and the situation, I didn't expect to find one. There *was*, however, a picture of Glad with straight, shoulder-length blonde hair, looking pale but stunning in a matching royal blue jacket and skirt. She was standing next to Bobby Munch, who was in a light-blue suit and tie.

Bobby was a few inches shorter than Glad. A bit thick in the middle, he sported dark, nearly black hair and long, mutton-chop sideburns. Bobby might have been handsome, and even passed for a close relative of Elvis if not for one thing. His teeth. He was as buck-toothed as a road-flattened jackrabbit. The picture of Glad and him in their dress-up clothes appeared to have been taken in the generic lobby of a church or government building. Both Glad and Bobby looked more distracted than happy. There was no way of telling for sure what the occasion had been.

My mind went to thoughts of Glad as I had known her, so happy and at home with herself, sprawled out on her beach chair in her Gilligan hat and bug-eyed sunglasses. It was weird to see images of her looking so prim and proper and...*pinched*. I picked up a photo of her sitting at a picnic table wearing pink pedal pushers and a matching gingham top buttoned up to her neck. Another picture of her outside a white revival tent showed her in a plain, modest dress down to her knees, a sweater over her arms. In every photo she flashed a big, beautiful smile. But on closer inspection, all of her smiles looked identical—and her eyes didn't reflect a matching happiness.

They reflected something else.

Disappointment? Regret? No. It looked more like a faraway...*longing*.

By being with Bobby, free-spirited Glad had probably missed out on the hip, free-loving counter culture of the 1960s altogether. I could only imagine how bitter a pill it must have been for her to view that social revolution from within the cage of a forced marriage.

I put the photos back in their correct date slots and pulled out the only paper filed under 1974. It was a hand-written receipt from William N. Jonson to Gladys K. Munch for the transfer of title to a 1966 Minnie Winnie Winnebago. Clipped to the receipt was a picture of Glad at the beach, standing next to the RV in a bikini that would have made a Bond girl grind her own teeth to dust. Glad had bought the Minnie Winnie off Jonson for a cool hundred bucks. I could just imagine her wheeling that deal.

That guy never stood a chance!

The receipt for the RV was dated May 12, 1974. I was recording it in my notebook when the phone rang. It was Jorge. Apparently Lieutenant Foreman worked fast.

"Val, hola! I got some news. Glad's mom's maiden name was Eunice Thelma Alford. She married Roy Gerard Kinsey in 1939. You already know Glad was born April 24, 1945 at Hawesville Memorial in Kentucky. And the letter from Tony to Glad in care of Mrs. H. E. Wannabaker? Turns out she was the wife of Harold Earl Wannabaker. He owned the house on Coolidge Street until he died in 1992. The obit said he was laid to rest next to his beloved wife. So I guess that's a dead end."

"Sounds like it. Got anything else?"

"Jes. But you're not gonna like it. There was no record of a baby being born to Gladys Kinsey in 1963, 64 or 65 in Hawesville or any other hospital nearby."

"That's not good."

"No. But listen to this. Tom said when he was doing the search he noticed a lot of the records from 1964 were duplicates. He called the city's records department to ask why. They told Tom that all the Hawesville birth records for the last two months of 1964 had gotten lost. The records had to be recreated by hospital files or the original documents given to the parents."

"That's strange."

"Tom thought so, too. He told me to ask you if you knew anyone who would want to get rid of all the records of the baby's birth."

I could think of a few to start. Glad's parents? Tony's parents? Tony, perhaps? Maybe even Glad herself...? No, I couldn't believe that.

"Not off the bat, Jorge," I answered. "Thank Lieutenant Foreman for me. I may need a few more favors from him before this is through."

"Okay, Val. See you tomorrow?"

"Sure."

Jorge clicked off and I began to ponder the lieutenant's question. *Who had the most to lose from the birth of Glad's baby being made public?*

A mechanical sound jerked through the drooping air. Suddenly, everything electrical in my apartment coughed back to life. The ceiling fan began to spin anemically and the light above the stove flickered on. I padded into the kitchen to check the status of my microwave. Dead as a doornail.

Dang it.

After about twenty minutes, the monsoon rain subsided to a drizzle, then petered out completely. I hauled the dead microwave down the wobbly wooden stairs to one of the huge black trashcans that lined the grimy, red-brick alleyway. As I set it down beside the container, I could feel the steam already rising from the old clay bricks like the breath of an underground dragon. Even after a deluge, the respite from the summer heat never lasted long in St. Pete.

The shoulder-high lid on the waste bin was as big and round as a Hula Hoop. I hoisted it up and peeked inside to discover my microwave was not the only victim of the storm. I wrestled the bulky white box up the side of the trashcan to the lip and pushed it in. I watched it smash into a cheap plastic blender and an ancient metal toaster.

A sudden thought twisted through my mind, and I slammed the trashcan lid down with all my might. Another of Glad's lessons echoed in my head.

It didn't pay to get too attached to anything.

I climbed the stairs, grabbed another beer from the fridge and flopped onto the lumpy, old couch. I needed to organize all the information I'd discovered about Glad so far. I started with narrowing down the timeframe of possibility for Glad to have given birth. Tony's letter had been postmarked December 12. He had asked Glad if it was a boy or a girl. So chances were, the baby was already born by then, but not necessarily. The missing records had included November and December, so Glad's baby must have been born between November 1 and December 31, 1964, or it would still be in public records.

Since all the records had disappeared for both months, they must have gone missing at the end of December 1964 or early January 1965. Sometime during Christmas holidays through New Year's. With everybody potentially on vacation at the time, anyone could have taken the records. But why would they?

Tony had sent his letter to Glad in care of Mrs. Wannabaker. Why? Glad's parents had gone on vacation to Florida. Did they take the baby with them? Had they left Glad in the care of Ms.

Wannabaker? Was she some kind of midwife? Maybe the head of a place for unwed mothers? Did she work for an adoption agency? The hospital? Was she, herself, adopting Glad's child?

And what about this Mrs. D. B. Meyers, Glad's father's cousin in Tallahassee. The one Glad's parents were visiting when they died in the car crash. Could she know something?

Then there was Tony's family. It was crystal clear they weren't thrilled with the situation. They'd sent Tony off to boarding school. Had *they* done something with the records? Maybe even with the baby? Tony had mentioned his father had influence over the faculty. Was he a big shot in politics or high society? That would offer some pretty good motivation for a cover-up....

It was all getting way too confusing, with more loose ends than a bowl of spaghetti. I needed someone used to dealing with multiple motives and evidence. Maybe it was time for Jorge to come out of retirement. Or call for backup. I closed my notebook and rubbed my eyes. It was *definitely* TNT time. I hauled myself up from the couch and headed for the fridge.

I WAS AT THE BEACH with Glad. The sun hung lemon-yellow in a crazy purple-blue sky. Glad's beer can glinted a full spectrum of rainbow colors as we raised our beers to toast. The tinny clink of the aluminum cans morphed into laughter as a boy around four years old wandered by us, a pile of seashells in each hand. He dropped one shell. As he bent over to pick it up, two more fell out of his overstuffed palms. He tried to pick those up, and even more shells tumbled loose from his grip. Glad thought the whole thing was hilarious.

"See? It ain't good to hold on to too much," she said. Glad cackled and sat back in her pink lounge chair. "After a while, memories can get to be like elephants, Val. Better to forget 'em than tote their heavy memories around."

"How can you forget when there's so much pain attached?" I asked.

Glad laughed and took a swig of beer. "Them's the best ones to forget. What'cha winnin' by holding on?"

"People should suffer for what they do to others."

"Have it your way, kiddo. So who's doin' the sufferin'?"

"Me, okay? You happy?"

"Yes, I'm happy," she said, beaming at me through smeary red lips. "Are you?"

I started to speak, but a man came running up the beach with a machinegun, firing at random. He looked right at me and fired. Bam! Bam! Bam!

The sound of gunfire startled me awake.

Bam! Bam! Bam! The shots came in rapid fire, like an automatic weapon.

"What the...?" I grumbled, trying to kick-start my tipsy brain. I ducked my head and crawled off the couch.

Bam! Bam!

I snuck a peek through the blinds.

Boom! Bam! Bam. Bam!

Flashes of color lit up the sky, taking eerie snapshots of the Vinoy Hotel's Greek temple of a tower. The rush of adrenaline finally kicked my brain into gear.

Ah! Fireworks.

I had totally forgotten it was the Fourth of July. I sat up and sighed, then debated whether to walk the two blocks to the park for a better view of our fine nation's Independence Day celebration.

Naw.

I lay back on the ugly couch and scratched my flabby stomach. I wondered if, somewhere out there, Glad's son or daughter was celebrating, too.

I snuggled into the sofa and thought about Glad and all the things I'd been forced to let go of in the last year, including her. It was a long list. But it was just a postscript, really. Since I'd popped out of my mother's womb I'd created three, maybe four separate lives already. And I'd wiped the slate clean of each of them like yesterday's blackboard lesson.

Glad was right. I *had* learned a lot. And each life had had its value, for sure.

But boiled down to its essence, I had almost nothing to show for all that living in terms of what could be seen with the naked eye. What had proven worth holding onto so far in my four-and-a-half decades of life had been precious little indeed.

Geez. Maybe that was the whole point.

Chapter Fourteen

The next morning, I was still spooning with my melancholy memories. I was supposed to meet Jorge and Lieutenant Foreman at Caddy's at 8 a.m. The clock said I had half an hour to drag my butt out the door. I showered and pulled on my official Florida business attire: flip-flops, a one-piece, tropical-print bathing suit and an aqua skirt that fell mid-thigh. I padded to the kitchen to blow a kiss to my boyfriend, Mr. Coffee.

"Hey, I love you dude, but variety is the spice of life," I said to my stoic companion. "Just wanted you to know your services are not required today. I'll be cheating on you with some strange restaurant brew."

Great. Now I'm talking to appliances. I really need to get out more....

THE DRIVE TO CADDY'S was a straight shot west down Central Avenue that took about twenty minutes. Along the way, I sat back and smiled at the puffy, pink clouds dissipating in the soft, morning sky. Like a pile of fluffy pillows, they offered a soft start to the day, and for the first time in a long while, I felt appreciated and loved by some all-knowing source. A giddy joy traced across my heart. I stepped on the gas. Maggie's dual glass-packs roared out like thunderous applause.

The fossilized shells that comprised Caddy's parking lot made a breakfast-cereal crunch under my tires as I slung Maggie into a space. I spotted Jorge and Lieutenant Foreman standing together by a picnic table in the sand. Each held a cup of coffee in their hands, the sight of which made my stomach gurgle with envy. Jorge spied me and we exchanged quick waves. I studied the men as I walked through the lot in their direction. The sun hung midway in the sky like a melty, red-rubber ball. The friendly pink clouds were gone, and I could smell the salt of the Gulf of Mexico just a hundred yards away.

Lieutenant Foreman was dressed in a clean, white muscle tee and blue surfing shorts. Definitely off-duty attire. He looked shockingly shiny and brand-new compared to the shorter, slump-shouldered Jorge in his faded Hawaiian shirt and fraying, grey cut-offs. The contrast made me study the cop with fresh eyes. He was actually pretty darn hot!

"Nice to see you again, Val," Lieutenant Foreman said. "I've never seen you in a bathing suit before."

"I have," said Jorge. His eyes studied the sand. "Plenty of times."

"Lucky you," the cute cop said, never taking his sea-green eyes off me.

Eye contact with the lieutenant sent a jolt of surprise through me, mixed with something I wasn't able to define. I'd be the first to admit that life had whittled me into more of a realist than a romantic. I was in pretty decent shape, if you didn't count my upper arms. And considering my age, I garnered my share of attention from men, albeit most of it unwanted.

"Thanks for coming out, Lieutenant Foreman," I said, trying hard to quit making a mental inventory of my body parts. "Why don't we go for a walk on the beach? I'm afraid Winky might show up if we stay here."

"Don't chew worry, Val," Jorge said, bobbing his head. "Goober's got babysitting duty this morning."

"Oh. Great!" I said, genuinely relieved. "So, should we sit down or should we walk?"

"My vote is for a walk," said the cop. "Please, call me Tom."

"Okay, Tom. Looks like you get out to the beach a bit," I said as the three of us twist-stepped our way through the sugary sand toward the gulf. Tom's blond hair shone golden in the sun. His smooth skin was a rich, golden brown. Even the hair on his legs and arms was sun-bleached to a glimmering gold.

"Being a native, it's in my blood," he said. His grin activated a fine web of crinkles at the corners of his eyes and mouth.

"Yeah. Tom's a native just like us," said Jorge. He arched his thick, black eyebrows and gave me a rare look directly in the eye.

"Go figure," I said. "Three Florida natives in a row. Do we get eggroll with that?"

Tom flashed me a grin, then turned to scan the shoreline up and down. The tide was coming in. Lazy waves lapped at the sand, making tentative grabs at the coquina and cat's paw shells stranded by last night's high tide. "Looks like another perfect day in paradise."

"Except for the ninety-nine percent humidity," I replied as the first trickle of sweat worked its way down the center of my back. "I think I'll test the waters."

"Let me hold your shoes," Tom offered.

Tom took my flip-flops and our fingers touched briefly, sending a mild tingle up my arm. The sight of this handsome man holding my shoes suddenly seemed very personal. Intimate even. I probably would have blushed if I could've remembered how. I wiggled out of my skirt and he held that, too, making something inside me squirm. I sucked in my gut and put my toes in the warm gulf waters.

Distracted by vanity, suddenly I was sidelined by a blast of seawater from my left. It soaked me from my neck to my waist, causing me to abandon my held-in breath with a gasp.

I looked to my left. Tom and Jorge were laughing at the culprit. A boy about three years old stood motionless in the water a few feet away. He stared at me wide-eyed, mouth open, still clutching the empty plastic pail he'd used to douse my fledgling flame. I fished around and found a smile for the boy.

"What's your name?" I asked.

"Miguel," he answered shyly. Then he dropped his pail and ran through foamy seawater in the direction of a Hispanic woman and a dark-haired girl who looked to be about six. They were both wading their way toward shore. "Momma, Momma!" he yelled.

"No, no Miguel!" the woman cried. She looked up at me. "So sorry!"

"It's okay," I replied.

"Kids. They're a blessing and a curse," the woman said.

I watched Jorge flinch at the woman's words, then lower his eyes to the sand. The woman herded her brood up the beach toward a big blue umbrella. Jorge watched them for a moment, then said, "Uh, I don't feel so good. You guys go on without me. I'll see you back at Caddy's."

"Are you sure?" I asked.

"Jes. I think I jus' need a beer or something."

Jorge didn't wait for a reply. He turned sharply and walked back toward the beach bar, head down, shoulders slumped.

"Okay, see you soon," I called after him, trying not to sound sympathetic. Tom and I turned back toward the turquoise water and walked in silence along the shore for a minute.

"He and I used to be partners, you know," Tom said, breaking the quiet tension between us. "I've never seen anyone so devastated as he was when he lost his family. He's still just a fraction of the person I used to know."

"A fraction. That's sad. Tell me, where do our missing pieces go?"

Tom stopped walking and looked me in the eyes. "That's a darn good question. I wish I knew the answer."

"Me too."

His eyes studied my soul for a moment, then shifted back to this mortal plane. "I guess we better stick to questions we can answer, Val. What have you got for me so far?"

"Just a bunch of jumbled up theories, mostly. With the Hawesville records missing, I'm not a hundred percent sure Glad even had a child, or, if she did, that it survived."

"What does your gut say?"

"My gut?"

"Yes. In my line of work, I've learned that facts can only get you so far. You'd be surprised how often it's intuition—a gut feeling—that fills in the missing pieces, connects the dots, and solves the case."

I stopped walking and looked at Tom, incredulous. "Really?"

Tom stopped, too. He turned to face me, and the wind off the gulf fluttered his golden bangs over his forehead. "Yes, really. I'm going to ask you a question, Val. Don't think about the answer. Just let yourself kind of relax and float instead. Then say the first thing that bubbles up from your throat. Ready?"

"Uh...I guess."

"Close your eyes." He reached toward me and removed my sunglasses, then slid them into his shorts pocket. He touched his fingertips to my cheeks, then gently placed his thumbs on my eyelids to close them. Hot electricity shot through my body.

"So Val, did Tony and Glad have a baby?"

I shivered. "Yes," I heard my mouth say.

"And did it survive?"

"Yes," formed on my lips again.

Spooky.

"And is it still alive?"

Goosebumps broke out on my arms. "Yes!"

"Boy or girl?"

I overthought it and the tingly feeling evaporated. My gut quit on me. I frowned. "I don't know."

"No worries," he said gently.

I opened my eyes just in time to see Tom wink at me. He pulled my sunglasses out of his pocket and handed them back to me. They were warm from his body heat.

"How about we head back? I don't want to leave Jorge alone too long," he said.

I nodded in agreement. We turned and began the walk back toward Caddy's. It was barely nine in the morning and the sun was already hot enough to make me sweat without exertion. At least, I thought it was the sun. I watched the sun do its diamond shimmy show with the gulf, and listened as the seagulls heckled out their gratitude for another gorgeous morning.

For some reason, I felt so light I worried I might lift off and float away. Tom's deep voice brought me back down to Earth.

"So, now that we feel pretty sure they had a baby, Val, do you think Tony or Glad would have wanted to harm the child, or get rid of it?"

My gut reaction was instant. "No! In my heart of hearts, I have to say no, Tom. The Glad I knew...I just can't see her being capable of that. And based on Tony's letter to her back then, I don't think he wanted anything bad to happen to her or the baby either. You saw Tony's house. He never let go of anything. He couldn't even bear to throw garbage away."

"Fair enough, Val. But hoarding is a sign of psychological trauma. It can stem from a big loss...or a guilty conscience."

I thought about Tom's words as I watched a black-backed skimmer fly by. It maneuvered so close to the water that its blood-orange bottom mandible touched the surface and made a shallow rivulet in the calm, lazy gulf.

"I'm sure that's true, Tom. But when they died, Glad and Tony were living together as a couple. I just can't see her staying with a man who would take her baby from her. She always talked to me about letting go and forgiving as the way to freedom. I'm sure she could have let go of hating the people who did this to her. But I don't think she'd subject herself to the punishment of living with one of them. She wasn't into self-flagellation."

"Just self-medication."

I smiled and shrugged. "Hey, nobody's perfect."

"But some are more perfect than others." Tom's hypnotic green eyes slowly traced my body, beginning with my toes. When they reached my face, they settled in for a long look into my brown eyes, making me sweat a little more. Tom seemed to sense my discomfort and abruptly switched gears. "So, have you found a marriage certificate for Tony and Glad in all that shoebox stuff?"

"No. Not yet. Is that important?"

"For inheritance rights it is. But if they lived together for more than seven years in Florida, she could be considered his common-law wife whether they were married or not."

"For some reason they kept their relationship secret, Tom. From the people at Caddy's, anyway. I don't know if anybody else knew they were together. Could you check public records for a marriage certificate?"

"Sure."

"In the meantime, I'll check the shoebox files. If I can't find a certificate, maybe there'll be wedding pictures, or something else that might prove how long they lived together."

"Okay. But make it quick, Val. We need to return all that stuff to Tony's house by tomorrow."

"Why tomorrow?"

"Tony's memorial service is tomorrow. So far, nobody's turned up to make a claim on his estate. But that could change at any moment. I think it would be prudent to have everything back in its proper place. It's my neck on the line, you know."

"Yes. I know. And I'm grateful, Tom."

I smiled at him softly. He returned the favor.

"You think Tony's relatives might show up at his house?" I asked.

"It could happen. Usually, the only ones that snoop around the property are the ones named in the will. Or ones who hope they are."

"The newspaper article said that one person was named as sole heir. Thelma G. Goldrich."

"What's the "G" stand for?"

My eyebrows scrunched together. "That's what I was hoping you could tell me."

"Ah." Tom nodded and turned toward me with a wry smile on his lips. "I'll see what I can do. You going to Tony's ceremony tomorrow?"

"Yes."

"I'll see you there, then."

"Okay."

As we approached Caddy's, Jorge was at a picnic table drinking beer and talking to himself. As we drew closer, I realized that he was actually conversing with a couple of brown lizards, another subset of Florida's burgeoning transplant population. Descendants of stowaways that arrived from Cuba decades ago without their papers, the little reptiles had quickly made themselves at home, and now counted in their millions from Tampa southward.

The little lizards looked like miniature dinosaurs as they perched on the table, licking precious moisture from a forgotten chunk of watermelon.

"Hey Jorge," I said.

He looked up from the lizards and smiled. "Nature, Val!"

"I think I'll have a beer with my buddy," Tom said, secreting me a sympathetic glance. "Care to join us?"

"No thanks. I've got work to do. Shoeboxes and all. What time is the ceremony tomorrow for Tony?"

"Shix aclack," Jorge slurred, his drunken head cocked sideways, supported by the palm of his hand.

"Okay, then. You guys have fun."

I mouthed the words, "thank you," to Tom. He just smiled at me and shrugged.

"See you tomorrow," was all he said.

I STEPPED OUT OF THE shower and slathered some coconut oil moisturizer on my sunburned shoulders. Without the protection of a strong sunscreen, the sun's intense rays had turned my olive tan to ripe pink in under an hour. I grabbed the last beer out of the fridge, then cut apart each of the circles of opaque plastic that had held the six cans together. I read somewhere that those things floated, and could loop around the necks of birds and turtles, choking them to death. More bad karma was something I didn't want or need.

I tossed the cut-up plastic into the recycling bin. It was time to get to work.

I flopped on the couch and peeled back the tape on the second shoebox labeled 1974 to 1985. It was empty.

Weird. Why was the stuff for those years missing?

With no answers at hand, I turned my attention to the box Jorge had been looking through in the bedroom at Tony's place. It was labeled 1986 to 2009.

The first thing under 1986 was a dried-up pink rose, taped together with some brown, crumbly baby's breath. In better days, it had been either a corsage or a boutonniere. Next was a photo of an older, happy Glad in a long, pastel, Hawaiian-print dress. Tony stood next to her, looking proud in white pants and a Hawaiian shirt that matched Glad's dress. Both were barefoot, standing in sand at a beach. Then I noticed a pink rose in Glad's hair. This had obviously been a special occasion for them. A wedding, perhaps? Or maybe someone else's? The back read simply, October 7, 1989.

The rest of the box was full of vacation mementos and photos. Snapshots of Tony and Glad together, looking happy somewhere in the Southwest. One on a ferry. One in front of a giant redwood tree. The photos of them in Hawaii in 1998 that Jorge had spoken about. The little yellow and blue drink umbrellas. A Route 66 refrigerator magnet. A cruise ship luggage tag. A paper napkin from a restaurant in Oregon.

Strangely, not a single picture had anyone else in it besides Glad and Tony. Didn't they have any friends or relatives? Or did they keep their relationship a secret from everyone? Maybe it was just a coincidence, and these were just normal "couples" pictures. They were mostly travel photos, after all.

I was putting the photographs back in the shoebox when a green glint from the bottom of the box caught my eye. I turned the box over. A little piece of jewelry about a half-inch long fell into my hand. It was a silver oval about the size and shape of a pinkie nail. Tiny green stones dotted the entire front surface of the oval. From a rough edge, I could tell it must have broken off a larger piece. A brooch or a necklace charm, perhaps? I couldn't be sure. But it was in the box, so it must have meant something important to Glad. Why else would she have held on to it? Unless perhaps it was just another travel memento....

The phone rang. It was Tom. "Hey Val. Any luck with the marriage certificate?"

"No. Just the one for Bobby. But I think there's plenty of evidence to show that Glad and Tony had been together for more than seven years. Probably since the late 1980s."

"What kind of evidence?"

"Photos, mostly. One even looks like it could be an informal wedding. On a beach in 1989."

"Interesting. It'll take a few days to check public marriage records. In the meantime, I ran the name Thelma G. Goldrich through the DMV database."

"Yeah? And?"

"I got three hits."

"Any in Kentucky?"

"No."

"Any born between 1963 and 1965?"

"Yes. All three, actually. But Val, we don't even know if this Thelma person named in the will is Glad's child. Tony could have left his estate to anyone. It's more likely Thelma G. Goldrich is a niece or a cousin of Tony's, not their long-lost love child."

"Crap. You're right," I said, suddenly deflated. "I really hadn't considered that. I guess I was just hoping that it would be that simple."

"If it was, don't you think Glad and Tony would have found her themselves?"

"Maybe they did. Maybe.... Hey! You said *her!*"

"What?"

"You said they would have found *her* themselves."

"Yeah. I guess I did."

"Does that mean you think their child is a girl?"

"One better. It means *my gut* is telling me she is. See? There I go again. She."

"I hope you're right, Tom. I'd like their child to be a girl. A woman just like Glad. The world could use more people like her."

"I didn't know Glad myself, Val. But if you vouch for her, that's good enough for me. See you tomorrow, then?"

"Yes, tomorrow. Goodnight Tom."

"Goodnight Val."

I hung up the phone and drifted off to sleep on the couch, the gentle whisper of Tom's "Goodnight Val," tickling my ear and making my lips curl upward.

Chapter Fifteen

The memorial for "garbage man" Tony was to be held at Caddy's that afternoon, so I skipped my morning beach ritual. I couldn't afford the double sun exposure—or the double drive out to Sunset Beach. Shabby Maggie sucked down the go-juice to the tune of twelve miles to a gallon—on a good day, going downhill. So I traded a beach stroll for my alternate walking route, the downtown waterfront.

I stepped outside at 6 a.m. sharp. The air was already as wet and stale as a day-old puddle of beer. Not a flicker of a breeze. The moist air clung to my body thick and soggy, like a wet hamburger bun.

I resigned myself to becoming drenched in sweat and power-walked along the sidewalk skirting Beach Drive. At Seventh Avenue, I crossed the street by the Episcopal Church and headed east toward Tampa Bay. Immediately, my nose was assaulted by the smell of crap from the dog park, still a full city block away. It hung in the air like a portent of some giant pile of crap to come.

When I reached the water and saw the sky over the bay, I knew this morning's sunrise was going to be something special. An inverted pyramid of creamy white shone like a searchlight from the water's horizon line. Reaching heavenward, the off-white cone widened to encompass half the sky before it dissipated into the misty blue of the stratosphere. In the center, rectangular clouds of differing heights formed skyscrapers in a mock cityscape backdrop. The overall effect was one of a city rising from beneath a spotlight under the sea.

Amazing!

As I walked along the open water, the sun began to rise behind the blue-grey cloud-buildings, backlighting them with a molten orange crust of fire. It was as if a fantastic stage was being set for a fabulous day to come.

I stopped and drank in the view for a moment, then rounded the bend at Coffee Pot Bayou. I stretched my legs on a park bench by Eighteenth Avenue, my halfway mark. As I did, a brown pelican glided past, mere inches from the water, suspended by some unknown anti-gravitational force. I smiled again and turned toward the direction of my apartment, my thoughts on Glad...and a double-espresso cappuccino.

I GUESS LIKE EVERY other material thing in this world, legal documents didn't hold much weight with Glad. After looking through her treasured mementos, I had precious little to connect her with anyone but Bobby and Tony. I still wasn't even sure of her last name. Was it her maiden name, Kinsey? Her married name, Munch? Or had she married Tony Goldrich and taken his name? I looked at my notes. Besides Thelma G. Goldrich, I had only two other names to work with: Mrs. D. B. Meyers of Tallahassee and Mrs. Harold Earl Wannabaker of Hawesville, KY. Actually, there was a third, if I counted Wallace Jonson who sold Glad the RV.

Time was running out. I had to give Glad's boxes back today, and the thought made my heart hurt. I flopped onto my crappy couch and took a final glance through the photos in the shoeboxes. I made a mental picture of Glad in her Easter dress. Glad in a bikini next to her RV. Glad with a rose in her hair standing next to Tony at the beach.

I couldn't bear to look at the photo of Glad holding her baby again, so I didn't. I wanted to remember her happy, like she was when I had known her. I put the photos back in their proper places and started to tape the boxes shut, but my apartment got all blurry and my heart began to ache like a sore tooth.

Sorting through Glad's lifetime of memories had hit me hard. Harder, even, than her farewell service had. The stolen glimpses into her life had become a very private affair between me and Glad. I lined up the boxes beside me on the couch. They looked like three little coffins. I sucked in a breath.

Coffins! Oh my word! The contents of these boxes aren't just a chronological measure of years. No. Like me, Glad had segmented her time on this Earth into separate and distinct lives!

Box one, lifetime one, spanned from 1945 to 1974. From her birth until she left Bobby. Box two, lifetime two, was a mystery that stretched from 1974 to 1986. She'd bought the Minnie Winnie in '74 and, as far as I could tell, she'd lived the simple, quiet life of a beach bum. Box three, lifetime three, began when she hooked up with Tony again, and lasted until the day she died. A little coffin for each of her three lives.

Should there be a fourth one for her child?

The grievous thought grabbed me by the throat and squeezed. I hugged the shoeboxes to me like long, lost children. Huge, hot tears leapt from my eyes, hitting the boxes with hollow, drum-like thuds.

This was the last time I would ever be this close to Glad. And it hurt like hell to know it.

I'D PROMISED THE STOOGES I would meet them at Caddy's an hour before Tony's ceremony. My eyes were still puffy and I was in no mood for socializing. But I didn't have much choice. I had to hand over Glad's boxes to Tom. I'd put them in a pretty gift bag covered with images of daisies.

No garbage bag this time for my precious Glad.

I hit the gas and Maggie hummed west along First Avenue North toward the beach. Along the way, I watched the eclectic parade of modest homes file past, mostly wooden cottages with open front porches and a few stucco Spanish revivals thrown in the mix. Over the years, some had been converted to offices for lawyers, accountants and ad agencies. Most, though, were still private residences made urban by St. Pete's rapid growth spurts. As I drove the seven miles from downtown to the beach, the facades of the structures slipped from posh to poor, then back to posh again.

Crossing the bridge over the Intracoastal Waterway put an end to the historic architecture tour. I didn't mind. The sparkling water lightened my mood, and I blew out a calming sigh. By the time I passed Treasure Island's kitschy pirate mascot and his booty chest full of oranges, I was feeling good enough to smile again.

Decked out in a new white sundress that accentuated my figure, I'd pulled out most of the stops to look my best today. I'd told myself it was out of respect for Tony, but I knew that was a lie. Tom would be here to take the boxes, and I'd glammed up for him.

God help me, I was actually wearing foundation makeup!

I hoped Tom would get here before my mascara melted. I glanced in the rearview mirror.

Too late.

"It's Val Pal!" shouted beer-bellied Winky from his perch on a bar stool adjacent to the porch railing that framed Caddy's beach bar. Winky was also decked out in his finest—the same blue, button-up shirt he'd worn at Glad's service, but with shorts this time. He raised his beer can in my direction and belted out an ear-piercing wolf whistle. "Nice gams, Val!"

"Nice shirt, Winky," I replied.

"What, this old thing?" Winky grinned, looked down and tugged on the front of his shirt with his free hand. His inattention caused him to slosh beer down the side of his shorts.

"Where's the rest of the gang?" I asked.

"Huh?" Winky swatted at the wet spot on his shorts, as if that would make it go away.

"Goober and Jorge."

"Oh. In the john. But Tom's right behind you."

A shiver ran up my spine. I turned around and smiled at the blond cop. "Hey, Tom."

"Hi, Val."

Tom was dressed in a blue button-down shirt, too, but beyond that, the two men bore no resemblance whatsoever. For starters, Tom's shirt was ironed. In St. Pete, a handsome man in an ironed shirt was almost as rare a sighting as the mythical skunk ape. I swooned a little.

"I've got the boxes in the car," I fumbled.

"Okay. Should we make the transfer now?" Tom shot me a devilishly crooked smile.

"Sure. I just want to step into the ladies' room for a minute."

"What boxes y'all talkin' about?" Winky hollered, already halfway to tispy-town.

"Official business," Tom said, saving me from having to come up with a lie.

Winky looked us up and down suspiciously. "Looks purty official to me."

Tom turned back to face me and raised his eyebrows an inch. I shrugged and headed toward the restrooms. Unfortunately, the two oval mirrors that hung in the ladies' room at Caddy's weren't into telling nice lies. My mascara had morphed into black, under-eye crescents reminiscent of an NFL quarterback's. I cringed at the thought that Tom had seen me that way.

"Aw, hell!" I said, and reached for a paper towel.

"Watch your mouth!" said a woman in the handicapped stall.

"Sorry," I replied.

The door to the stall flew open as if it had been kicked by a mule. A short woman as round as a bowling ball waddled out. She studied me for a brief second and said, "Yep, I'd say that about sums it up."

"Excuse me?" I asked, dabbing at my eyes and catching glimpses of her reflection in the mirror. The woman had the round head and jowly scowl of a French bulldog. Her white hair was secured in a ponytail pulled so tight to her scalp that at first glance she appeared bald. Her long, albino locks continued to her waist, pinched tight in short sections, making the three-foot-long ponytail resemble a string of white sausages hanging over a fat, rounded shoulder.

"Sorry. Yep, I'd say that sums up what *you* are." The woman sneered back at me in the mirror. Her beady eyes were aflame with menace.

Caught totally off guard, my mind raced to understand her meaning. In the South, to be called "sorry" was to be labeled as being worthless. Surely that wasn't what I'd just heard from this stranger?

"I don't understand," I said, "I...."

"Yeah, women like you never do," she spat. She turned her nose up like she smelled a fart. "You're Tony's girlfriend, aren't you."

It was more an accusation than a question.

"What?"

"I know your kind, tramp. Always lookin' for a man to latch on to. Well, you can forget it. You ain't gettin' a dime of Tony's money."

Oh, no she didn't!

That woman had put her fat foot on my last nerve.

"I'm not after Tony's money," I hissed. "And you'd better not be either, you witch." I threw my mascara-stained paper towel in the waste bin and stormed out the door. The bowling-ball shaped battle-axe waddled after me.

"I won't be havin' a tramp like you insult me!" she screeched.

I whipped around on my heels, and was startled to see her red, bulldog face just inches from my own. "Who the hell do you think you are?" I asked.

"I'm Tony's *wife*," she said as her fist smashed into my face.

The air around me turned red, then black, and I felt myself falling into a hole in the floor.

Chapter Sixteen

I cracked open my right eye. I was lying sort of halfway on the floor of Caddy's restaurant. Tom was on the floor with me, his back up against a wall. He'd pulled me to his chest and was holding my head up. His legs were sprawled out on the concrete beside mine as he staunched my bloody nose with a handkerchief.

I'd fantasized about being in Tom's arms. This scenario wasn't exactly what I'd pictured.

"Wad happened?" I asked, and wriggled around to look up at Tom's face.

"Seems the jealous wife turned up." He dabbed tenderly at my throbbing nose with the handkerchief. "Be still for a minute. You okay?"

The hair on the top of my head stood up. "His *wife*? The paper sed his wife wad dead!"

"Newspapers have been known to be inaccurate. Besides, they may have meant Glad."

I tried to sit up a bit more. The movement made my nose pulse with pain.

"Be still!" Tom commanded again, then softened his voice. "Try to think of something else right now. Like maybe *yourself?*"

I grabbed the handkerchief from Tom's hand. "I'm fine. But I'll be darned if I'm going to let that horrible woman get her hands on Glad's money. It just wouldn't be right!"

Tom laughed. "You're a feisty one! Why do you care?"

I stopped being angry for a second and cocked my head. "I don't know. I...I just *do!*"

"Okay, fair enough. Can you stand up?"

"I think so."

Tom put his hands on my waist and hoisted me to my feet. My new sundress looked like a bloody butcher's apron.

So much for beachside glamour.

The three stooges were sitting at a table six feet away, watching intently from their front-row seats.

"There she is, back on her feet!" Goober quipped. He took off his sunglasses and put up his dukes. "Ready for round two?"

"Val, you look like one a them there zombie brides on TV," Winky said, shaking his head.

Jorge shoved an elbow in Winky's ribs. "She's beautiful. She's always beautiful." He smiled at me, then quickly looked down at his beer.

"Well, compared to that other one, sure," Winky said. "That old woman's uglier 'n' a box a chicken turds."

I laughed, causing my nose to explode with fresh pain. I winced and hobbled over to join the gang. Tom helped me onto a stool. I grabbed a handful of paper towels from a roll on the table and handed the cop back his gooey, blood-soaked hanky. He took it without so much as a flinch.

"So, where did Godzilla go?" I asked, looking around.

"One of my guys is questioning her now," Tom said. He pointed a finger at the parking lot. "I figured it would be better if I stayed out of it."

I nodded and looked over at the car lot. Bulldog Woman was shaking her fat finger in a black cop's face. The cop had his hand on his thigh. Probably where he kept his pepper spray. I secretly hoped he found grounds to hose her with it.

"Lookit that idjit," Winky said. "Gaul-dang it, I think Tony would a married *me* before he got hitched to that ol' buffalo bag."

"Is she really Tony's wife?" I asked, looking over at Tom.

"Who knows at this point," Tom replied. "And I've got some more news that doesn't look good for the home team."

"What?"

Tom reached in his breast pocket and pulled out a small notebook. He thumbed through it. "We ran Glad's name through public marriage records and got a hit. Actually, we got two hits. Glad was married to Tony Goldrich in 1989. But before that, she was married to a guy named Bobby Munch."

"Yeah, we knew that," I said, daubing my nose.

"*I* didn't know it!" Winky yelled. His eyes darted around suspiciously at the four of us.

"The problem is," Tom continued, "there's no record of the Munch's ever getting a divorce. So legally, Glad's marriage to Tony isn't valid."

"Crap!" I said.

"Unless Bobby died before she married Tony," Jorge said. Surprised, we all turned to face the shy Hispanic as if he were a talking cat.

"Right! Good thinking, partner!" Tom beamed at his old friend. "But here's the thing, Bobby Munch was convicted of felony assault in 1975. While he was in there, the church he'd been working with added embezzlement to his charges. All together, he did twelve years in Apalachicola Correctional Institution. He got out in 1987 and disappeared. He hasn't been heard from since."

"So unless we can prove Glad divorced Bobby or he died before she married Tony, that bulldog-faced witch over there might get her paws on Tony's estate?" Goober asked.

"I've seen stranger, more unjust things happen," Tom said.

Goober whistled and shook his brown, peanut-shaped head.

"But none of that matters if we find Tony's heir," I said, touching my swollen nose tentatively. "The one in his will. Thelma G. Goldrich."

"That's the other fly in this ointment," said Tom.

"What do you mean?"

Tom hitched a thumb in the direction of the parking lot where Bulldog Woman was still arguing with the cop.

"That woman over there with the mean right hook? Her name is Thelma G. Goldrich."

Chapter Seventeen

How could a day that had started with so much promise turn to crap so quickly? I stared at my reflection in the bathroom mirror. My nose looked like an overripe peach. My front right tooth was loose, but still hanging in there. Thankfully, my lip wasn't busted.

Count your blessings. That's what Glad would say. God, I wish she was here to tell me what to do next.

I'd missed Tony's memorial service. I figured I was more of a sideshow than a help with my big fat nose and bloody dress. But more than that, I couldn't bear the sight of that smirking Bulldog Woman's face for another second. After the cops were done with her, she'd made a beeline right toward me. Goober and Jorge had kept her at bay long enough for Tom to walk me out to my car so I could make my escape. Following Tom's advice, I'd decided not to press charges...for now. Who knows? Maybe she'd wanted to thank me. But from the evil, self-satisfied grin on her face, I seriously doubted it.

I was back at my apartment, alone again, without even so much as Glad's boxes to keep me company. When I'd handed them over to Tom, my heart had begun to throb worse than my nose. Tom had wanted to drive me home, but I'd insisted on going alone.

To tell the truth, I'd felt ready to burst into a million pieces. A torrent of emotions had swirled around inside me like a tropical storm. Sadness. Anger. Embarrassment. Fear. I wasn't sure which was going to get me first, but I knew a good cry was coming down on me like a bad case of swine flu. I'd managed to make it home and inside the door before the flood hit. But then I let the dam burst.

I fell face-first onto my ratty old couch and cried until I passed out.

BUSTED NOSE. BROKEN dreams. A ruined dress bought with money I couldn't afford to waste. And worst of all, I'd been made a fool of in front of just about everybody who meant a darn to me. My phone buzzed. It was Tom. I sat up on the couch and debated whether to answer. Then I figured, what the hell. Time wasn't going to heal this wound anytime soon.

"Hi, Tom."

"Hey, Victory Val."

"Ha ha," I said, unamused.

"You made it home okay, I see."

"Yes. You should have seen the looks I got, too. A woman in a convertible wearing a bloody white dress. Some idiot actually asked me if I was going to a Halloween party. It's July, for crying out loud."

"I've learned to never underestimate the stupidity of the general public."

I snickered, then winced from the pain shooting through my nose.

"Okay, enough of that. I thought you could use some good news, Val."

"That would be brilliant."

"It turns out Bulldog Breath is not Thelma G. Goldrich. She's G. Thelma Goldrich."

"So?"

"That may be enough to delay her claim on Tony's estate."

"Oh," I said without enthusiasm.

"I know it's not much, but it could buy us some time with the lawyers. Especially if we can come up with a reasonable doubt that Tony's house and stuff really belongs to someone else."

"How much time?"

"I don't know. But we have to do something fast. I caught her snooping around Tony's house when I went to put the boxes back."

"What!" My blood pressure soared and pounded on my nose.

"I was in uniform. I don't think she recognized me. I told her the house was under surveillance and that no one was allowed on the property without a court order."

"Is that true?"

"Technically, no."

"You lied?"

"It was for a good cause. Besides, it's *kind* of true. If there *is* another heir, she has no business poking around the place. I'm really starting to dislike this woman as much as you, Val. It's obvious she's no Miss Congeniality. But why do you seem so sure she isn't Tony's real heir?"

"Tom, you saw her in action! I can't imagine Tony leaving that woman a pile of his own excrement, much less his estate! If I was him, I'd have burned the place down before I gave it to her!"

"Since you put it so eloquently, I'll concede your point, Val. But the slight name difference could have just been a clerical error. Do you really think Glad and Tony's child could be this mysterious Thelma G. Goldrich?"

"Yes."

"Why?"

"Let's just say I have a gut feeling."

I heard Tom blow a sharp breath through his nose. "I guess that just leaves one option."

"What's that?"

"We've got to find Thelma G. Goldrich, and fast."

"No crap, Sherlock. Got any ideas?"

Tom laughed. "We can start with the three hits that came up on the DMV."

"But Tom, if Glad's baby was adopted, it might not even have that name."

"I know, Val. But it's all we've got at the moment. It's still possible that one of them is the heir. We might as well start with the obvious and rule things out from there. And, like I said, if we're going to put Bulldog Woman on a leash, we need to throw a bone into the works, and pronto."

"Now look who's being eloquent."

"What can I say, you bring out the best in me."

A tingly feeling shot through me.

Tom and I were flirting!

It was time to slide into my usual motif operandi and set about sabotaging myself. "Me, bring out someone's best? That's a first!" I snorted.

"I guess you just never barked up the right tree before."

"So now I'm a dog, too?"

Please, please, shut the hell up, Val!

"That's not what I meant...."

"All right, enough with the canine crap. How do we get these other Thelmas into the catfight?"

"So, now we're into cats, are we?"

"Meow."

God, I'm such a jerk!

"I'd say we need to call these women and tell them they may be heir to a fortune. Whether it's true or not, who knows. But that ought to get their attention."

The last comment did it. Tom was back to business.

Satisfied with yourself, Val?

"I guess all we need now are the phone numbers, Tom."

"I'm on it."

"Call me when you've got them. I'll do the dirty work."

"Okay."

"And Tom? Thank you for your help. I mean it."

"My pleasure, Val. Sleep on your back tonight. Goodnight."

"What?"

"Your nose."

I'd forgotten all about it.

"Okay. Roger that. Goodnight, Tom."

Roger that? Seriously? I really am *a jerk!*

Chapter Eighteen

I woke up the next morning with the left side of my face stuck to my pillow. I winced and stumbled to the bathroom mirror for a look. During the night, blood had drained from my nostrils down the left side of my face, leaving two paths like dark-brown slug trails that crossed my cheek and disappeared into my matted hair.

Ugh!

I reached for the shower dial, turned it all the way to the left and waited for steam to fill the air.

I'D JUST STEPPED OUT of the shower and was toweling off when the phone starting ringing. I checked the number and cringed. I took a deep breath and clicked the green answer button.

"Hi Jamie!" I said, in a tone ridiculously cheerful for a naked woman of my age and build. "You're up early!"

"Hi, Val. This is just a wake-up call."

"I'm awake," I said more seriously, and wrapped a towel around my torso.

"This is a wake-up call that your chance at a career is going down the crapper, girl! You need to submit that story outline by Monday. And it better be good."

"Okay, already. I promise."

"I'm holding you to it," Jamie barked. Her tone smacked of mistrust. "Call me tonight. Give me a rough outline. Let me sleep tonight without having to take a Xanax."

Jamie reminded me of my mother. She had a knack for making me feel both loved and guilty at the same time.

"Okay," I acquiesced.

Today. Tomorrow. What difference does it make? Squat was squat.

"Call me at six. Sharp!"

"Okay, okay! Talk to you then."

I clicked off the phone and felt a trickle run down my back. Was it shower water or sweat? When the summer heat was on, it was hard to tell. As I hung my towel on the rod, the bathroom mirror reminded me that I was probably better off not being seen in public. My nose was as big as a plum.

A bum with a plum.

"Just call me plum bum," I said to my reflection. Neither of us looked amused.

I got dressed, plugged in the computer and had a conjugal visit with old reliable, Mr. Coffee. I was steaming the milk when it frothed over and scalded my hand.

"Really? You too?" I hissed at the appliance. But he just sat there like an inanimate object, as if he had nothing to do with my sour mood. "Typical man!"

I spooned the milk foam over the espresso and took a sip. My sour mood sweetened on contact. I logged onto my computer and opened a new file. I named it *Double Booty*, since I had absolutely, positively *no* other ideas. I needed five hundred words for the book synopsis. Only four hundred and ninety-eight more to go....

STARING AT A BLANK computer screen always made me itchy. I needed a break. I checked the freezer. The Tanqueray bottle was as empty as I was. But I knew where I could get a pocket flask really cheap.

I climbed aboard Shabby Maggie. She flew west on First Avenue North, like a homing pigeon, toward Water Loo's. I didn't even try to stop her.

Screw it.

I had to admit it. I wanted some company. I missed Glad something awful.

So what if the only people in my life happen to be dumpster divers? What's the big deal?

I rationalized that I was going there to conduct research. I would turn this coffee break into a working meeting. Yes! I would pump the stooges for theories about Thelma G. Goldrich. Hopefully they could give me some ideas, crazy or otherwise, that I could use in my book outline. God knew, at this point I had nothing to lose.

As I drove into the lot, I could see the gang was all there, safely huddled together in their greasy brown corner of the world. I opened the glass door and stepped inside. The lukewarm air wheezing from the asthmatic wall-unit air conditioner was thick with the aroma of burnt coffee and desperation. But it didn't seem as overpowering as usual.

Geez. I hope this place isn't growing on me....

Winnie the waitress squinted at me through her red, cat-eye glasses as I entered her greasy domain. But when she saw my nose, her face softened into a milder-than-usual look of disgust. I flashed her a red-nosed smile and wondered how it could be that a girl half my age would even *think* of being jealous of me. Sure, she was a little plump. But she was also cute and stylish in her own funky way.

Then I remembered.

Of course!

The age-old, feminine Achilles' heel: low self-esteem. Since time immemorial, the insidiously female plague had knocked down women around the globe. Weirdly, most men appeared to have developed an immunity to it, either through mama's love, work achievement, self-delusion, or sheer stupidity.

Lucky them.

I glanced around the restaurant. Water Loo's was nearly empty, save one old man at the bar and three lunatics in the corner booth. All three stooges were present and at full attention, waving and smiling at me. I smiled and waved back. As I did, I felt something inside me relax and go slack. I think it was the final shreds of my ambition.

As I picked my way around sticky tables and crusty linoleum stains, I studied Winky, Jorge and Goober. Each looked genuinely...what was the word for it? *Content!*

Screw me. It never failed to surprise me that a man could be fat, bald, ugly, broke, missing teeth or other body parts, lack personality, charm and erectile function and *still* think he's god's gift to womankind. The male capacity for self-delusion almost made me wish I had a pair.

Almost.

"Do you guys live here?" I teased. My simple joke caused the stooges' smiles to evaporate into thoughtful, blank stares. Apparently, my lame attempt at humor was taken as a serious inquiry. Heat stung my face like a swarm of killer bees, as I felt the full force of the enormous social gulf between us.

I had an apartment to go home to. Perhaps they were here because they had nowhere else to go.

Red-faced and humbled, I set my jaw to lockdown and slid into the booth next to Winky. He reached over to give me one of his signature armpit headlocks. I blocked his attempt with a defensive, Karate-style chop to his freckled forearm.

"Hey, not cool, Val Pal," Winky sulked, looking genuinely hurt.

"Gotta protect the old schnoz, Winky," I said, reminding him of the obvious.

"Oh, yeah. Sorry 'bout that." His face brightened as he studied mine. "She's a real beaut!"

"Thanks."

"To answer your question, Val, no, we don't live here," said Goober. He removed his mirrored aviator shades. "But Winky here might if he ever gets the gumption to put the moves on Winnie."

"Shut your pie hole!" Winky bellowed. His bright mood evaporated. He slumped into the booth and stared at his coffee mug.

"You're a grumpy one today, bud. Somebody piss down your tent hole again?" Goober punched Winky good-naturedly on the arm. Winky swatted Goober's hand away.

"Wait. You guys live in *tents*?" I asked.

"Just me and Winky," Goober answered. "Jorge over there's got it good. His mamasita lets him live in the garage at her house."

"Jus' until I get back on my feet," Jorge said defensively. He shot Goober a dirty look, then glanced shyly over at me with his huge, blackish-brown eyes and smiled brightly. "It's got air condition an' everything!"

"A regular Taj-a-Maholic," Winky sneered.

"At least it's got a roof and walls," Jorge sneered back.

"So where do you guys camp?" I asked.

Goober nearly choked on the spoon clicking around in his mouth.

"Camp? You make it sound like a vacation, Val. Living in a tent for a week is camping. For a month it's an adventure, maybe. Any longer than that and you've got to admit to yourself that you are just one thin sheet of fabric away from being homeless."

I swallowed hard. "So you and Winky camp...uh...are neighbors?"

"Yeah. There's a makeshift camp out in the woods nearby. About half a dozen guys call it home. I'd tell you where it is, but then..."

"You'd have to kill me, right?" I joked.

"No. I wouldn't want to be woken up with you bothering me every night for a quickie." Goober grinned luridly at me from under his moustache. His tongue worked the handle of the spoon in his mouth, making it move rapidly up and down. The spoon clinked against his teeth with a tinny, hollow sound as his eyebrows made their own set of obscene movements.

Jorge and Winky snuffed back grins and snorts, as my expression morphed from dumbfounded to disgusted and back again. Goober's contorted face was both hilarious and horrifying, making me unable to decide whether to laugh or scream. So I did neither. I opted to smile calmly, look away and change the subject.

"So, what do you guys think of Tony's wife?" I asked Jorge and Winky.

"That bulldog witch can kiss my behind," Winky said sullenly.

"What I mean is, do you think she's really Thelma G. Goldrich?" I asked. "The one in the will? If not, what's her motivation?"

"What's her motivation? What are you, some kind of detective?" asked Goober. "With your big, swollen nosy-nose we might start calling you Stephanie Plum."

"I think that's been taken," I said snidely.

"No kidding."

Goober's retort bucked me off my high horse.

Val, you're being a jerk! These guys aren't dumb. At least Goober isn't. But why, then, do they live their lives on the edge? Just one short step away from oblivion?

I saved my questions for another time, swallowed my snooty pride, and returned to the topic of discussion.

"So, really, do you think she's Tony's wife?" I asked meekly.

"At one time, apparently," said Jorge. "Tom did say her name was Thelma Goldrich."

"Speaking of Officer Foreman, how's it going with Tommy dearest?" Goober interjected. He leaned over the booth until his face was just inches from mine. The close-up view and accompanying aroma made me flinch involuntarily.

"Nothing to report," I said.

"No man *down* yet?" Goober asked. He sat back and pretended to write in an imaginary notepad.

"Absolutely not."

"Won't be long, now." Goober's eyes glanced up from his imaginary notebook just long enough to shoot me a lewd look.

The three men burst into a cacophony of raunchy laughter. Winnie must have felt sorry for me. The waitress walked up and actually *handed* me a cup of coffee. Her face was almost as red as mine.

"A toast!" I said, raising my mug.

I was on a mission to kill this conversation and get the hell back home.

My words caused the men's laughter to sputter out like an engine taking on water. Each put a left hand over his heart and raised his cup to meet mine.

"WHAT A TOTAL WASTE of time," I muttered to myself as I stomped across Water Loo's parking lot toward my car.

What did I expect? That these burn-outs would have ideas? I must be getting as demented as they are.

I climbed into Shabby Maggie, cursed the red-hot-lava seats, and twisted the key into the ignition. I was about to shift into reverse when I nearly jumped out of my skin. An old man was standing beside my driver's-side door. I gasped at the short, wiry man with a full head of straight, steel-grey hair.

"Can I help you?" I asked curtly. The man nodded and took a tentative step toward the car. I slid Maggie into reverse and kept my hand on the shifter.

"I don't mean you no harm," he said, and raised his open palms in an effort to demonstrate that he was harmless. Dressed neatly in a clean white t-shirt and white plaid shorts held up with a white leather belt, white socks and white tennis shoes, he looked like he might have just dropped out of heaven.

"What do you want?" I asked.

"I heard you talking in there about Glad and Tony Goldrich," he said.

"Yes."

"I knew Glad and Tony pretty well."

My heart skipped a beat. "You did?"

"Yep," the old man said. He nodded his head slowly, as if stirring up the memory in his brain. "I knew Tony from way back. College days."

"Who are you?"

"Oh. Excuse me! My name is Jacob. I used to be Tony's roommate at school."

Something clicked in my brain. Tony's letter to Glad from the academy. He wrote that if she received the letter, it was because his roommate Jacob.... *Jacob!* "You're the Jacob who smuggled Tony's letters out?"

"Uh...yes. How did you know that?"

I shifted Maggie back into park. This was just the break I'd been looking for. "Oh my god! Mister, have you got time to talk?"

He glanced at his naked wrist, then back. "Miss, I've got nothing *but* time."

For a split second, I thought about going back into Water Loo's with Jacob. But then I remembered how hopeless it was to try to get serious with the stooges around. I sized up Jacob. He seemed harmless enough. I decided my best chance would be to make a clean getaway with him.

"Great! Why don't you hop in?"

Chapter Nineteen

"You hungry?" I asked Jacob.

I studied the immaculately white man as he climbed into the passenger seat. Everything about him seemed neat and orderly, including his movements. He strapped Maggie's after-market seatbelt across his lap and settled himself in. Only then did he turn to me and speak.

"I could eat."

"You like beer?"

"I could drink." He smiled at me wistfully and looked away.

"I know just where to go."

I shifted gears and pointed Maggie south on Gulf Boulevard in the direction of Bill's Sand Bar. It was a small, open-air beach bar butted up to the sand behind the nostalgic Bon Aire Motel on St. Pete Beach. By nostalgic, I meant the motel was the kind of place that still advertised rooms with air conditioning and color TVs.

Bill's Sand Bar wasn't much to look at, either. But as that old saying went, looks could be deceiving. The scruffy little dive happened to have the coldest beer and the best fish spread in town. The view of the gulf from the barstools wasn't half bad, either.

"So, what are you doing down here?" I asked as we tooled down the tourist strip. With the top down, we both enjoyed an unbroken view of the summer sky, clear and blue as a sapphire. The purity of the blue made the puffy clouds seem whiter, as if they'd just been laundered.

"Well, I saw Tony's obituary online," Jacob explained. He held his hands in front of him in an apologetic, open-handed gesture as he talked. "I know it sounds weird, but it's kind of a hobby for me. Online obituary surfing. There's not much else to do when you get to be my age."

Jacob looked over at me as if seeking forgiveness. I shrugged at him. That must have been enough, as he smiled painfully and continued talking.

"Anyway, I saw Tony's obituary about a week ago. I came down for the memorial service. Were you there?"

"Briefly. I was the one in the bloody white sundress."

"What?" Jacob asked, his eyebrows raising an inch. "I must have missed that. What happened?"

"I got punched out by Tony's ex, Thelma Goldrich. Haven't you noticed my big schnoz?"

"I have, young lady. But I've learned not to comment on such things. I got to say, her taking a swing at you also doesn't surprise me much. I guess nothing does anymore. I saw her myself, you know. Thelma Goldrich, I mean. At Tony's memorial. She's changed on the outside, for sure. Almost unrecognizable except for that string of sausages she calls a ponytail. But from what you say, she's still as rotten as ever on the inside."

"Wait a minute! You *know* her?"

"No, not personally. But I know *of* her. From Tony."

I pulled Maggie into the parking lot of the low-slung, 1950s-era Bon Aire Motel. Jacob continued sharing what he knew as we walked along a sidewalk that skirted the motel's two-story, blue-grey walls. They formed a horseshoe-shaped, open-air courtyard filled with a veritable jungle of palm trees and colorful, tropical foliage.

"Tony and I were pretty good buddies in high school. The best, really. He was kind of shy back then. Always was. No ladies' man, that's for sure." Jacob laughed as if sharing a joke with the ghosts of his past.

"Then he met Gladys. Or should I say, *Glad?* It was spring break. Middle of May, I think, 1962 or three...something like that. Anyway, Tony and me were cruising for girls. That's what we did back then before this blasted online dating and texting stuff. Anyway, we were feeling hungry and stopped at Duffy's Burgers. It was a kind of drive-in place you just don't see nowadays. Except maybe for Sonics."

The sidewalk led us to a knee-high concrete wall abutting the sugar-white sand of St. Pete Beach. A short row of old-fashioned, concrete picnic tables embedded with smooth, pastel-colored tiles offered uncomfortable but scenic places to sit and enjoy the stunning views of the gulf from under the cool shade of beach umbrellas sponsored by Corona beer.

"A cold one?" I asked Jacob.

"Just an iced tea will do me." He forced a smile onto his tired, sad face.

"Okay then."

Jacob chose a table while I walked over to the half-circle of peeling laminate countertop ringed by barstools that was known as Bill's Sand Bar. I ordered the smoked fish spread and an iced tea for Jacob. Despite the overt advertising attempt, I chose Fosters over Corona. The day was blistering hot. But a nice breeze off the water and the shade of the umbrella made it pleasant weather for Florida, considering we were nearing mid-July's triple-digit meltdown temperatures.

I handed Jacob his tea and set the fish spread on the table between us.

"Thank you, Miss...uh, I don't mean to be impolite, but I don't know your name."

"Oh! Sorry. I'm Val Fremden."

"Nice to meet you, Miss Fremden. Are you a relative of Glad's?"

"No."

"Oh. I just thought...well...I didn't see her at Tony's memorial."

"You don't know, then."

"Know what?"

"Glad is dead."

"What?" said Jacob, choking on a sip of tea. "I didn't see her obituary. I thought she was still.... What happened?"

I thought about explaining that the reason there was no obit was because Glad died with no ID, and how I'd falsified her name to claim her from the morgue, but then I remembered what I'd done was probably a crime. I wasn't sure I could trust Jacob. Besides, I just wasn't in the mood to think about Glad being dead.

"It's a long story. But she's at peace now. Ashes sprinkled in the Gulf of Mexico. Same place as Tony's."

Jacob shook his head. "That's unbelievable. When did she die?"

"The last day of June."

I felt a familiar tightening in my throat. I needed a change of topic. "How about a toast?" I held up my beer.

"Sure," Jacob said, clinking his plastic cup against mine. "To what?"

"To what's to come."

Jacob looked at me sharply. "Sure. To what's to come."

"But for now, let's get back to what has already come and gone, if you don't mind."

Jacob nodded and took a big gulp of tea.

The thought that Jacob had known Tony and Glad in their youth sent a nostalgic longing washing over me. "Please, Jacob, tell me how Glad and Tony met."

"Let's see," Jacob began, then cleared his throat. "We were at Duffy's. Yeah, we were at Duffy's eating burgers one day when this hot number walked by in a pink sweater and pants cut to her knees.

What did they call them? Ah yeah. Pedal pushers. Flowery ones. I remember because she was a sight pretty hard for a man to forget. Blonde, beautiful smile, big bazong... uh. Nice figure, you know? Hourglass." Jacob grimaced and glanced my way.

I smiled. "I think I get it."

Jacob blew out a breath and his face relaxed.

"Okay. So I looked over at Tony and he was just staring, open mouthed, like he'd just been hit over the head or something. Guys being guys, I couldn't let it go. I laughed and grabbed his arm and started waving it like a gorilla. I yelled, 'You want a hamburger to go with that shake?' Then I let go of Tony's arm real quick. Glad turned around and saw Tony with his hand still in the air, staring at her like a deer in the headlights. Ha ha! I'll never forget it! Glad started walking toward him. I thought Tony was gonna faint! She marched right up to him and said something like, 'So, handsome, are you going to give me a bite of that burger?' I know it sounds pretty tame nowadays, but back then that was pretty suggestive talk, if you know what I mean."

He looked at me as if waiting for a response. I nodded and he continued.

"That Tony...he was smitten like a kitten in a mitten. Ha ha! They started dating. Those two together was truly something to see. Glad was like Miracle Grow for Tony. He opened up and bloomed like a rose that summer. I never saw him so happy. He came from a kind of tough family, you know."

"No, I didn't know."

"Bunch of highfalutin jerks, if you ask me."

Something dark flashed over Jacob's face, then faded. He shook his head and picked up a Saltine cracker from the plate of fish spread.

"Glad got pregnant. But if you read that letter, you already know that part. And you know Tony got shipped off to private school. But what you probably don't know is that Tony wasn't just a student at that place. He was a prisoner. I know because I was hired to be his guard."

I sucked in a deep breath and held it as Jacob absently ground the cracker to dust between his fingers. "His father paid my tuition. I sold my soul for an education. I got one, too. But not the one I'd planned on. Kids today with their hundred-grand student loan payments. God, if only my debt had been just money. I'd trade with one of them in a heartbeat."

Jacob looked surprised at the pile of cracker dust on the table. He wiped it away and stared out at the gulf. "I was on the payroll as Tony's enemy. Reporting back to his father for my next meal ticket." Jacob blew out a breath and swallowed hard. He looked at me with eyes full of anger and regret, then pursed his lips and pressed on with his confession.

"Tony wrote Glad every day. He counted on me to mail the letters, but I only mailed the first one. The one you read. I also stole all the letters Glad wrote Tony. It was easy. Tony never suspected me. When he didn't hear nothing back from her, I watched Tony wither away, wild with guilt and pain and sorrow. His hateful father kept telling me it was for the best. That Tony would get over it.

"When that took too long, the dirtbag told me to do whatever it took to *make* Tony get over it. I didn't know what to do. When Mr. Goldrich realized I didn't have any natural talent for making people miserable, he gave me some from his ample supply."

Jacob stopped for a moment and looked out at the water. "God help me, I tried pretty near all of that devil's suggestions. I told Tony that Glad had another beau. I told him that when her parents died, Glad confessed to somebody that the baby wasn't his. When Glad hooked up with that traveling preacher, I told Tony the kid was really that guy's. I said Glad had been seeing the preacher for months and was using Tony to cover her sins and get a big payoff, because she knew Tony's family was loaded. Then I told him one thing that wasn't a lie. I told him Glad had taken her baby and run off with that preacher. A shyster named Bobby Munch."

"Wait a minute," I interjected. "You're saying Glad had her baby with her when she left with Bobby?"

"Yeah. She couldn't bear to give it up."

"How do you know?"

"I'll get to that."

"Okay, Jacob. But tell me now, I'm dying to know. Was it a boy or a girl?"

Jacob coughed out a cynical laugh. "As bad as I was to Tony back then, I just had to know, too. So I pretended to get chummy with Tony's father. I asked him if Gladys' kid had been a boy or a girl. I honestly didn't think he'd tell me. But I guess up in his golden palace, Glad was nothing to him. As insignificant as a flea. I remember that jerk Goldrich laughed like a demon and told me that Glad had a baby girl. I remember his words exactly. He said, 'The witch named the little brat Thelma, after her own tramp of a mother.' His pompous voice still rings in my ears whenever I think about it."

Jacob shook his head as if to clear away the lingering remains of the noxious memory. He wiped his eyes with a napkin and sucked in a deep breath, then took a sip of tea and looked me straight in the eyes. What he said next set my own ears to ringing.

"Tony and Glad's baby girl. Thelma. She's the one named in the will. I'd bet on it."

A surge of excitement caused my heart to thump. "So where is she, Jacob?"

His face deflated.

"I was hoping you could tell me."

Chapter Twenty

M y heart sank. Jacob didn't know any more than I did about the whereabouts of Glad and Tony's daughter. He couldn't even tell me whether she was still alive or not.

"Do you know any more?" he asked.

"I've only got some theories, a few documents and some sketchy clues," I said. "What do *you* know, Jacob?" I reached for a cracker and smeared some fish spread on it.

"What kind of documents?" Jacob asked.

"Birth notice. A marriage license. Stuff like that."

I could tell Jacob wanted to know more. But so did I, and *I* was buying.

"How in the world did Tony end up marrying that ponytailed witch?" I asked, then popped the cracker into my mouth so that Jacob was forced to fill the silence.

Jacob eyed me carefully. "Well, I'm not saying I'm innocent in all this, but all my lies about Glad failed to break Tony's love for her. Nope. It was the truth that finally did that. When I told Tony about the baby being a girl, and that Glad had named her a combination of his, her, and her mom's name, Thelma Gladys Goldrich, he got all excited. He told me he was going to escape that prison of a school and get himself back home and marry her. But I had to tell him it was too late. Glad had already up and married Bobby. I've never seen anybody shatter like that. Hope I never do again.

"After I told Tony about the marriage, it was like something just broke inside him. He started drinking, and got busy making some big-ass mistakes of his own. Marrying Thelma Cornish—the woman who punched you in the nose—was by far his biggest one. Believe it or not, Thelma kind of looked like Glad back then. Blonde hair, big boobs...uh. And her name...Thelma...Tony said he took it to be some kind of sign." Jacob shook his head wistfully. "Too bad he didn't read the fine print. Thelma had a nose for money, and didn't mind taking one for the cause, if you know what I mean."

My mind tried to go there but I slammed on the brakes and thought about kittens playing with yarn balls instead. "I think I get the picture."

"Okay. Enough said on that," Jacob said. "At any rate, Thelma acted the part real good. She pretended to love Tony and—here's the genius part—*she pretended to hate Tony's father*. It was a double-whammy combo that swept Tony right off his feet. She fooled Tony into marrying her and signing up for law school, just like his daddy wanted. Funny, the same day Tony told me he was gonna be a lawyer was the same day my tuition money dried up. Heh. I'd been replaced. My services were no longer needed. Tony went off to law school. I went home and got a job selling stoves and TVs. Their sham marriage didn't last a year. Just long enough for Thelma to get a BMW and a monthly living allowance. Conniving witch."

Jacob's eyes met mine, then he hung his head. "Who am I to talk? I was no better than her. The only saving grace to this whole mess was that, back in the day, Tony never figured out that he was surrounded by his father's henchmen—me being the main one of them. It would have killed him for sure. He was just too trusting. Too pure of heart to realize what a heel I was."

Jacob's glass was empty and so was mine. I needed another beer. I thought maybe he could use one, too. I smiled at him sympathetically and picked up his glass.

"Wanna upgrade to a beer? My treat."

"Thanks, Miss. But these days I'm a teetotaler. After going back to Hawesville, I hit the bottle hard. Johnny Walker became my best and only friend. The secrets I'd kept from Tony twisted in my guts like maggots. Nothing I could chase or screw or drink ever came close to making me feel okay about selling out my best friend. Long, boring story short, I hit bottom and went through AA's Twelve Step Program. My last confession was to Tony. In 1980. Back then, he was just about as hollowed out a shell as I was."

I reached over and touched Jacob's hand. He winced and turned away.

"Jacob, you don't have to explain...."

"Let me," Jacob cut in. "I'll just get it out quick. I called Tony up and asked if we could meet. He sounded happy to hear from me. *Happy!* Can you believe it? I don't think I ever felt so low in my life. He invited me over to his place. I took him up on the invitation. I sat on his couch and spilled my guts like a slaughtered pig. I asked him to forgive me. He sat there, still as a statue. Didn't say a word. I begged him to punch me. Kick me. Anything he needed to get it out. But he was too much a gentleman. Honest to god I don't think he had any anger or love or anything left in him by the time I found him. He just crumpled to the floor and cried. I got on the floor and cried with him. When we both couldn't cry no more, he just said, 'Help me find her.' I vowed I would. It didn't matter to him that what I found wasn't pretty."

"What do you mean, wasn't pretty?"

"What Glad had suffered at the hands of Bobby Munch makes my sorry, self-pitying life look like a fairytale."

MY CLOCK RAN OUT JUST when it was getting good. I was desperate to know more, but I had promises to keep to both Jamie *and* myself. "I'll see you in the morning," I said to Jacob as I dropped him off at his car in the Water Loo's parking lot.

"See you back here, 8:30 sharp," he replied, climbing into his white Prius. The car matched his white t-shirt, belt and tennis shoes. *All white. A play for purity? Or penance, perhaps?*

I waved as he pulled out of the lot and I glanced at my phone. *Crap.*

It was already 4:30. I needed to get my butt home, write four-hundred and ninety-eight words, and email them to Jamie before she called at 6 p.m. Jacob's story and the afternoon sun had caused me to sweat through my clothes. I needed a shower, but that was going to have to remain an option for the moment. I hit the gas and Maggie's mufflers belched out a grey, smoky roar.

The lights on Central Avenue were kind and I made good time. It was five minutes to 5 p.m. when I pulled into my alley parking spot. I bolted up the stairs. As I fumbled with the key, my phone started buzzing. It was Tom.

Crap. Crap. Crap. I don't have time for this!

"Hi Tom!" I said sweetly into the phone, then changed my tune. "Make it quick. I'm a woman on a mission."

"Woah, there, tiger lady. What's the hurry?"

"I can't explain right now. What's up?"

"I got the DMV lowdown on the three Thelma G's. Got time for that?"

"No. But sure. Let me have it."

"Turns out one lives in Chicago. She's African American. Another is local. Hispanic. The other one Caucasian –"

"It can only be her, the third one," I said, cutting Tom off.

"Why?"

"Like I said, I can't explain right now. Where is she?"

"Well..."

"What, Tom? I'm begging you, I'm in a hurry!"

"Slow down, sister! She's in a hospital for the criminally insane. Chattahoochee State Mental Hospital in North Florida."

"Screw off!"

"I'm serious!"

Time slowed down as my mind sped forward. "Didn't you say Bobby was incarcerated nearby up there? At Apalachicola Correctional?"

"Yes."

"Didn't he go missing or something?"

"Yep. Right after he was released."

"Tom, the hospital and correctional facility are in the same town."

"Yeah. Interesting, huh?"

"I really don't have time for this right now."

"Hot date?"

I smiled despite myself. "Something like that. Meet you for lunch tomorrow? Ming Ming's?"

"Roger that."

I clicked off.

Roger that. Great. Now he's stealing my romantic lines.

I sat down at the computer and opened the file named *Double Booty.* I forced myself to type despite the fact that my hands were shaking like a woman on the lam.

I TOOK A BITE OF FISH taco and listened to Jamie over the phone as she read through my story synopsis. From her vantage point in New York, she couldn't see that I was at the Taco Bus on Central Avenue. She also couldn't see the odd dozen or so people milling about in line, waiting to place their orders.

For the uninitiated, the Taco Bus restaurant really *was* in a bus. It was also painted the same hideous orange as the local Pinellas County school buses. Originally a food truck, it was now permanently parked on Central Avenue in front of a plain-Jane, single-story concrete block building painted the same scholastic shade of rusted-out dreams.

After Taco Bus caught on with locals and tourists alike, it expanded its main kitchen into the ugly building behind the bus. Customers ate their tacos and burritos on dark-green, metal-mesh tables under the shade of big, beach-style umbrellas. Or they opted for dining in a carport-like area tacked onto the right side of the building. Like a lot of hole-in-the-wall places, the Taco Bus put out some seriously good food. It even earned a spot on that TV show, *Diners, Drive-ins and Dives,* though I'm not sure which of the three categories best described it.

As I ate my taco, I became mesmerized by the sight of an enormous black man in blue overalls shoving a whole burrito in his mouth. A tinny beeping in my ear made me realize Jamie was yelling into the phone, saying my name over and over.

"Val? Val? You still there, Val?"

I detected bad news woven into her tired, pinched voice.

"Yeah, I'm here."

"I don't know about this synopsis, Val. It needs work. Major work."

"What's wrong with it?"

"It just doesn't seem plausible."

"But Jamie, it's all based on true events!"

Jamie's voice morphed into a sneer. "That's the rub about writing fiction, Val. Unlike real life, fiction's got to make sense."

Chapter Twenty-One

All I needed was a miracle. One teeny-tiny bit of inspiration. I stared blankly at my blasted book synopsis.

Double Booty. Ha! Double Doody was more like it.

Even my morning walk and canoodle with Mr. Coffee had done nothing to raise my enthusiasm. The only bright spot was that it was Saturday. I still had today and tomorrow to come up with something good for Jamie. But working on it would have to wait a bit longer. I was running late for a date with an angry, alcoholic, neat freak old enough to be my father.

It was the best offer I'd had in a while.

JACOB WAS WAITING FOR me in the parking lot when I pulled up to Water Loo's. He saw me and waved through the squeaky-clean window pane of his Prius. He climbed out of the car, shut the door, tested the handle to make sure it was locked, then ambled over my way.

"Mind if we go somewhere else?" he asked, holding his hands open and to his sides in what looked like a weird truce gesture, just like the day before.

"No problem," I said. "Don't like it here?"

"Not my favorite. Do you know anyplace with a good cup of joe?"

"Starbucks?"

"I'd rather not. I don't know what all the fuss is about. That stuff tastes like burnt plastic to me."

"We've got options. Get in."

Jacob smiled and buckled himself in tight. "Your car. She's a real beauty."

"My Maggie? Yeah, she sure is. You seem like a man who appreciates the classics, Jacob. How about we go to a real, honest-to-goodness diner for breakfast?"

"That's the best idea I've heard all day."

I maneuvered Maggie onto a southbound lane of Gulf Boulevard in the direction of Corey Avenue and Gayle's Diner. Jacob and I sat silent for the ride, enjoying the relative coolness of the early morning breeze on our faces. A few minutes later, we were sitting across from each other in a cozy booth for two, a waitress filling our white ceramic cups to the brim with piping hot java. Jacob took a tentative sip from the steaming mug.

"Ahhh, now that's what I call a good cup a joe!"

"Glad you like it, Jacob. And I want to thank you. Breakfast is on me today."

"Thank me? For what?"

"For coming forward. For sharing your stories with me. For being honest. You didn't have to. And I know it's not easy."

"You two ready to order?" asked the round, shiny-faced waitress. "I see somebody here appreciates my coffee. I'll be back to top you off in a minute, young man. Now what'll it be?"

Being a Southern girl at heart, I ordered biscuits and gravy. Jacob followed my lead. While we waited for the food to arrive, Jacob continued his story from the perspective of a man who knew his part in it all too well.

"I realized I could never go back and make things right for Tony, but I was the only one holding enough cards to try and deal with what had gone wrong. You know what I mean?"

I didn't, but I nodded anyway.

"Tony was a pushover, but he was no dummy. He'd already figured out some of the facts before I filled in the missing pieces for him during my AA confession. His father had died of lung cancer a couple of months before I caught up with Tony. The old man confessed on his deathbed that he'd paid Bobby Munch five grand to get Glad out of town and make the baby disappear. Back then, that was a fortune! He didn't care how Bobby did it and he never asked questions later. The old man had one of his flunkies steal the hospital and county files to erase any record of the birth. He had 'em take a couple of months' worth just to cover their tracks. He told Tony he got the idea after Glad's parents and brother got killed in that traffic accident. He figured no one would go looking for a baby with no kin."

"No kin! What about Glad herself? She was the *mother*, for crying out loud!"

"What can I say, Val? Back then things were different. Women didn't have many rights. Especially fallen women. They kept their traps shut and did what their husbands told 'em. Either by choice or by force."

"Geez! Wasn't Tony's father the least bit sorry for what he did to them?"

"I don't know. Tony said his father thought it was the right thing to do at the time, to save the high and mighty Goldrich family from scandal. But Tony said the bum broke down in the end and said if he could do things over, he would have let Tony marry Glad."

Jacob huffed out a sarcastic laugh. "It's amazing what people will do to unload their guilt. Especially at the last minute when they won't be around no more to witness the damage."

"What do you mean?" I asked. "It seems to me like he'd already witnessed the damage he did to his son and to Glad. The only thing he missed out on was the chance to be forgiven. To make things right."

"Maybe. But his confession didn't help either one of them. Both Tony's and Glad's lives were pretty much ruined by then."

Jacob's words pinged a memory from our prior conversation. I cobbled the fragments together into a question while the waitress placed our breakfasts on the table and topped off our coffees.

"Jacob, yesterday you said Glad had suffered at the hands of Bobby. That your life was a fairytale in comparison. What did you mean?"

Jacob's jaw tightened. He glanced out the window and swallowed hard, like he was trying to get a pill down with no water.

"Put it this way. Bobby was a man of convenient morals. Learned it from preaching, I guess. A pretty picture of Glad and the thought of five grand in his pocket was all the motivation he'd needed to get the job done. I'm sure Bobby poured on the charm. Crap. He probably didn't even *need* charm. Glad was a woman with no real options."

"I could imagine."

"No you couldn't, Miss. No woman in America today could imagine what it was like back then. Picture this. Glad gets wheeled out of the hospital with a new baby, no husband and no place to go. Parents dead, boyfriend disappeared, she ends up at a 'mercy home' for unwed mothers. The place is run by holier-than-thou society women looking down their noses at her like she smells of crap. They tell Glad the best thing for everyone is for her to give her illegitimate baby to some decent folks and pray that she can weasel her way back into moral acceptability someday by kissing every butt she sees. Mercy home my behind! Those scumbags!"

Jacob rapped his knuckles hard on the table, causing me to flinch. He seemed to catch his own self off guard. "Sorry. I didn't mean to be impolite."

"It's okay. Finish your story."

"So Glad's taking turns nursing her baby and crying her eyes out when some bucktoothed bozo of a preacher takes notice of her. He says it's love at first sight or some such horse hockey. Then he offers her a way out. Glad can marry him and keep the baby. He's fine with the kid. Says he'll adopt it, raise it as his own. Only thing is, the revival tent is packing up and heading out of town in a day or two. She's thinking it over when a snot-nosed society shrew tells Glad they've found a decent couple who wants her baby. They're coming by tomorrow for a look-see. The clock is ticking in Glad's ears like a time bomb. What would *you* do?"

"Did that really happen?"

"I don't know, but probably. More or less. So, Miss Val, what would you do?"

"I'd keep my baby...and go with Bobby."

"Bingo. Glad told me herself she didn't have any choice, really. Bobby convinced her he would take care of her. She married him and they took off with the baby. For a moment she even thought she was lucky. Lucky! Geez. She had no idea what she was getting into. She didn't know she was sealing her fate."

"How do you know all this?"

"Because I kept my promise to Tony. I was the one who found her."

Part of me wanted to know what came next. Part of me didn't. I swallowed hard and thought of Glad in her pink lounge chair, sprawled out in the sun. I glanced at the time. The vintage chrome clock on the wall at Gayle's Diner said it was ten after ten. I was supposed to meet Tom at noon. If I pushed it, I could stay another hour with Jacob. I hoped it would be long enough for him to share everything he knew.

"Something else, Jacob? Slice of pie, maybe?"

"No thanks, Miss Val. Mighty nice of you."

"Okay. So tell me, how did you find Glad?"

"The truth be told, I didn't have to look. I already knew where she was. I didn't tell Tony because she'd begged me not to. I'd run into Glad nearly six years before. I think it was sometime in 1974. She and Bobby were in Hawesville with that traveling circus they called a revival. I drove by the church while they were setting up the tent. I recognized Bobby right away. He'd built himself up a belly over the years, but he still had that ridiculous Elvis hairdo and jackrabbit teeth. He was arguing outside the tent with a woman about as thin as a sheet of paper. I watched as he grabbed her arm and jerked it so hard I thought it might break it in two. Call it whatever you want, but something inside me made me pull over."

I fiddled with the packets of artificial sweetener, not wanting to make eye contact with Jacob. I braced myself for what might come next and glanced quickly into his eyes, then back down to the pink and yellow packets. I gave a quick nod.

"I guess Bobby thought no one was looking. That buck-toothed piece of crap pushed the woman so hard she fell to the ground. He laughed at her, then got in a truck and drove off. I got out and ran over to the poor lady. I asked if I could help her up. That's when I saw her eyes, Val. Dead, zombie eyes. Like her soul was already gone from her body. Still, her face looked familiar. I wasn't sure it was Gladys, but I said her name anyway. You know what she said back?"

"What?" I looked up from the packets, dread mixing with the biscuits and gravy in my stomach.

"She said, 'Yes sir.' Like I was her freaking commanding officer or something." Jacob's voice cracked and he looked away for a minute. He took a deep breath and continued.

"I said, 'Gladys, it's me, Jacob.' She said, 'Yes sir,' again, like a ro-bot. I helped her up and saw her arm was covered with bruises. My heart nearly broke. So I told her to come with me, right then and there. She said she couldn't. She told me she was cursed. She said the devil had killed her baby and if she left the church he'd get her, too."

"Geezus!"

"Jesus had nothing to do with it, Miss Val. Bobby had screwed her up almost beyond recognition. I told her I was from the church and I was here to take her to a better place. That made her smile a lit-tle, but her eyes stayed dead, like she was in a trance."

Jacob's voice cracked again. "Val, she wasn't even 30 yet and she had dentures. That no-good bum had knocked every one of her front teeth out. I took her by the hand and said 'Let's go.' She said, 'Yes sir,' again and followed me to my car like a lost child. I told her she looked tired and should take a nap in the back seat. She laid down and I fired up the engine and took off, wondering what the hell I should do next."

"What *did* you do?"

"I ended up taking her home to my place. I showed her the spare bedroom and told her to get some rest. She got a little hysterical say-ing there was too much air in the room or something like that. I gave her a shot of gin and a piece of toast. She drank the gin and laid down. I left her for the night. The next morning I found her sleeping under the bed like a whipped dog.

"It was awful. Glad had such a nervous stomach she couldn't hold anything down but booze and bread. I knew I was out of my league, so I called my sister Angela. She was big into women's lib in those days. Gloria Steinem and all that happy horse hockey. I ex-plained the situation. Ang said she'd take her in on one condition. That Glad pressed charges against Bobby Munch."

"What did you say?"

"Well, I was in no position to argue. And why should I? I lured Glad into the car with a Stolli miniature and the promise we were going to visit one of Jesus's angels. I popped No-Doze and drank Pepsis all the way down to my sister's little place here in St. Pete. I didn't dare stop for nothing but gas. Glad was afraid of everything. But when I introduced her to Angela, Glad fell to her knees and wept like she'd seen the Virgin Mary. I remember my sister getting teary-eyed, too, but I whispered in Angela's ear that angels don't cry. Ang caught on quick and spoke to Glad like she thought an angel would. Kind. Gentle. But with authority, you know? From that moment on, Ang—or Angel, if you want—had the last word with Glad. That poor, broken woman followed her 'angel' around like a donkey follows a carrot."

"Your sister really *does* sound like an angel."

"Yeah. I guess our mom got it right when she named her."

"So what happened next?"

"Glad stayed with Angela for a few weeks. I called every day to make sure everything was going okay. Ang said Glad was no problem at all except when it came to going to bed. She said Glad feared open spaces. She was afraid that 'all that air' was going to get her. Well, one day Ang called me and said she was expecting a friend for a visit. An old friend of Ang's who'd recently lost his wife and was feeling pretty low. He was in the area camping and had called to see if he could stop by. She wanted to know if it was okay with me. She was worried that Glad might freak. You see, there hadn't been no man at Ang's house since I left. I told her I thought it would be all right, since Glad didn't seem to be bothered much by me. Besides, Glad was beginning to eat better by then and was actually talking a bit."

I glanced at the clock. Five minutes to eleven. Jacob noticed me check the time.

"Long story short, Miss Val, Ang's friend turned out to be her old high-school flame. It was love at first sight all over again for them. He

moved right in and they took up where they'd left off. As good heart-
ed as Ang was, it was awkward having Glad in the house with them
all the time. But I guess Ang's angels were looking out for her, too.
You see, this fella had driven over to Ang's in an RV. His late wife had
been a butterfly freak. The whole RV was covered inside with fake
butterflies. They were on the curtains, the bedspread, wind chimes,
knick-knacks. You get the picture. Well, the guy was going to sell the
RV. But Glad took a look inside, climbed in and didn't want to leave.
So Ang and her boyfriend moved the RV into the backyard and Glad
moved in for the duration."

"So that's how she ended up in the Minnie Winnie!"

"How did you know it was a Minnie?"

"I saw the receipt of sale. Some guy sold it to her for a hundred
bucks."

"You mean Billy Jonson, Ang's boyfriend. Ang told me he'd given
the RV to Glad. I didn't realize he'd transferred title, too. I don't
think he charged her anything. How could he? Glad didn't have a
dime."

"Wow. None of this even remotely resembles the stories Glad
told me."

"Well, Val, can you blame her? Who would want to remember
any of that horrific stuff? Glad was so messed up back then she spent
nearly a decade cooped up in a fantasy world of butterflies and angels
in a tiny RV."

I thought back to the empty shoebox Glad had labeled 1974 to
1985. It started to make sense now. The box was empty because she
had been, too. I grabbed my purse and wiggled out of the booth.

"Thank you, Jacob. I've got to be somewhere at noon. Let me
give you a ride back."

Chapter Twenty-Two

I left Jacob in the Water Loo's parking lot with a promise to meet up again that evening. I wanted to find out if he knew any more about Glad's baby, but we'd run out of time again. My head was spinning. So much to take in. But there was no time to ponder. If I was lucky, I had just enough time left to make it to Ming Ming's by noon.

I hit the gas and headed south toward 107th Avenue. The road morphed into Central Avenue once it crossed the Intracoastal Waterway. Ming Ming's was on Central, right in the middle of what had to be the ugliest little strip center in the world. The low-rent, grey concrete structure with unpainted metal siding for awnings was home to the usual suspects: A nail salon, a tax-prep service, a florist and, of all things, a British restaurant.

Who in the world ever got a hankering for kidney pie or blood pudding?

When I pulled up, I could see through Ming Ming's shiny glass storefront that Tom was already seated inside at a table for two. He was facing the parking lot and could see me through the large panes of glass. I shut off Maggie's ignition and discreetly checked my face in the rearview mirror. No amount of powdering my nose was going to help the red schnoz shining like a beacon in the center of my face.

I sighed and stepped out of the car, right into a steaming pile of dog crap.

Really, universe?

I could see Tom grinning at me through the window as I scraped the sole of my sandal on the curb.

So much for making a grand entrance.

"Having a crappy day, I see," he said as I came through the door.

"Let's hope it doesn't get any crappier," I shot back.

Tom laughed. "I can't make any guarantees."

My stomach flopped. "What do you mean? Don't tell me you've got bad news."

"I wouldn't call it *bad*, exactly."

"What would you call it?"

"Whoa there, Val. How about we start with some social niceties. How are you today?"

I blew out a breath and smiled apologetically.

"Sorry. It's just been a pretty *interesting* day so far. I'm fine, Tom. How are you?"

"Feeling a bit fishy. How about we share a sea creature roll and a seaweed salad?"

Tom held up the shiny, laminated menu and I remembered why I liked Ming Ming's so much. Not only was the sushi fantastic, the menu was simple—almost like a children's book—all pretty pictures and large print. No overwhelm. And, even better, *no old-lady reading glasses required*.

But my favorite thing about Ming Ming's *that* day turned out to be the tiny tables. The table Tom chose was so small that his knees brushed against mine whenever he shifted his legs. As pathetic as my love life had been lately, it wasn't long before this cheap thrill had me almost drooling.

When the waiter came to take our order, I sobered a bit and studied Tom as he talked and laughed with the guy. I realized then that it hadn't been my overactive imagination. Tom really *did* look like a blond Adonis. And the blue in that button-down shirt he was wearing really accented his eyes....

"Val?"

It was Tom's voice.

"What?"

"Where were you? I was asking if you wanted anything else."

"Oh. Uh...an order of edamame, please."

The waiter scribbled in his notepad and left. Tom turned his attention to me, making me squirm in my chair.

"So, interesting day, you said?"

"Yeah. I met a guy who knew Tony and Glad. He was a friend of theirs. He knows their whole history."

"Wow. That *is* interesting. What's his name?"

"Jacob."

"Jacob what?"

"Uh, I don't know."

"Nice detective work, Miss Plum."

I shook my head and pursed my lips. "Not *you*, too. Have you been talking to Goober and his Raisinets?"

Tom smiled coyly. "Among others."

The waiter delivered the edamame on a beautiful square china plate along with two tall glasses of house-blended iced tea. I took a sip and savored hints of blackberry and orange. I reached for a soybean pod and noticed Tom playfully watching me.

"So, what's your news, Tom?" I asked matter-of-factly.

"News?"

"What did you find out about the 'Caucasian candidate' named Thelma G. Goldrich?"

Tom's face shifted gears. I'd managed to nip our blossoming flirtation in the bud again.

Great going, Val.

"Besides the fact that she's in a prison for the criminally insane, you mean?"

"Yes. Besides the fact she's in Chattahoochee State Mental Hospital."

"You remember the name from yesterday. Good work, Miss Plum."

I sneered. "Call me that again and you'll be Mr. Glum."

Tom's eyebrows shot up and dimples dented his cheeks. "Duly noted."

"I've got relatives up there."

"Up where?"

"In the Chattahoochee area," I said.

"You? Miss Snooty Two-Shoes?"

"Yeah, copper. You found the skeleton in my closet."

"Chattahoochee? That's some skeleton!"

"My relatives aren't in the *mental hospital*. They're in the *area*. My mom's from Greenville. My aunt lives in Two Egg."

"Two Egg?" Tom asked. "That's not even grammatically correct!"

"Now you know why I had to escape."

Tom laughed and picked up a bean pod and squeezed it. A soybean shot across the table onto the floor. I giggled.

"Letting another perpetrator escape justice, I see."

"Hey, nobody's perfect."

"True enough. So, tell me, Tom. Why is this Thelma Goldrich in a hospital for the criminally insane? Did she kill somebody?"

"No. Nothing that bad. Just garden-variety craziness, mostly. And she likes to set fires."

"Great."

"I've got her mugshot if you want to see it."

"Of course!"

Tom reached in his shirt pocket and pulled out a piece of paper. He unfolded it and laid it on the table in front of me. I wasn't sure what to expect, but it sure wasn't this. Thelma looked like Miss Piggy after a bar fight and a bareback romp in the hay. Despite her angry, dirty and disheveled appearance, some aspects of her reminded me of Glad.

"A real looker, wouldn't you agree?" Tom quipped.

"She's blonde. Big boobs. Like Glad."

"Still, it doesn't automatically make *her* the one. Val, I still don't understand why the Thelma you're after can't be one of the other two women on the DMV list."

"Because Mister...because *Jacob* confirmed that Glad's baby was definitely Tony's, and that Glad had named her Thelma...after her own mom. Tony and Glad are both white, so that rules out the other two, obviously."

"Obviously," Tom agreed. "I guess Jacob didn't have any information on where the daughter is, or you'd have led with that."

"No. He told me a lot about Glad and Tony, and what happened with her and her first husband Bobby. But we ran out of time. I'm meeting him later this afternoon to find out what he knows about their daughter. When I dropped him off at Water Loo's, he told me he didn't know much about her. But he's been known to tell lies."

"What do you mean?" Tom asked. He sat up and looked serious for the first time.

"Long story. Just take my word for it. Of course, if Jacob doesn't know where Thelma is, he also doesn't know if she's dead or alive."

"I'm rooting for alive."

I smiled at Tom. "Thanks. Me too. What makes you so positive?"

"Tony and Glad. Think about it. If they had known for sure their daughter was dead, why would they have made the will out to her?"

"You know, you're pretty smart for a cute guy."

Tom sat back and showed me his perfect, pearly whites.

"Thanks, Val. You're not too dumb yourself. You know, I'm off until Tuesday. We could go up there and meet this crazy Thelma woman. It's just a five- or six-hour drive. We could spend the time getting to know each other."

My neck flushed with heat and my brain slammed into sabotage mode. "I'm picky about who I spend my time with, Tom."

Tom grinned back at me. "So, pick me."

A knot of panic clogged my throat.

Why did he have to be so cute and *charming?*

"I'm not sure I'm ready for another relationship, Tom."

"Whoa, Val. I'm just talking about a long drive here."

"Yeah. Every relationship I've ever been in began with a long drive and ended in a long, painful death."

"Wow. That's pretty heavy, Val. You know, if you don't stop carrying that giant chip on your shoulder, you're going to turn into Quasimodo."

Chapter Twenty-Three

I jerked on the handle of my overnight bag, trying to dislodge it from between two boxes on the top shelf of my bedroom closet. For the first time since I could recall, I was actually *busy*. Triple-booked, even. A synopsis to write. Jacob to interview. And now this trip with Tom.

What happened to my quiet little life as a washed-up writer wandering the beach and getting wasted?

Tom was going to pick me up at eight tomorrow morning. I was supposed to meet Jacob at six this evening. It was already after two. I had about three hours to pack and take a final stab at *Double Booty*. I needed to focus. I needed a clear head.

I needed a TNT.

I gave a final tug. The bag let loose, sending me careening to the floor along with it. The seismic tremor created by my medium-large bottom hitting the wooden floor sent a small, blue box tumbling off one of the shelves. As it hit the ground, the lid flew off. A tiny object fell out, ricocheted off the floor and landed on my lap. I stared at it and shuddered. It was the broken-off piece of jewelry I'd found in one of Glad's shoeboxes.

It was as if my evil deed had come back to haunt me.

I'd kept the silver oval embedded with green rhinestones as a memento. I'd figured no one would miss it. That's what I'd told myself at the time, anyway. Now I could feel the full weight of the real truth on my conscience. I hadn't *rescued* it. I'd *stolen* it.

After looking through Glad's shoeboxes of memorabilia, my heart had ached to keep a little piece of her with me. It had felt right at the time to take this little memento of her. Who would care about a worthless, broken little piece of junk? But now I realized that maybe this piece of junk belonged to someone else. Maybe that crazy woman in Chattahoochee. It might mean the world to her, for all I knew.

I turned the tiny object over and over in my hand, feeling as lost and out of place and incomplete as it was. Then I remembered something. I didn't have time for all this sappy sentiment!

I grabbed the blue box and placed the broken piece of jewelry back into it. I hauled myself up off the floor, unzipped my overnight bag, and dropped the little box inside.

RUNNING SHORT ON TIME, I'd told Jacob to meet me in Straub Park this afternoon. I could walk there from my apartment in under five minutes.

Situated on the waterfront downtown, Straub Park was a long, rectangular patch of green grass dotted by statues and skirted by sidewalks and benches. It was sandwiched between the small shops and restaurants lining Beach Drive on the west and the expansive blue water of Tampa Bay on the east. The Vinoy Hotel sat at the northern end of the park. St. Pete's Museum of Fine Arts completed the rectangle to the south.

Designed with the intention of being a respite for city dwellers, the north end of Straub Park was almost entirely shaded by beautiful, old, oak trees. Their canopies provided a natural refuge from the blazing Florida sun, and made sitting outside tolerable most days, even in summer.

I recognized Jacob's thick head of steely-grey hair from a hundred feet away. He was waiting for me on a park bench under the trees. I'd made some progress on *Double Booty*, but I knew it was nowhere near ready for prime time. I needed to hit pay dirt during this meeting with Jacob. Something juicy for my novel, and hopefully something useful for my trip with Tom. As I passed the corner sidewalk lined with miniature azalea bushes, flop sweat trickled down my back.

What if Jacob had nothing worthwhile to tell me about what happened to the baby?

Jacob was facing the water. Intently watching the boats in the bay, he didn't notice me walk up.

"Hi, Jacob." My voice caused the old man to jump.

"Oh! Hello there, Miss Val."

I smiled. Jacob's Southern upbringing was showing. Adding the term "Miss" before my name was what a polite Southern man did out of respect for an unmarried woman of uncertain age. He was dressed again in a saintly uniform of mostly white—white t-shirt, white tennis shoes and socks, and a white belt to hold up his white-and-plaid shorts.

"Any problem finding the place?" I asked.

"Huh? Oh, no. None at all. How was lunch with Tom?"

"Fine." I thought about telling Jacob about the trip I was taking tomorrow, but my gut told me to withhold the information, for the moment, at least.

"This certainly is a neighborhood for the 'haves,'" Jacob said. He pointed to the collection of opulent pleasure boats and catamarans bobbing in the Vinoy Club yacht basin across the street from the snooty, pink, wedding cake of a hotel.

"Yeah."

"So, Val, are you a 'have' or a 'have not?' "

"Depends on what you mean by 'have.' I 'have' bills. I 'have' doubts. I 'have not' money, if that's what you mean."

Jacob eyed me almost suspiciously, then gestured for me to sit down on the bench next to him. As I did, my eye caught on the sharp contrast between the grey, faded wood of the bench and the fresh, clean wood of the new armrest recently installed in the middle of it.

How ingenious. And apropos.

St. Pete had found the perfect, politically correct solution to keeping penniless people from turning the benches into bedsteads. The new armrests made it impossible to lie down across the bench.

Score another one for the "haves."

"So how about you, Jacob? Are you a 'have' or 'have not?' By the way, what's your last name?"

"Oh, I'd say I'm a 'have not,' on the way to being 'have not-er,'" Jacob joked, then laughed dryly. "You said you're short on time, Val. Should we get to it? What else do you want to know?"

"I need to know everything *you* know about Glad and Tony's baby. What could have happened to Thelma? Where she might be. I guess I was hoping to hear about whatever clues you might have picked up along the way."

"You want the long version or the short one? Either way, it doesn't add up to much."

I sighed. Then I remembered Tom's words. He said cases often get solved by gut feelings. I had a gut feeling Jacob had some of the answers, whether he knew it himself or not. The more information I could get out of him, the more data I'd have to sort through myself.

"I guess I'll take the long version."

"Okay. Where'd we leave off? Oh yeah, Glad moved into the RV. Wait. Before I forget, when she first got to my sister's, Ang and I took pictures of the bruises on Glad's arms and legs. It was awful. Glad was dang near a walking skeleton. Ang had one of those old 8mm cameras at the time, so we made a movie of Glad, crazy as she was, talking about how the devil had done all that damage to her. Well, we all knew who the *real* devil was. So would anybody with half a brain, we figured.

"So Ang and I got the paperwork and filled it out for Glad to press charges against Bobby. We didn't mention the baby in the court proceedings. We thought it would have been too much for Glad at the time. The real focus was to get Bobby in the slammer and pronto. The last thing we needed was him to come snooping around and find her. So, Glad signed the papers and, well, we showed the judge the pictures and the home movie, and it was pretty much a slam dunk. Bobby went to jail for felony assault and Glad went back to hiding in that RV."

"Wow. Do you still have the pictures or the home movie?"

"Yeah, somewhere I guess. At Ang's probably. Do you really want to see them?"

"Maybe." My gut flopped. "Not really. You know, Jacob, Glad never mentioned having a baby to me. What happened to it?"

"I'm getting to that. Like I said, Glad was in real bad shape when we found her. Not just physically. She was scared as a whipped puppy. It took her a good three months of living in the RV before she felt safe enough to peek her head out. She still believed that devil Bobby was coming back to get her. Anyway, Ang called me one day saying she'd had a breakthrough with Glad. I drove down to see what she was talking about."

"So, what had happened?"

"I don't exactly know for sure. It was like that RV full of butter-flies was some kind of magic chrysalis or something for Glad. Ang had a routine of checking on Glad a couple of times a day. She'd bring meals to her in the RV. When she did, Glad was usually staring off in-to never-never land or sleeping. But one day Ang walked in and Glad sat up and started talking. It was still kind of crazy talk, but any talk-ing was good in Glad's case."

"What did she say?"

"Mumbo jumbo, mostly. Bobby must have brainwashed her good. She said crazy religious stuff like the devil was after her. That the devil himself had chosen her virgin child among all others or something like that. One thing I remember for sure was that Glad said Jesus sent 'the butterfly' to save her."

"The butterfly? To save who? Glad or her baby?"

"Hmmm. I don't rightly know."

"How had a butterfly saved her?"

"As far as I could tell, it hadn't. She was crazy. But you know, Val, there's moments in life you can hardly believe, even though you lived through 'em yourself. I asked Glad pretty much the same question—how had a butterfly saved her? You know what she did?"

"What?"

"She reached a hand into her mouth, pulled out her top dentures and handed them to me. I was so floored I couldn't do anything but take 'em. Glad stared at me for a minute, then she told me to look on the back of her teeth. I did, and I'll be darned. Glued to the back of her dentures was a little silver piece of jewelry with tiny green stones in it. She told Ang and me that the butterfly had left it for her so she could find Thelma again."

I shivered despite the late afternoon heat.

"That...that doesn't make any sense, Jacob."

"I told you. Glad was crazy back then. It took another year of coaxing for us to sort out that Glad's mom had given her a pin shaped like a butterfly. Glad had worn it all the time in memory of her dead mother. But one day Bobby punched her on the shoulder and broke it. After that, Glad kept the main part of the brooch pinned to the inside of baby Thelma's diaper. The broken part she kept glued to her dentures."

"Why would she do that?"

"Because she was crazy—like a fox," Jacob said, and touched a finger to his graying temple. "Glad said her dentures were the safest place to keep something because Bobby had quit hitting her in the mouth by then. He didn't want to have to pay for another set of new teeth. Probably wouldn't have bought the first set if he didn't have to keep up appearances with his customers...the church people. And he sure as hell wasn't going to change the baby's diaper. Pretty clever of her, if you think about it."

I thought about it. It really *was* clever.

"Anyway, from then on, Glad kept the main part of the brooch on the baby and the broken-off piece glued to her dentures so that they would always be connected. I guess she thought it was some kind of talisman against harm. Maybe she thought the butterfly was her mom protecting her from up in heaven. Whatever she thought, I guess it didn't work, because one day, baby Thelma just up and disappeared."

"What do you mean, *disappeared?*"

"That's the saddest part of all. Years later, when Glad was a lot better, almost back to herself even, she confessed to me that she wasn't sure what happened to her daughter. She said she woke up one day and baby Thelma was gone. She didn't know if she'd done something with her, or Bobby had. When she confessed that to me, Glad broke down and cried like nothing I've ever seen before or hope to see again."

Jacob looked away for a moment and studied the boats in the harbor. A fat grey squirrel ran by carrying a peanut in its mouth. Jacob watched it run along the edge of the sidewalk past our bench. He turned back to face me and continued.

"Glad had blanked out a lot of memories. Self-preservation, I guess. Anyway, she said she could have been the one who got rid of Thelma. She could have given her away or left her somewhere. She knew first-hand that Bobby was a ticking time bomb. She remembered fearing for Thelma's safety so much she could hardly sleep or eat. Giving Thelma away for her own good might have won out over Glad's own desire to keep her. Considering Bobby's violent temper and the sheer misery of their situation, Glad confessed she thought that maybe those people at the mercy home had been right. She should have given Thelma up for adoption."

I tried to picture Glad back then. I couldn't imagine how desperate she must have been. I didn't *want* to imagine it. "Poor Glad! Do you think she did? Get rid of her baby herself, I mean?"

"Who knows? She could have. But my money's on Bobby. After all, he was paid five grand to make the baby disappear. And after Thelma vanished, Glad said Bobby took great delight in torturing her by saying he saw the devil himself come and steal her illegitimate child away. One time he even told her he *saw* the devil tear Thelma to shreds and eat her. He gave Glad a lock of blonde hair as proof. Glad hid the hair away, like she did the butterfly pin. She showed the hair to my sister Ang, but it turned out to be plastic threads like from a Barbie doll head."

My heart sank. "So Thelma's probably dead."

"Probably. But I'll tell you something I haven't told anybody, Val. I wanted proof, and the only person I figured knew for sure was Bobby Munch, the devil himself."

"What are you saying, Jacob?"

"Bobby did twelve years at Appalach'. Part for what he did to Glad, the other for embezzling church funds. When I found out Bobby was getting out, me and a friend of mine made a plan. Bobby didn't know neither one of us. When he came marching out, wasn't nobody waiting for him. I told that buck-toothed jerk that my friend had just got out of the slammer, too. We invited Bobby along for some whiskeys and beers to celebrate. Believe me, he didn't need much convincing. After we got him good and drunk we threw him in the back of the truck. You know, there's lots of woods up there near Chattahoochee. Lots of places no one can hear a man scream."

Another shiver went down my spine. I scooted a few inches down the bench away from Jacob. I watched his face grow cold and bitter as he spoke.

"When morning came around, we were about as far from earshot as a man can get. Bobby woke up on the ground hog-tied and hungover. Now Val, I'm a Southern gentleman. I asked Bobby politely what he did with baby Thelma, but he wasn't talking. Well, I'm a man who believes in Old Testament justice. An eye for an eye. A tooth for a tooth. I figured Bobby owed Glad about eight teeth. So I got out a set of pliers and got to work. I was fair about it. I gave him a chance to talk between each tooth. He hollered plenty. But he never confessed. I guess prison taught him how to tolerate pain. Or maybe he figured losing his choppers was better than another stint in the hoosegow. Or death row for murdering the baby."

Jacob laughed bitterly and looked out toward the harbor again. He turned back to face me with a sadistic grin that made my spine squirm.

"Just for fun, I left Bobby's two front teeth alone," he said coolly. "When we untied him and drove off, he looked like a bloody, bucktoothed water rat. He tried to cuss us, but he couldn't say squat with that mangled mouth. We might not a got any information out of Bobby Munch, but we sure as hell got our revenge."

"What happened to Bobby after that?" I asked, trying not to sound horrified.

Jacob's smile evaporated. "What do I care? At that point, he was worthless to me. I didn't have any more reason to see his worthless face again."

"Did you tell Glad what you did?"

Jacob shook his head almost violently. "No! I figured there was no use opening up old wounds. Glad was in pretty good shape by then. A little skittish, but well enough. For years she'd begged me not to tell Tony that I'd found her. She'd needed all that time to recover, you see? But a week or two before Bobby got out, she'd asked to see Tony for the first time. I didn't want to set her back and mess that up."

"I get it. But tell me Jacob, if things were so bad with Bobby, why didn't Glad just leave him?"

"If you'd seen her, you wouldn't be asking. I'm sure she figured no one would have her. Bobby made darn sure she was no looker no more."

I gazed across the street at a small sailboat as it bobbed in the harbor. Its long, thin mast pointed up to a pale blue sky already fading to pink at the edges. Jacob's story had drained me of something vital. It was getting late and I still had to pack for the trip tomorrow. In the hot, humid twilight, the white lights strung in the oak canopies glistened eerily, like Christmas Eve in hell.

"I've got to go, Jacob."

"Sure. Just one more thing. You said you found papers. Was one Glad's birth certificate? Or her daughter's?"

"Uh...no. Just a marriage certificate."

Jacob's shoulders straightened. "So you still don't have any proof her daughter existed. Except for what I told you and that letter from Tony to Glad."

"Right."

Something in Jacob's eyes changed that made me even more uncomfortable. I stood up to go.

"I'll touch base again next week," I said and took a step toward home.

Jacob reached out and grabbed my arm. My skin crawled to the top of my head. I wanted to scream, but held my breath. Jacob stared intently in my eyes and said, "Just wanted to shake your hand goodbye."

I blew out a breath of relief.

You've watched too many scary movies, you silly twit!

I tried to convince myself nothing creepy was going on. Still, Jacob's capacity to hurt someone had chilled me to the bone. Now, contact with his hand was sending ice cubes up my spine.

"Goodbye, Jacob."

I let go of the old man's hand and walked quickly through the park, my relief expanding along with the growing distance between us. Jumpy, I fought the urge to look back as I waited for the light to change at the corner of Beach Drive and Fifth Avenue. Like a kid who just heard a story about a hook-handed murderer on the loose, I scurried my way north on Beach as if I was being chased by the wind.

Just a block from my apartment, I passed a row of cars parked across the road. In the fading light of dusk, I made out the form of a person sitting in the driver's seat of one of the cars. The plump figure turned its face away from me as I walked by, and I thought I saw a row of white, sausage-like links trailing down its back.

I TOLD MY BODY TO KEEP walking like nothing happened. It probably wasn't *her*. But my body wasn't listening. My right knee buckled. I nearly fell, face-first on the sidewalk.

I recovered in time to save my healing nose from certain annihilation, but it cost me a turned ankle. My heart thumped like a drum in my ears. I limped as fast as I could the rest of the way to my apartment. My thoughts whooshed by blankly, like a speeding car down a pitch-black stretch of country road.

What is the world is going on here?

My aching ankle made climbing the stairs arduous and painful. Getting the key in the lock was even harder. My hands shook so badly I dropped the rattling bundle three times. Finally, I took a deep breath to steady myself.

With the focused intensity of a well-hammered drunk, I managed to get the right key in the hole and hobbled inside. I slammed the door and jerked the deadbolt in place—the first time I'd used it since moving in. All I could think of was to call Tom.

I nervously punched in his number. He answered on the second ring.

"I saw her! I think I saw her!"

"Val? Is that you?"

"Yes, it's me! I think I saw her!"

"Okay. Slow down. Who did you see?"

"Thelma Goldrich!"

"The daughter? That's great!"

"No! The other one. The one who punched me in the nose!"

The line was silent for a few seconds.

"Where?" Tom asked. His tone had turned dead sober.

"On the street near my apartment. In a car."

"How do you know it was her?"

"I'm not one hundred percent sure, but I saw her ponytail. I mean, I think it was her ponytail." I fought rising hysteria. "How many people in the world have a ponytail like that?"

"Okay, Val. Calm down. I got you. I'll check it out. Where did you see her exactly?"

Tom's calm demeanor caused something inside me to relax. The whooshing inside my head stopped. I took a breath. It felt like the first one in a long time.

"She was parked on Beach Drive. Between Seventh and Eighth."

"I'm on it. Now get some rest, Val. You're going to need it for the trip. See you around eight tomorrow morning. Good night."

"Good night, Tom. And thanks."

"You're welcome. One more thing. Make sure all of your doors and windows are locked."

Tom clicked off the phone. The whooshing sound roared back inside my head.

I scrambled around my tiny apartment and double-checked each window lock. Then, for good measure, I hooked every chain-latch on the front door.

Spent both physically and emotionally, I grabbed a beer from the fridge, plopped onto my hideous couch, hugged a lumpy brown pillow, and tried not to think.

Chapter Twenty-Four

I had to hand it to him, Tom was a man with a plan. Overnight he had set quite a few gears into motion, including a scheme to keep an eye on the whereabouts of "bulldog witch" Thelma Goldrich so we could drive up to meet "loony-bin" Thelma Goldrich.

I never realize irony could get so weird.

"More coffee?" I asked.

Tom leaned back, relaxed and comfortable on my wrinkled old lump of a couch. The contrast between the ugly brown sofa and his clean, shiny good looks was almost blinding. Tom's white sport shirt and crisp ironed jeans made him look like Mr. Clean—with a really good blond toupee. In fact, compared to Tom, everything in my apartment looked dull and dingy and faded. Including me.

"Sure. That's good coffee, Val."

I reached for Tom's cup. He gently caught my hand in his and tugged me toward him.

My apartment shrank to the size of a closet. My heart pounded in my ears. I pulled my hand away.

"I'm glad you like it," I said. "It's my special blend."

"I like your special blend," Tom teased.

I cringed out a smile and padded over to the coffee machine in my tiny kitchen. My neck was as hot as the coffee carafe. I forced myself to take deep, yoga breaths while I filled his cup and bit my lip. I was resolved not to make a fool of myself.

"Here you go," I said, and handed Tom his coffee.

He patted the sofa next to him, but I didn't dare sit down. A crappy voice inside my head said it was too good to be true. Unfortunately, I listened.

"So what's the plan, specifically?" I asked.

Tom's face shifted to neutral. My mood switched to disappointed self-loathing.

"Goober's going to drive his dodgy Dodge over to Bimini Circle and stake out Tony's old house," Tom explained. "Jorge will park his Buick on your street and keep an eye on your apartment. Anyone sighting Bulldog Goldrich is to report back to me, then try to follow her discreetly back to her hideout."

"Why?"

"We need to find out where she's staying so we can keep track of her," Tom said.

I cringed. "Do you think she was *stalking* me?"

"I don't know, Val. But I'd rather be safe than sorry."

I nodded. "Thanks. How did you get the guys to do it on such short notice?"

Tom laughed. "Let's just say their schedules were free at the moment. And the incentive was right."

"Incentive? Did you pay them? I'll pay you back...."

"Val, the incentive was *you*. They're doing it for *you*."

Unexpectedly, hot tears filled my eyes. Tom stood up and hugged me. Suddenly, I couldn't breathe. My legs began to wobble like a drunk in an earthquake. I felt weak and vulnerable and awkward. Freefalling into feelings was not my forte. I needed to find a branch to grab onto. I pushed away from Tom's embrace and reached for an old standby.

I tried to crack a joke.

"Your plan makes sense," I quipped hoarsely. "Goober and Jorge both have cars, and they're both used to living in them."

Tom studied me as I plastered on the worst fake smile ever and carefully wiped my runny nose with a tissue. I'd had one in my hand perpetually since receiving Bulldog Woman's face-rearranging right hook.

"So, what did you come up with for Winky to do?" I asked.

"Oh. He's coming with us."

"What?" Dashed expectations dropped my stomach three inches.

"Yeah. Jorge should be here with him any minute."

"But...why?"

"Because Jorge is coming here anyway to stake out your apartment. Remember?"

"Yes, I remember!" I groused. "Tom, I didn't mean, 'Why is Jorge the one bringing Winky.' I meant, 'Why does Winky have to go with us?'"

Tom grinned, and his sea-green eyes sparkled with mischief. He'd played me like a cat with a string. My feelings for him had been tricked out of me. Part of me was embarrassed. But another part of me kind of liked it.

I snorted out a laugh. Tom took my hand in his, and rubbed the back of my hand gently with his thumb as he spoke.

"Winky's from up there, Val. He knows the area. He might come in handy."

"I'm from up there, too. Remember, Mr. Detective?"

"I do remember. But Winky has a certain, how can I say it, *redneck flair.*"

"You mean he's a good-old *boy*?"

Tom smiled and kissed the back of my hand.

"Precisely. And we might need that kind of *man*power."

"But...."

"No buts, Val. Somebody's got to babysit Winky. Would you rather we take Jorge and leave *Winky* to guard your place?"

Dang. He had a point. I wasn't even sure if Winky was potty-trained.

I was trying to come up with a snappy response when Tom's cell-phone jingled.

"Buena dias, amigo," Tom answered, then hung up. "They're here."

"They're coming up?" I asked, slightly horrified.

"Don't you want them to?"

I felt too guilty to say no. After all, they were doing me a huge favor. But still. *Two homeless guys in my apartment?*

Tom studied me for a moment. "You don't have to let them stay, Val. But it would be nice if Jorge could come up and use the restroom once in a while. Maybe make a sandwich?"

I felt like such a jerk.

"Of course!" I said, beating back every instinct in my body and brain. I reluctantly handed Tom a key.

At least Jorge was domesticated. He'd been married, once.

Tom smiled and took the key. Someone knocked on the door. Tom let go of my hand and opened it. Jorge and Winky came tumbling in like...I hated to say it...*two stooges.*

"Nice digs, Val Pal! Use your crapper?"

I stood there, stunned.

Winky didn't wait for an answer. He barreled across my tiny living room straight into the bathroom. He shut the door, but the close proximity lent no privacy other than visual. As Winky grunted and farted on the throne, I took the time to show Jorge the ropes. Or in the case of my miniscule apartment, maybe it was just the strings.

"Here's the coffee machine," I said. I reached into the kitchen cabinet and pulled out the coffee and filters. "I'll leave these on the counter for you. Help yourself to coffee and anything else in the fridge."

"Tank you, Val," Jorge said, looking at the floor. "Berry nice of you."

"No, Jorge. It's very nice of *you*. Thanks for doing this for me. You can sleep on the couch, if you want."

"Tanks, but I like my car. The Buick's backseat is really comfy. You should try it sometime."

I was pondering how to respond to that when Winky emerged in a cloud of stink reminiscent of my beer-and-bratwurst days in Germany.

"Woo hoo! I wouldn't go in there for at least an hour," Winky said proudly.

"I'd say better make it at least two days," Tom quipped. "Let's get out of here before the mustard gas kills us."

"Road trip! I call shotgun!" Winky hollered.

"Dang it!" I griped.

"That's right. Dang it, Winky," Tom said. "Val's already beat you to it."

Winky wilted like lettuce in a microwave.

"I'll dang it, all right," he sulked. "Dang it, dang it, dang it. But them's the rules."

I smiled at Tom. He winked back at me, then took my overnight bag in one hand and shook Jorge's hand with the other. "Take good care of the place, mi amigo."

"I will," Jorge replied. "Via con Dios."

"Will do, padre," Winky shot back. "I got your 'vehicle-deos' right here." Winky held up a small green piece of cardboard shaped like a Christmas tree. "Took it right off your rearview mirror, Jorge. Figured we'd need it more than you."

"I can't argue with that," Jorge said.

None of us could.

WINKY CLIMBED INTO the backseat of Tom's silver 4Runner. I hopped in the passenger's side next to Tom. As I buckled my seatbelt, my foot scraped against a grey case that looked like a fancy tackle box.

"What's this?" I asked Tom.

"Nothing mysterious. Just where I keep envelopes and bags for collecting samples from crime scenes and suspects. I *am* a cop, you know."

"I know. Why did you bring it along?"

"I always have it with me. Besides, it might come in handy. Nothing says 'daughter' like a matching DNA sample."

"What! You're going to get a DNA sample from Thelma?"

"If I can. You got a problem with that?"

"Well, uh...," I started, but was cut off.

"Tom, you gonna cut a chunk off'n her or stick a Q-Tip down her throat?" Winky bellowed from the backseat.

"Not sure, yet, Winky."

"I'll hold her down if you need me to, buddy. You can count on my co-operation."

"Thanks for the offer, bud. I'll keep it in mind."

"I thought we were just going to visit her," I said.

"We are," said Tom. "But we might as well try for DNA. Chances are, she won't even notice."

Something inside me contracted.

This crap was starting to get real.

Chapter Twenty-Five

Traveling with Winky was like transporting a wild orangutan without a cage. He whooped and hollered and bounced around in the backseat of Tom's silver 4Runner until I was afraid we might be pulled over for reckless endangerment. Something had to give. We were driving on I-275 just north of Tampa when I made an executive decision.

"Tom, why don't we stop at Westley Chapel and get some refreshments?"

Tom looked over at me, then followed the downward movement of my shifting eyes toward my lap. Inside my open purse, I held a bottle of Dramamine up for him to see. He looked at me quizzically. I shifted my eyes to the left and gave a quick nod toward the backseat. His eyebrows relaxed.

"Roger that, Val."

Tom hit the gas and the exit for SR54 came into view a few minutes later. Tom made a right and pulled in to a Lil' Champ convenience store. As he parked the car, visions of a fat, freckled chimp going wild in the snack aisle made my stomach flop. I started to speak, but Winky beat me to it.

"I can't get this gaul-dang door open!"

It was Tom's turn for shifty eyes. He arched his right eyebrow and cocked his head down toward his left hand. His finger was on the child safety lock.

Man, this guy thinks of everything.

I smiled and turned toward the backseat. Winky's face was flushed with frustration.

"Winky, we need you to stay in the car and guard it while we go inside."

"Dang it!"

"We'll only be a minute. What would you like? My treat!"

Winky's savage beast was instantly soothed. "Really?"

"Really."

"Woohoo! All righty, then, Val! I'll have me a RC Cola and a moon pie. 'Naner-flavored if they got it."

How appropriate.

"I'll check it out."

I found the RC Cola on the bottom shelf of the glass cooler case in the convenience store. I popped the cap on a bottle and dropped in two Dramamine tablets as Tom watched.

"I could have you arrested for that, you know," he smirked.

"I suppose you'd rather hear him read every road sign from here to Chattahoochee—complete with sound effects?"

Tom laughed. "God, no. I don't even want to imagine what he'd do with those sexy billboards near Ocala."

I put my thumb over the bottle lip and shook the cola. "Happen to see any moon pies around here, Mister?"

"No. How about a pecan log, Miss?"

Tom held up a monster-sized candy bar and eyed me lasciviously.

"Maybe later," I said nonchalantly, causing his eyebrows to rise nearly to his scalp. I giggled. "Hmmm. No moon pies. That calls for redneck plan B."

I grabbed a bag of salted peanuts and poured half of them into the RC. The cola foamed up and out of the bottle, spilling onto the floor.

"What the heck are you doing?" Tom asked. He grabbed a handful of napkins from next to the hotdog roasting machine and helped me wipe up the mess.

"Better here than in your car," I replied.

"Got-cha. Good thinking, partner."

"So we're partners now?"

"If you play your cards right."

I grinned and grabbed a Dr. Pepper out of the cooler.

"Hey, I'll take one of those," Tom said.

"Finally, something we have in common," I quipped. I handed him a Dr. Pepper, then fished around in my purse for my wallet.

Tom touched my shoulder. "Forget it. I've got this."

"Thanks," I offered gratefully.

He paid the cashier, and we climbed back into the 4Runner. Before I strapped in, I reached over the backseat and handed Winky his foamy reward for good behavior.

"Sorry, no moon pies, Winky. But I fixed you up real good anyway."

Winky's eyes widened with delight.

"All right! I ain't had me one a these in a coon's age! Thanky, Val!"

Winky flung his head back and took a giant slug out of the bottle. He swallowed hard to get the foamy soda down, then crunched on a mouthful of peanuts. "Mighty dang good!"

I turned around to face Tom and slid into my best Southern drawl.

"That there's the original country-man dinner, don't cha know."

Tom shifted into reverse and grinned.

"I stand corrected. You really *do* speak redneck."

WITH THE ORANGUTAN fed and sedated, we were faced with a new problem. Winky had a snore that could rattle the windows on the Concord. Between our charge's thunderous blasts, Tom and I took turns sharing our life histories.

I learned Tom had grown up in Orlando, and had a degree in business from the University of Central Florida. Fresh out of college, he'd tried a desk job for almost a year. But he couldn't adjust to life confined to a cubicle, no matter how big or fancy it might have eventually evolved into.

"I guess you might call it failure to thrive in the business environment," he joked. "But it just seemed pointless...shuffling papers around. I'm not much of a theoretical guy. I'm more hands-on."

"I've noticed."

Tom grinned, then reached over and put his hand on my thigh. Electric heat shot through my entire body. I mean my *entire* body.

"It's a long drive. Better pace yourself, tiger," I said, and peeled his hand from my leg.

Tom grinned, shrugged, and focused on the road.

"So how did you end up in the police force?"

"Process of elimination, mostly," he replied. "I wanted a job that would get me outside. I tried landscaping, but I needed more adventure—and less sun. I would come home from mowing lawns all day so dehydrated all I could do was lie on the couch, drink water and watch TV. In a way, I guess that led me to my next career move. I watched a lot of those TV detective shows and thought, what the heck. I'll give that a try. I went to the police academy and, voilà, here I am."

"How long have you been a cop?"

"Twenty years this month. Seems like a lot less. Crazy, but I can still remember my first case."

"What was it?"

Tom took his eyes off the road for moment. "Are you really interested, or are you just trying to pass the time?"

"Does it have to be one or the other, officer?"

"Fair enough. The Buckaroo Bandit."

"Huh?"

"My first case. I called it The Buckaroo Bandit. Back then, I was a little less jaded and a lot more creative."

"I can see that. So tell me about it," I said as the exit sign for Dade City passed by.

"When you're first on the force, you're low man on the totem pole. You have to go where there's a job opening. I ended up spending six months in Chiefland, Florida. Pretty podunk little town back then. Still is, probably. Can't say, as I haven't been back. But as small-potatoes as it was, that town still handed me my butt in a beer can. A pretty weird case I never did solve."

"Weird?"

"*Really* weird. Some local farmer was trawling for catfish in the Apalachicola River that summer and snagged a skull. A human one. He fished it out and brought it to the station in a Piggly-Wiggly grocery bag. I'll never forget it. I felt just like Barney Fife on *Mayberry RFD*. I took one look inside the bag and nearly crapped my pants trying to keep from laughing."

"Laughing? Why?"

"The skull only had two teeth left in it. Two front teeth as bucked out as teeth can be. The guy must have been half rabbit. Maybe that's why we never found his next-of-kin. They were hiding in a hole somewhere eating carrots."

"You've got to be kidding me!"

"Nope. You just can't make that stuff up."

"No. You sure can't. Tom, pull over. I've got something to tell you."

Chapter Twenty-Six

"Wow, Val. If what you're saying is true, Jacob could have murdered Bobby Munch."

"I know."

We'd stopped at a Steak & Shake in Ocala for an early lunch. Winky was still sawing logs in the backseat of the 4Runner. Tom and I were sitting in a shiny black booth with a shiny chrome jukebox. A shiny pink waitress took our order.

Why did everything have to be so freaking shiny?

"As far as I know, my old Buckaroo Bandit case is still open, Val. I've got to report this. What's Jacob's last name?"

"Crap. I think he told me. Maybe not. I don't know."

"Phone number?"

"I only gave him mine. But wait. He called me yesterday. His number should be in my phone."

"Okay. Give me your phone and I'll get someone working on that."

I handed my phone over and went to the restroom while Tom placed the call. As the squeaky door closed behind me, I suddenly felt trapped inside a bad horror movie. Even my reflection in the bathroom mirror looked odd and unfamiliar.

What the hell am I doing here? Busted nose. Traveling alone with two strange men—to meet a woman in the loony bin! And last night....

Oh my word! I may have spent time chatting up a murderer! *My life isn't going down the drain. It's going down the toilet!*

"It's all right, kiddo."

Glad!

I grabbed the stall door next to me and jerked it open. It was empty.

What did you expect, Val?

I let go of the door. As it creaked to a close, something caught my eye. On the top right corner of the stall, exactly where my hand had been, was a dragonfly sticker. A chill shot through me.

Okay. Maybe I'm the one that should be in the loony bin.

Fighting back rising panic and tears, I pushed myself out of the restroom and into the shiny red, white and black world of ecstatically happy hamburgers and shakes. Tom was watching me from the booth. I scrutinized his face for telltale signs that he might be a serial killer, too. But then I realized I had no idea what to actually look for.

"They're on it. Shouldn't take long," Tom said. He looked at me closely. "You okay, Val? You look like you've seen a ghost."

"No. Just heard one."

"What?"

"Nothing.... It's just a lot...to take in."

"Never been that close to a potential murderer. I get it."

"Do you think he wants to kill me, Tom? Jacob, I mean?"

"I doubt it. If he did, you'd probably already be dead."

My mouth fell open and tears quickly filled my eyes to their brims. Tom reached over and took my hand.

"Geez. Sorry, Val. Cop humor. I don't see any reason why Jacob would be after you. We don't even know for sure he's involved in the Buckaroo case."

"How many bucked-tooth skulls can there be out there?"

"I don't know. They could be breeding like bunnies." Tom contorted his upper lip in a maniacal imitation of a rabbit. "Ehhh, what's up, Val?"

I snorted with frantic laughter, forcing runny snot to pour from my tender nose.

Tom jerked a couple of napkins from the chrome holder and handed them to me. I carefully honked my nose on one.

"She thought I was his girlfriend, you know," I said.

"What? Who?"

"Bulldog Thelma. She thought I was Tony's girlfriend. That's why she punched me in the nose."

"Oh." Tom's eyebrows knitted together and his smile drained away.

"There's something else, Tom. Jacob didn't know Glad was dead. When I told him, he wanted to know when she died. Then he wanted to know if I had her birth certificate. He also asked about a birth certificate for her daughter. Does all that mean anything?"

"I don't know. Anything else you haven't told me?"

I thought about dragonflies and broken brooches and Glad's voice in my head. "Nope."

"All right then. You ready to blow this burger joint?"

"I sure am."

Tom grabbed a handful of napkins on the way out.

"Just in case," he said with a wink.

WE TRAVELED NORTH ON I-275 to Lake City, then headed west on I-10 toward Tallahassee. The trip was half over. Winky was still sawing logs in the backseat. Now it was my turn to answer Tom's questions.

"How did you end up in St. Petersburg? Isn't your family from the Panhandle area?"

"I never lived up there long," I answered. "In Greenville, I mean. My parents moved around a lot. I grew up a bit of a redneck, and finished high school in Lakeland. Then I astonished everyone and moved to Tampa to get a bachelor's degree from the University of South Florida. After that, I worked for an insurance company and married a guy. We moved to St. Pete. Things didn't work out. I moved to Germany. Blah blah blah. Lather, rinse, repeat. Now I'm back home."

Tom shot me a look. "A real romantic, aren't you?"

I cringed. "I used to be. Now I guess I'm just...cynically optimistic."

"Cynically optimistic? No wonder you love irony, Val. You *are* irony!"

I was trying to think of a clever comeback when Tom's phone rang. I watched the pine trees and oaks whiz by on the side of the interstate while he listened for a minute, then hung up.

"It was a burner."

"Huh?"

"Jacob's cellphone. It was a pay-as-you-go. Disposable. Untraceable."

"Oh."

"Doesn't necessarily mean anything. But it doesn't help his case *or* ours. What's he doing down in St. Pete, anyway?"

"He was a friend of Tony's. Down for the funeral."

"The funeral was last week. So why's he still there?"

A good question for which I had no good answer.

I shrugged and looked out the window again. Sunday afternoon was ticking by. I thought about the new synopsis of *Double Booty* I'd emailed to Jamie this morning. It seemed like a year ago.

Would it be good enough to win me a publishing contract? Would I be able to pay my rent next month?

Tom poked my leg. "Hey. Where'd you go?"

"Lady Lala Land."

"*Okay*. Go there often?"

"According to Goober, yes."

Tom's phone rang again.

"Hola, amigo." Tom looked at me and silently mouthed the name, "Jorge."

"Uh huh. What did he look like? Uh huh. No. Yeah. Go ahead and follow her. Call me when you know something. Ciao."

"What's up?"

"Jorge said he saw Bulldog Thelma and some guy drive up your street. They stopped for a minute in front of your place. The man got out, took a picture of the house, then got back in and they took off. Funny, Jorge said the guy was an old blanco. White shirt, white belt, white shoes."

Jacob!

My whole body started trembling. "Tom, that sounds like Jacob. He and that Bulldog Thelma woman...*they're working together!* And they're *out to get me!*"

"Hold on, Val. Why would they be out to get you?"

"I don't know! *You're* the freaking detective!"

I lost it and started bawling my eyes out.

"It's going to be all right, Val," Tom said gently. "You're safe with me."

Tom sat in silence and let me have my cry. I took my time moaning and mulling over my situation.

Why did I ever let myself get involved with these crazy people? I should have kept to myself. Relationships never worked out for me. People are hard. People are pain. People are dangerous!

My pity party lasted a good half hour. Then I shifted back to cynically optimistic. *Dang it!*

Tom saw me come up for air and flashed me a reassuring smile.

"You're cute when you're terrified. I'd kiss you if I weren't driving seventy miles an hour down I-10 through the middle of Tallahassee."

"*Now* look who's the romantic." I sniffed and blew my sore nose carefully. "Where are we staying tonight?"

"I thought we would get a hotel in Chattahoochee."

I snorted a laugh. "You've obviously never been to Chattahoochee. There's no hotels there. They barely have a traffic light. We better stop in Quincy and check for rooms. Take the next exit once we get past Tallahassee, city boy."

"Yes ma'am. You feeling better?"

"I guess," I muttered.

"I'm serious about not worrying about Jacob and that woman you call Bulldog, Val. Statistically, you have a much greater risk of dying in an automobile accident than getting murdered."

I shot Tom a dirty look. "Is that supposed to make me feel better?"

Tom grimaced. "Somehow it sounded a lot better in my head."

"Thanks for trying, Tom. Just do me a favor. Keep your eyes on the road. Our exit is coming up."

Tom took a right off the interstate and soon the ugly, hardscrabble town of Quincy came into view. "I hate Quincy," I said. "I got my one and only traffic ticket here from a mean old cop when I was seventeen."

Tom laughed and tried to talk like a redneck. "Maybe I can make it up to you, sugar doodle."

"That's the worst Southern accent I've ever heard."

"Thanks," Tom said, pretending to be crestfallen.

He pulled the 4Runner into the parking lot of the town's only motel, The Sandman Inn. "Wish me luck," he said, then hopped out and went inside a rust-red door labeled "Motel Office." He was out and tapping on my window not much more than a minute later. I rolled down the pane.

"Bad news, sugar doodle," Tom said, his bad accent making an unrequested encore. "It's the annual Flea Across Florida Festival. Manager said there's no rooms to be had 'round these parts' for fifty miles."

"Great. Just when I thought things couldn't get any worse."

Crap. I guess desperate times really did call for desperate measures.

"I'll call my mother and see if she's got room for us. But first I'm going to need a drink."

Tom looked at me warily. "Come on. Your mom can't be *that* bad."

"Sugar doodle, you have no idea."

Chapter Twenty-Seven

The sun was fading in the sky ahead of us. Tom was driving fifty-five on I-10, and I was chugging down my second Budweiser. Suddenly, Winky came to life with a snort, then commenced to yelling like a stuck pig.

"Where the hell am I?" he bellowed. He hoisted himself up and rubbed his radish eyes. I swigged my beer and watched the redheaded redneck in horrified fascination as he felt around on his freckled face with both pudgy hands, found a peanut stuck to his cheek, peeled it off and ate it.

"Just outside Greenville," Tom answered. "We're waiting for Val's liquid courage to kick in."

Winky looked at me and nodded. "Well hurry up. I'm so hungry I could eat a possum."

"Here, have a hoagie instead." Tom tossed Winky a greasy white paper bag. "Picked up beer and dinner at the Junior Store down the road. Sorry. They were fresh out of possum."

"What's a dad burned Hokie?" Winky asked. He snatched the bag and ripped into it. "This here's a summarine sammich, Yankee boy."

Winky chomped on the sandwich like a hungry gator. The grunts and groans he made as he crammed it into his face were almost pornographic. Still, they were preferable to what I knew was coming as soon as I stepped inside the door at dear old mom's.

I drained the second Budweiser and set my jaw to lock-down. "Let's roll," I hissed.

MY MOTHER LIVED IN what I semi-affectionately called, "The tristate area of denial." Denial about how filthy her house was. Denial about how lazy she was. Denial about how mean-spirited and petty she was. But I had to say *this* for her—she'd give you the shirt off her back if you needed it.

You'd just have to wash it first.

She and my father divorced nearly thirty years ago. He died a decade later. She remarried three years ago and now lived with her perfect match—a legally blind guy with the patience of a snail on Prozac. His name was Dale, but my sister and I affectionately call him, "The Hostage." I was explaining all this to Tom when we pulled up in their front yard and ran over something metal hiding in the foot-tall grass.

"What the hell?!" Tom cursed his luck and jumped out of the 4Runner to assess the damage.

My mother must have heard the commotion. The front door cracked open and a little white-and-tan, mixed breed pooch came shooting out into the yard. It disappeared in the grass, yapping its head off. A second later, the silhouette of my rotund mother in a faded old shirt and worn-out stretch pants appeared on the porch. She made a visor over her eyes with a pudgy hand and peered out at us.

"Ragmuffin!" she hollered. "Is that you? Y'all come on inside. Don't you have no sense? It's too hot to be out this time a day!"

I popped a breath mint and sighed. "We're coming!"

"Ragmuffin?" Tom asked, his right eyebrow up to his hairline.

"Zip it, copper." I wasn't joking.

Tom and Winky followed me into the house. My mom offered them a seat on a couch even uglier than mine. She carefully positioned her extra-wide derriere, then leaned backward and fell into her worn-out recliner. The whole house smelled faintly of old farts, urine and Jergens hand lotion. A hodgepodge collection of Olan Mills family portraits hung on the wood-paneled wall above the sofa like a gallery of the doomed. I was there as well, in my glorious missing-front-tooth stage, along with big-hair prom night and mascara-meltdown college graduation. A few open spaces on the wall between frames offered tell-tale clues to marriages that were no longer to be mentioned.

"Mom, these are my friends Tom and Winky."

Tom nodded and smiled. Winky bowed and curtseyed.

Unbelievable!

"Guys, this is my mom, Lucille Jolly."

Mom scrunched her face at me. "I ain't Jolly no more, Val. I'm *Short*. Since me and Dale got married."

"Oops. Sure, Mom. Sorry. This is my mom, Mrs. Short."

"Nice to meet y'all," my mother said. "Would y'all like some sweet tea?"

"Yes ma'am," answered Winky before anyone else could speak.

"Vallie, why don't you get in there and make us some."

Here we go.

"Sure," I replied sweetly, then picked my way around mom's hopelessly cluttered kitchen. Amongst the ruins, I found an ancient, rubber-handled saucepan and a box of Lipton tea. I filled the pan with water from the tap and set it on the stove to boil. Then I pretended to be busy while I eavesdropped on the conversation going on in the living room.

"Nice place you have here," said Tom.

"Thanky, Tom. How do you know my other girl, Val?"

"We're both friends of Winky, here."

Nice dodge, Tom.

"Winky. Ain't you one a them from the Alford clan in Grand Ridge?"

"No ma'am. But I'm kin to the Jeeters in Graceville."

"The Jeeters, huh? I know'd you was from around here. You got good manners, son."

I stifled a laugh and nearly busted my nose open again. *Ouch!*

"Tom, where's yore family from?"

"Maryland, ma'am."

"You a *Yankee?*" It was more an accusation than a question.

"Oh. No, ma'am. I was born in Florida. My family moved from Maryland before I was born."

"Hmmm," mom growled.

The water started to boil. I dropped in four tea bags and watched the clear water turn to brown sludge. I switched off the burner, then tugged at an old plastic pitcher in the drain board until I could get it out from under a mountain of Cool Whip containers without causing an avalanche. I rinsed the stained interior of the yellow pitcher and scooped a full cup of sugar from a bag on the counter. I poured in the sugar, then the hot, brown brew. I filled the pitcher to the top with tap water and was done. Sweet tea just the way my mother taught me.

I rinsed out four miss-matched jelly jars, filled them with ice and tea, and carried them out to the living room.

My mother took a sip and scrunched her upper lip. "Kind of weak, but you never did know how to make good tea, Val."

"Sorry, Mom. Where's Dale?"

"Already gone to bed. Here, take this for me." Mom placed something wet in my hand. "It's my bridge. I don't like to wear it when I'm drinking tea. Might stain my teeth."

I looked down at the u-shaped piece of metal embedded with two false molars. I reset my jaw again. "Where do you want me to put it?"

"In the bathroom on the toothbrush holder. Don't you know anything? Oh, I forget. You ain't been to visit in a long time."

My yoga breathing was about to get a lot of practice.

More pictures of unfortunate souls stared at me from cheap brown frames as I walked the sculptured-carpet gauntlet to the bathroom. I thought about dropping mom's bridgework in the toilet, but her familiar hammer of guilt slammed down on my conscience. I rinsed her dental work and hung it in a hole on the toothbrush holder next to tubes of denture cream and hair tonic, then made my way back to the scene of the crime in progress. Mom was laughing at something.

"Ha ha ha! Val, are y'all really here to visit some crazy lady in the Chattahoochee nuthouse?"

I shot an angry look at Tom. He pointed a thumb at Winky. I blew out a deep breath.

"Yes. Thelma Goldrich. Do you know her, Mom?"

"Never heard of her. What's she in for?"

I shot out an answer before anyone could say a word, leaving Winky's and Tom's mouths hanging open like stranded goldfish.

"She just has spells. Like everybody else around here."

My mother nodded knowingly. "Yep. I guess by now all of us has seen the inside of that place from one side or the other."

Tom looked at me with eyes as big as fried eggs. I pointed a thumb at my chest and shook my head no. Tom sighed, then laughed out loud with relief. I could almost hear the thud of his good impression of me as it hit the skids.

"She might be a millionaire," Winky blurted.

"Who?" my mother asked.

"That crazy lady. Thelma. We gonna steal some a her DNA and see if she's heir to the throne of Goldrich."

"You don't say," my mother said, leaning in now that the gossip had gotten good. She cocked her ear toward Winky. "How come you don't already know if it's her or not?"

I wanted to stop this train wreck, but it had already traveled too far down the tracks. I resigned myself to my usual role around my mother—horrified spectator.

"'Cause she up and got herself lost a long time ago, when she was just a baby," said Winky. He sat up straight, relishing his position as the deliverer of juicy news. "Her folks wat'n rich back then. But they are now. I mean, they was. They's both dead now. Anyway, it's what you might call complicated. Val says it's got to be her. Ain't nobody else fit the bill."

"I'll be," my mother said, and sat back in her faded, beige recliner. "A millionaire in a nuthouse. Now that's a cryin' shame waste a good money if I ever heard a one."

"Amen to that, ma'am." Winky lowered his head.

I shot Winky a look. "We don't know if she's actually a *millionaire*—"

"Oh well. Enough of that. It's time for Matlock," my mother chirped, switching gears as smoothly as a long-distance trucker. "Val, you wanna fix up the guest room for the fellers? You can sleep on the couch when I'm done with my programs."

"Sure, Mom."

"I think they's some Jello pudding packs in the fridge if anybody wants one. Val, could you get me a v'niller? If they ain't no v'niller, I'll take a butterscotch."

"Okay, Mom. Where can I –"

"Shhh. Program's startin'. I just *love* me some Matlock."

Mom turned to face the TV, as mesmerized as a lizard caught in the stare of a great blue heron.

I got Mom her pudding pack and fished around for bedclothes in the overstuffed linen closet full of mismatched sheets and towels. Tom helped me change the sheets on the rickety old full-sized bed in the guestroom.

"Sorry about the mothball smell," I said sheepishly. "And the Smurfs."

Tom laughed good-naturedly. "I've lived through worse. Don't worry about it, Val. I've got relatives, too, you know." Tom took my hand and tried to kiss me, but I turned my head away. Tom looked puzzled and a bit hurt.

"Don't take it wrong, Tom. It's just that...if this relationship *does* go somewhere, I don't want to remember this house as being the first place we kissed."

Tom grinned and sighed. "Got it. But I want a raincheck."

"Okay."

"Promise?"

"I promise." I squeezed Tom's hand, then let it go and walked to the bedroom door.

"You know, I'll be happy to take the couch, Val."

I turned around in the doorframe and smiled. "I wouldn't do that to you. I like you too much. Winky? Now he's another story. He knows how to fend for himself in the land of the skunk ape. Speaking of Winky, where is he?"

"Passed out in the back of the 4Runner would be my bet. He found the remainder of your six pack. The rest, as they say, is history."

Tom smiled and studied me with those sea-green eyes of his. He looked as out of place in my mom's house as a wristwatch on a T-Rex. I really *did* want to kiss him. But not here. This place held too many screwed-up memories. The last thing I wanted was to jinx my chances with him.

"Good night, Tom."

"Good night, Val. Oh, just one more thing."

"What?"

"Was your mother's last name really *Jolly?*"

"Yes. Now you know where I get my love of irony. I inherited it from my mother."

"That must be all you inherited. You don't look anything like her."

"Thanks," I said coyly. "You sure know how to sweet talk a girl."

Tom grinned.

I shut the door behind me, and tried to brand the image of his impish smile and handsome face into my memory banks.

Chapter Twenty-Eight

A vulture circled overhead. It landed and pecked me on the forehead.

I groaned and struggled to wake myself, but my limbs felt trapped in an impenetrable cocoon. For a moment, I thought I was on my couch in my apartment. Then I heard a familiar voice, and memories of yesterday came rushing back into my mind like floodwater into a dry riverbed.

I was at Mom's house...and an old man named Jacob was trying to kill me!

I cracked opened my eyes just in time to catch sight of a red blur heading right for my face. Before I could scrounge up enough energy to react, it landed on my forehead.

"Vallie, wake up."

My eyes flew open. Mom was standing over me. She tapped me on the forehead again with a dirty red flyswatter.

"I'm awake, Mom," I grumbled.

"Good. I need you to make the coffee. I got a new can of Maxwell House and I can't open it a'cause a my author-itis."

"Sure, Mom. Gimme a second."

I rubbed my eyes and watched the backside of my mother's pink housecoat disappear into the kitchen. She'd worn that fuzzy, floor-length coat for as long as I could remember. I guess some things never changed...especially when it came to moms.

I stumbled into the kitchen where she was unloading plastic containers from the refrigerator. It never failed. Whenever I visited Mom, she declared it was a good time to use up the leftovers. But I knew it was just a ploy to get me to wash all her dirty dishes.

"It's a good time to use up the leftovers, Vallie, while we got two strappin' young men here."

"Sure, Mom. Everybody loves green fried chicken and fuzzy mashed potatoes."

"Don't get smart with me, young lady."

"Just kidding." I smiled at my mom and her face softened. "Where's your can opener?"

Mom turned her head and shook it slowly, gazing at me as if I were a hopeless mental reject.

"Hangin' on the wall next to the stove, like always." She pointed a finger toward the wall, then bent over to retrieve more containers from the refrigerator.

"Oh." I yawned. "Where's Dale? Still sleeping?" I asked in the direction of her large, pink, fuzzy behind.

"Nope. He run off to IGA to get us some donuts. You gotta get there early or old Tiny McMullen'll buy the whole store out. I seen him eat three dozen glazed one morning in six minutes. Dale timed him. Tiny's a donut-eatin' machine."

"Well, hopefully Dale beat him to it this morning. He must have left early to walk there."

Mom slowly stood up with a jumble of plastic containers balanced in her hands. She shut the old fridge door with a shift of her ample behind. "Oh no. He drove the golf cart."

"Mom, isn't he blind?"

"He's not *that* blind. Besides, you know I don't drive no more."

Greenville's mascot, a one-legged Mallard duck named Greenback, had been the straw that finally broke the back on my mother being able to keep her driver's license. She'd already put a dent in nearly everybody's car in town. But when mom flattened Greenback the day before Easter last year, the sheriff had confiscated her license and told her she no longer had the privilege to legally drive a car in Jackson County.

Knowing Dale was blind, the sheriff had informed my mother she could still drive a golf cart. But mom didn't take to the sheriff's decision too well. Out of stubborn pigheadedness and pettiness, she refused, and made Dale drive the cart instead.

Without my morning coffee, I couldn't think of a response anywhere approaching appropriate for her sending poor, blind Dale out on the loose, so I kept my mouth shut and turned my attention to opening the can of Maxwell House. I watched the can slowly twirl along with the tinny grinding of the can opener, then click to a stop. I threw the metal disk in the garbage and scrounged around in the cupboards for a coffee filter. Soon, the aroma of fresh-brewed coffee filled mom's dirty, dated kitchen.

"I love that smell," Mom said. She'd taken her place at the head of the table and prepared herself to be waited on by me.

"Me too," I said. I poured us both a cup and sat to her left.

"Where's my Bailey's creamer?"

"Ooops. I'll get it."

I was poking around the inside of the fridge for the creamer when Tom came in the kitchen. He strutted around, making a grand appearance in his white t-shirt, white tennis shoes and socks, and a pair of Bermuda shorts held up with a white, woman's belt that could have wrapped around his body at least twice.

"Good morning, ladies," he said, grinning proudly. "Remind you of anybody?"

Mom grunted and looked back down at the paper. She was reading the comics, or as she liked to call them, "The funny papers." Everyone in the family knew it was against the law to disturb her during this important quality time.

I wasn't amused by Tom's foolery either. "Definitely not funny," I replied. "Jacob could have killed me! Just for that, you can get your own coffee."

Tom looked crestfallen. "Hey! I was just trying to make you feel better, Val." He twirled around. "See? I'm harmless."

"The joke's not working, Tom. Drop it."

"Ouch! Okay. I can see you're not a morning person."

"Nope."

"Duly noted."

The living room door flew open. Winky and Dale tromped in together, laughing like old buddies. Each displayed telltale signs of premature donut devouring. Mom caught sight of the white powder around their mouths and lost track of her good mood.

"Y'all didn't eat my cream-filled, now, did yer? Or my cruller?"

Winky and Dale jerked back and shriveled up like schoolboys caught peeping in the girls' locker room.

"I...I don't think so..." Dale stumbled. The Coke-bottle-thick lenses of his glasses made his eyes look twice as big, and doubly terrified. He opened the donut box and groped around inside. "Nope! Here's your cruller!" Dale held up a glazed donut that looked like a little tractor tire. I guess he could feel the tread on it.

"Good," Mom barked. "Now where's the cream-filled?"

Winky licked his lips and made a beeline for the door, leaving Dale holding the bag...or, more accurately, the box.

"Now ain't that just great," Mom grumbled. "I can't rely on nobody fer nothin' around here. Sometimes I feel like I'm livin' with a bunch a Charlie Browns. Ever'body's a Charlie Brown. Charlie Brown! Charlie Brown! Charlie Brown!"

Tom ducked his head like a whipped dog and turned back to face the kitchen counter. As he poured himself a cup of coffee, I leaned over and whispered in his ear. "Better Charlie Brown than Hagar the Horrible."

Tom shook his head and blew out a breath. "I don't know how you survived it here."

"Who said I survived?"

Tom smiled. "I did."

I smiled back. "Just for that, you can have my cruller."

WINKY HID OUT IN THE 4Runner all morning. I guess he was smarter than I gave him credit for. I'd snuck him a cup of coffee and another donut when Mom wasn't looking. He was all sugared up and raring to go when Tom and I loaded up for the trip to Chatta-hoochee State Hospital. We planned on heading over to meet Thel-ma G. Goldrich and then hightail it back to St. Petersburg. Tom turned the ignition. The 4Runner sputtered, belched and died.

"So much for our great escape," I said.

While Tom poked around under the hood, I went back in the house and asked Mom who we could call to take a look at the vehicle.

"Tiny McMullen, a course. Number's on the fridge. But don't let on that Dale got the big box a donuts this mornin'."

I called the number and a man answered on the fifth ring. "Yellow?"

"Is this Tiny McMullen?"

"Yes ma'am. What can I do you fer?"

"Our 4Runner won't start. Can you come take a look at it?"

"Sure thing. Where you at?"

"Greenville."

"That your silver 4Runner over at Dale's?"

"Uh...yes."

"Be there in a sec. I just live across the street."

"Oh. Thanks."

Just like my mom to leave out a minor detail like that.

I hung up the phone and went outside. Tiny was already on his way over. One look told me his name was a huge misnomer. The only way he could have been considered tiny was if he was swimming with a school of blue whales.

"Hey y'all!" Tiny called out from the middle of the street. He hitched up his huge overalls as he half-walked, half waddled barefoot across the red clay road. Tom looked up from under the hood at him, then back toward me, his face one big question mark.

"It's the cavalry. Tiny McMullen," I explained.

Tom stood up and shook Tiny's huge paw.

"Nice to meet you Tiny, I'm Tom."

"Likewise, I'm sure," said Tiny with a grin. Then he dove his head under the hood. "Watcha got here? Them Ty-otees can be tricky."

"Won't start," Tom said.

"Give it a try," Tiny said.

Tom climbed into the vehicle and turned it over. It sputtered and died.

"Hmm. Let me have a look at her. I ain't got nothin' else goin' on today. Where was y'all headed, anyways?"

"To Chattahoochee," I said.

"In or out?"

"What do you mean?" Tom asked.

"In Chattahoochee nuthouse or out in Chattahoochee proper?"

"Oh. In, I guess," Tom answered.

"We're going to visit someone," I said.

Tiny looked over at Winky, who was helping Mom's yappy dog chase a squirrel up a pecan tree. Tiny nodded knowingly and winked. "Gotcha. *Visit* someone. Sure."

"I...uh..." I began, but Tiny cut me off.

"Seein's how it's kinda an emergency, y'all can take my truck if y'all wanner." Tiny hiked a thumb toward his yard full of dead and decaying vehicles. "She ain't a looker but she runs like a wet dream. Ooops. Sorry Miss."

I shrugged and looked over at Tom. "Beats hanging around here."

"Sure, why not," Tom said. "Thanks, Tiny. Can we bring you anything back from Chattahoochee?"

"You're a gentleman and a scholar," Tiny said. "I sure wouldn't mind havin' me a Chattaburger. And fries. Uh...and a Mountain Dew, if it ain't too much trouble."

"Deal," said Tom. "Where can we find this place?"

I stuck an elbow in Tom's ribs. "I know where it is."

Tiny grinned. "You ought to. Chattaburger's world famous 'round here."

The men talked about mechanical stuff while I rounded up Winky. Tom fished the grey plastic container that looked like a double-decker tackle-box out of his truck. We climbed into Tiny's rusty old red Ford pickup. I sat in the middle of the bench seat because Winky'd gone and called shotgun. I guess I couldn't win them all. But I wasn't complaining. Sitting in the middle put me dangerously close to Tom. He sidled in next to me and handed me the grey box.

"Hopefully we'll need it today when we meet Ms. Goldrich."

"Miss *Thelma G.* Goldrich," Winky said. "Got a nice ring to it. Tom, if I was to up and marry her, would I get me some a her money?"

"I don't know, Winky. First we've got to see if she's even related."

"Yeah, they don't take too kindly to marryin' inside the family no more."

"I meant if she's related to Tony and Glad."

"That too. And if she's ugly. Ain't no amount a money worth marryin' a butt-ugly person."

I looked over at Winky, a testament to the un-showered, un-shaven, unappealing and uncouth.

"Amen to that," I said.

Chapter Twenty-Nine

Getting in to see Thelma Goldrich was a lot easier than Tom and I had planned. When Tom showed his badge to the guard at the main gate, he'd simply waived us through and pointed us in the direction of the mental health buildings on the west side of the huge state hospital campus. Following the guard's directions, we arrived at a nondescript white building with black handrails leading up six concrete steps. After careful consideration, we left Winky in the old Ford with a Randy Travis CD, a six-pack of Bud and a carton of banana moon pies for company. I don't think I'd ever seen a grown person look so absolutely contented.

Winky was already tearing the cellophane wrapper off the first moon pie as I closed the truck door. Tom was halfway up the steps, waiting on me. I stumbled on the second stair. Tom grabbed my arm.

"Are you as nervous as I am?" I asked.

"Nothing to be nervous about, Val," Tom said with a shrug. "What will be, will be. That's all."

"I guess I can't argue with that."

We walked inside the front door of the long, narrow building. It opened directly onto a lobby area. I took a seat with a view down the hallway while Tom spoke with the bespectacled, middle-aged receptionist behind a glass window. As they chatted it up, I saw a skinny, butt-naked man walk down the hallway and disappear behind a doorway. Another woman in tight jeans and a grey sweatshirt came

down the hall and sat in the chair next to me. I smiled at her, thinking she was another visitor. She took my hand and launched into a
stream-of-consciousness babble about being able to chew gum again
after years of practice.

Oh boy.

I felt like an extra in *One Flew Over the Cukoo's Nest.* I took
turns fake smiling at the gum-chewing woman and stealing glances
in Tom's direction, hoping he would look back at me. When he finally did, I shot him my best "hurry up" look. He laughed with the
receptionist one more time and walked over with two visitor tags in
his hand.

"Here. Put this on. It turns out Thelma is in here on a voluntary
basis. They're going to get her now."

The receptionist ushered us into a small waiting room that
looked exactly as I pictured it would. The blank walls were that in-
dustrial shade of green found only in government buildings and the
inside of dill pickles. White, metal bars protected two curtain-less
windows, and dust swirls danced in the twin rays of sunlight they let
into the room.

The table and chairs were made of solid oak, and were heavy and
square. I figured that made them harder to pick up and throw. The
top of the table was tattooed with messages scrawled in black and
green and blue ink.

I was reading the inscription, "Screw you, Velda," when the waiting room door creaked open. A thin, shattered-looking blonde
woman poked her face inside.

"Y'all lookin' fer me?"

"Are you Thelma Goldrich?" I asked.

*She must have lost a lot of weight since that mugshot I saw of her
was taken.*

"Yes'm."

"Hi, I'm Val. This is Tom. He's a police officer."

"I ain't done nothin' wrong!" Thelma shrieked. Her head disappeared behind the door.

"Wait!" I called after her. "Thelma! We know you didn't do anything wrong! We're here to see if something belongs to you!"

The door creaked open again and Thelma stepped inside. She was thin and big bosomed, just like Glad. Her skin was white as milk. She had on a faded yellow sundress with a tiny daisy print. Her hair was a tangle of brownish-blonde straw, stacked in a loose bun that looked an awful lot like an abandoned bird's nest.

She spoke tentatively, keeping one hand firmly on the doorknob. "I ain't lost nuthin' as I recall."

"Well –" I began, not realizing she wasn't through.

"'Ceptin' my parents," she added. "That's all."

"You lost your parents?" I asked softly.

"Nope. *They* lost *me*. People 'round here said I was left on a doorstep with nothing but a diaper and a note with my name on it."

"Oh. How long ago was that?"

"Last November a hundred years ago."

Tom looked over at me and tapped his fingers lightly on the tabletop. I took it to mean hush, so I did. I thought he was going to lead the interrogation, but instead he just asked, "Thelma, would you like a cup of coffee or something?"

"What the –?"

Tom shushed me again with his hand, then patted his shirt pocket where I'd seen him put the plastic bag for collecting the DNA sample.

"I sure would like me some coffee," Thelma said. "You know they make us pay a whole dime for a cup around here? They think we's made outta money or somethin'." Thelma let go of the doorknob and took a seat across the table from us.

"It's my treat, ma'am," said Tom. "Do you take cream or sugar?"

"Yessir."

Tom did an almost imperceptible double take, but said nothing. He stepped out the door and left me alone with Thelma. Earlier, I'd thought of a whole list of questions to ask her, but now that I was face-to-face with her, my thoughts all skittered out the window like mice chased by a barn cat. Before I could get my brain and mouth in sync to say something, Thelma spoke.

"That's a purty necklace."

I touched the cheap dragonfly pendant hanging around my neck. "Thanks."

"It reminds me a somethin'."

The hair on my neck stood up. "What?" I asked.

Thelma raised her voice ten octaves. "I said it reminds me a somethin'!"

"No. I mean...right. What does it remind you of, Thelma?"

"What?"

"The necklace? The dragonfly?"

"Oh. It reminds me a them bugs that flies around outside. That's why I don't like to go out there. Too many bugs ever'wheres."

The door creaked open. Tom came in carefully balancing two paper cups in the flattened palm of his right hand. The sight of him sent relief flooding through my body.

"You said cream, Thelma?" he asked.

"Yes'm."

"And sugar?"

"Yep."

Tom nodded, and removed one cup with his left hand. He offered Thelma the second cup by lowering his right hand like a tray in front of her. She picked up the cup and took a sip. I looked over at Tom while she drank. He smiled at me and mouthed the word, "bingo."

"You want this one?" He offered me the other cup.

I shook my head. I couldn't take my eyes off Thelma.

Thelma seemed to disappear into another time and place as she drank the coffee. She closed her eyes and hummed between sips. Tom and I watched her, as mesmerized by her as she was by a simple cup of coffee. When she'd drained the cup, it was as if someone hit her "on" switch again. Her eyes opened. She returned to this plane of existence, and began to slowly tear the paper cup to pieces. She wadded it into a ball and threw it in the wastebasket beside her. Tom and I both tried hard to pretend we didn't notice.

"Mmmm. That was good," Thelma said. "So what y'all want again?"

"Thelma, you said your parents left you on the road," Tom said. "What were their names?"

Thelma looked hard into the left corner of the ceiling.

"Mickey and Memaw...or Minnie, I do believe. They was mouses, you know. I was only tiny as a mouse when they left me. They come back when I was fully growed, but I didn't want to talk to them folks no more. They was too crazy! I was nice to 'em and ever'thing. Even so, that old woman stole a piece a my hair! She reached out and cut it clean off with a pair a scissors!"

Thelma formed her right hand into a pair of scissors. Quick as a rattlesnake strike, she thrust her hand across the table and snapped her two fingers together just an inch from my tender, red nose. I flinched and sucked in a startled breath.

"You ain't got no scissors has ya?" Thelma barked at me, then stood abruptly.

I jerked backward, nearly tipping over in my chair.

"No, Thelma, we don't," Tom said in a calm, reassuring voice.

"You's all liars!" Thelma shrieked. "Liars, liars, pacifiers!"

Thelma covered her bird-nest hair with one hand and grabbed for the doorknob with the other. "I ain't gonna let you cut me again!" She jerked the door open, then disappeared behind it.

I looked over at Tom. I was still reeling with shock.

"I didn't know what to expect. But it sure as hell wasn't *that*."

"It's okay," Tom said. "It's over."

Tom got up and peered over the wastebasket. "Only three cups in here, and only one shredded to smithereens."

He took the plastic bag and a pair of tweezers out of his shirt pocket and gingerly placed the tattered remnants of the cup inside the bag. "Looks like we've got what we came for."

"Right," I said sadly.

Tom shot me a sympathetic smile. "Too bad she's such a loony-toon, Val."

"I don't know, Tom. There may have been some truth to what she said. You know, Jacob mentioned something to me about Glad saving a lock of Thelma's hair when she was a baby. Do you think Glad might have tracked down Thelma here and taken another sample...for comparison testing or something?"

"Could be. To be honest, I'd be surprised if she hadn't. Thelma wasn't *that* hard to find. But don't take too much stock in what the poor woman just said. Crazy people aren't renowned for their reliability."

I sighed. "I guess you're right."

Tom took my hand.

"Val, with Glad and Tony both dead, we'll probably never know for sure if they knew about Thelma. And there's really no use in wasting any time speculating about it until the DNA test comes back. If this poor, squirrelly girl *is* their Thelma, I wouldn't blame them for not making her part of the family. Geez. They'd probably have been better off never finding her at all."

I hung my head. "I guess you're right."

A thought occurred to me that should have long before then. "Tom, what are we going to compare the DNA sample to, anyway? We need Glad's and Tony's DNA, right?"

"Already on it, Val. At Tony's memorial ceremony, you made it pretty clear how sure you were that he wouldn't name his ex-wife as the heir. What was it you said? Something like, 'He wouldn't leave her a pile of his own fecal matter, much less his estate.' "

I cringed. "Yeah, something like that."

"Well, I have to say, the eloquence of your words stuck in my mind."

I knew Tom was joking, but for some reason it made me cringe even harder.

Tom grinned and let out a short laugh. "What can I say, Val? You inspired me. I decided to go over to Tony's house and get samples. You know, just in case. I found some good ones, too. A matted hairbrush and some fairly large toenail clippings. I sent them off to a private forensics lab in Tallahassee. My buddy Darryl there owes me a few favors."

I smiled coyly. "Wow. I didn't know a cop's life could be so *glamorous*," I teased. "You know, fairly large toenail clippings and all."

"How's *this* for glamorous?"

Tom grabbed me in his arms and kissed me hard on the mouth. The feel of his strong arms around me made my body tremble. His tongue circled the tip of mine until I forgot my last name. Hell, and my first one, too. When Tom finally unlocked his lips from mine, red and white stars swirled around on the pickle-green walls.

Holy Crap!

WHEN TOM AND I GOT back to the truck, Winky was curled up in the front seat of Tiny's rusty old Ford, sawing logs like a seasoned lumberjack with a brand new Black & Decker. Tom's kiss had softened my snarky façade. For the first time in forever, I felt all mushy inside. I peered into the passenger window at Winky. He looked as cozy as a baby bird, all snuggled in his jumbled nest of emp-

ty beer cans and plastic moon pie wrappers. I caught sight of my reflection in the glass. My sappy expression said it all.

Oh crap, Val. You're in deep!

I bit my lip and looked up. Tom was waving at me from across
the cab. A mischievous look crawled across his face, and he put a finger to his lips. I watched and tried not to giggle as he quietly opened
the truck's squeaky door. He stealthily leaned inside, and thumped
Winky right on the nose. The freckled little piggy snorted to life.

"What the gaul-dang-it is goin' on?" he bellowed. "Can't a feller
catch a nap around here?"

"Rise and shine, Winky-dink," I chimed from the passenger window.

Winky-dink? Really? Girl, you've lost it!

Winky wrestled his way up to sitting and scratched at his beer
belly. His faded red t-shirt appeared to have lost both sleeves in some
tragic accident.

"How was that girl? Thelma? Is she the one?"

"Can't tell for sure at the moment," Tom said. "But I got her
DNA sample right here."

Tom patted his breast pocket. He reached around Winky and
took a manila envelope from the grey box, then slipped the plastic
bag containing the mangled cup inside.

"Let's see if there's a Fed-Ex around here. I was planning on
dropping this off in Tallahassee on the way back this afternoon. But
there's no telling how long before Tiny has the 4Runner up and going again."

"Shot gun!" Winky called out.

I pretended to be disappointed and let Winky have his victory.

We got lucky and found a Fed-Ex carrier picking up packages
from a drop station just outside the hospital entrance. I watched
from the old Ford as Tom put the manila envelope containing the
cup inside an overnight package and filled out a delivery form. He

handed the carrier some cash and shook his hand, then headed back to the truck.

"That Tom there's got some green. *And* some balls," said Winky. "Let's just hope he don't got green balls!"

Winky snorted with laughter at his own joke, then grabbed me in his infamous headlock-hug. I almost suffocated in his armpit before I could escape. An untold number of days without a shower had raised Winky's body odor to near lethal. When he finally let me loose, I felt as if I'd been slimed by a dead catfish. I looked in the rearview mirror. My makeup was beyond repair.

Crap on a cracker!

"Good news. The guy said he's on his way to Tallahassee from here," Tom said as he climbed into the truck. He eyed us both like kids who'd been up to no good. "He said he could deliver it in an hour or two."

"That's great, Tom," I said.

"Yeah. The sooner the better. Florida heat doesn't do DNA any good. I sent the cup to that friend of mine at the forensics lab. We should know something in a couple of weeks."

"Thanks." I hugged Tom's arm and inched toward him in the seat, partly because I wanted to, and partly to get away from Winky's cloud of body odor. My move didn't go unnoticed by the foul-smelling redneck.

"Whoa nelly! You two hookin' up now?" Winky asked. He wagged his tongue at me like a deranged tequila worm.

I punched him on the arm. "Stop it, Winky!"

"Is that what she says to you, too, Tom?" Winky quipped.

Tom winked at me. "So far. But I'm not giving up that easy. Anybody else starving? I think it's time for a Chatterburger."

"It's Chattaburger, not Chatterburger," I said, then cringed when I realized how much I sounded like my mom. "But who cares?" I added, overcompensating with a syrupy layer of cheerfulness. "We better not forget Tiny's order. What was it again?"

"Burger, fries, Mountain Dew," Tom answered in his just-the-facts cop voice.

"Right you are, Tom!"

Geez! Cut the enthusiasm, Val. You're getting weird! It was just a kiss. Don't blow it out of proportion!

"I'm starving, too. Who knew that police work was so demanding?"

What? Shut up, for crying out loud!

"Tom prob'ly did, since he is one," Winky replied. His dry, obvious tone made us all snort with laughter.

Tom turned the ignition on the old Ford and pointed it east on Hwy 90. Chattahoochee State Hospital disappeared in the rearview mirror as we headed toward Chattahoochee proper, home of the world-famous Chattaburger.

Chapter Thirty

There was no way to have a real conversation with Winky in the seat beside us, so on the drive to the burger joint, Tom and I kept our thoughts to ourselves. We decided to save time and get our Chattaburgers to go and eat them on the ride home. Tiny Mc-Mullen's order was in a sack between my knees. It was my not-so-subtle attempt to keep Winky's dirty hands off of it.

"I have to admit, this Chattaburger is pretty darn good," I said, trying to make conversation to drown out the sound of Winky chomping and slurping mere inches from my right ear. "No wonder Tiny wanted us to bring him back one."

"Yeah," Winky agreed, smacking his lips. "Who would a thought a cheetah could taste so good."

"It's Chatta, not –" I began, then reminded myself that some battles weren't worth fighting. "How do you like yours, Tom?"

"Pretty tasty," he said, then nudged me and whispered. "But nothing compared to something I tasted earlier."

I blushed with an uncomfortable mixture of pride, embarrassment, and lust. To compensate, I did the only mature thing I could think of. I punched Tom on the arm. The impact made him drop his bag of fries. They scattered over his lap, putting grease marks all over his crisp, ironed jeans.

"Oh no! I'm so sorry!"

"You're going to have to clean that up, young lady," Tom said.

I looked into Tom's twinkling green eyes and smiled coyly. I shot a glance in Winky's direction. He'd already finished wolfing down his food and was in his own, well-fed nirvana. His head was sticking out the passenger window like a red-speckled hound dog—complete with open mouth and wagging tongue. With Winky distracted, I turned my attention back to Tom.

"Yes, sir, Mr. Officer," I whispered. "Should I start here?" I picked up a French fry from his lap and ate it slowly and suggestively.

"Uh...I see you like fries," Tom said, trying to keep one eye on the road and one on me.

"I *love* fries." I moved my hand slowly down the inside of his thigh on the pretense of searching for a stray fry. His leg felt strong and muscular. "I want to make sure I'm doing a good job, officer."

Tom inhaled sharply, then blew out a breath. "Believe me, you are."

"Why we goin' so gaul-dang slow?" bellowed Winky. He'd pulled his head in from the window.

I looked down at the speedometer and bit my lip to keep from laughing. We were going about twelve miles an hour.

"I like to take my time," Tom said a little too loudly. His face was scarlet.

"Me too," I added, smirking into his sea-green eyes.

"Well if that don't beat a goat a gobblin'," Winky said.

Whatever that meant.

NOT-SO-TINY TINY GRABBED the Chattaburger bag with delight and explained Tom's car troubles between mouthfuls of fries and slurps from a huge, half-gallon cup of Mountain Dew.

"It's the earl line," the huge man said. He leaned against the hood of the 4Runner and sucked some antifreeze-colored soda from the straw.

"The earl line?" Tom asked politely.

"Yep. Been cut clean in two. Earl nearly completely drained out. Good thing you didn't go nowhere. Would a blown the block. Need to replace the line. Gonna need a few quarts a earl, too. Take six or eight to fill her?"

"Oh. I'd say six quarts of oil should do it," said Tom.

"All-righty then. I got enough earl at the house. I done ordered the earl line. Should be here tonight. Or first thing in the morning. Won't take but a jiff to have her ready. I figure $30 and a box a donuts and we're square. Deal?"

Tiny wiped his right hand on the thigh of his filthy overalls, then held it out toward Tom. Tom shook it without hesitation.

"Deal."

Tiny eyed me and Tom, then whispered, "Wouldn't take him, huh?" He nodded his head in Winky's direction.

"Nope, too far gone," I said before Tom could answer.

Tiny nodded solemnly. "Yeah. Purty obvious. Prob'ly coulda saved you a trip by sayin' so."

"Don't worry," I said in a serious, hushed tone. "We got an aunt in Valdosta who'll take him."

Tiny pursed his lips solemnly. "You can always count on family."

"Okay then," said Tom, in a way that seemed to close the discussion. "Looks like I'm taking the day off tomorrow. I'll call the office and give them the heads up."

Tom walked off to make his call. I headed for the house, leaving Tiny and Winky standing in the shade of the pecan tree in mom's front yard. I walked in to find Mom and Dale sprawled out in their matching recliners, watching *The Price is Right* at five million decibels.

"Hey," I shouted to the backs of their heads, trying to trump the volume on the TV. "Looks like we need to stay another night. That okay with you two?"

"Sure," Mom said, her eyes never leaving the set. "What you wanna do about dinner?"

"I'll think of something."

"Good."

I poked around in the fridge. Off hand, I didn't know any recipes that called for pudding packs, Velveeta, or buttermilk.

"I'm going to the store," I hollered in their general direction, and tromped back outside. Across the street, I saw Tiny's large backside disappear behind a junked car in his yard.

"We're good to stay another night," I said to Tom. He gave me a thumb's up.

Winky was trying to aggravate that poor squirrel with a stick again. He heard the news and hurled the stick across the yard. He kicked the ground with his bare foot, making me wonder whether or not he'd been wearing shoes on our trip today.

"Gaul-dang it!" Winky grumbled. "I was hopin' to hightail it outta here!"

"Why? You got somewhere to be?" Tom asked.

"Not partic'lar. But I know when I ain't wanted." Winky looked me in the eyes. "Excuse me for sayin' so, Val, but right now I'm about as welcome with your mammy as a turd on a cherry sundae."

I laughed. "Don't worry, Winky. It'll blow over. I've been the human sacrifice for Mount Saint Mom's volcanic moods for over forty-five years now, and I'm still standing."

"And still smokin' hot, I might add," Tom said in a half-joking, half-sexy way that made my neck flush with heat.

"Well, I ain't used to gettin' such dirty looks," Winky whined.

"Really?" I asked, genuinely amazed.

"Ha ha, Miss Val Pal. Your humor ain't lost on me." Winky shot a sore glance over at Tom's truck. "Crap. Looks like I'll be settin' up camp in the 4Runner again."

"Sorry, Winky."

I felt bad about making *him* feel bad. "Look, let's take the golf cart up to IGA and get some donuts or ice cream or something. That'll get my mom in a better mood. I need to find something to fix for dinner anyway."

Winky's freckled face brightened at the prospect. He nodded and yelled, "Shotgun!"

I CHOSE TO FRY CHICKEN for dinner that night. Not because I was a good hostess, mind you. And not because I wanted to impress Tom with my Southern culinary skills. Nope. I chose to fry chicken because I knew it would take a long time, and it would keep me out of that familiar line of fire I called, "Conversing with my mother."

I smiled smugly at my own cleverness and dredged a raw chicken thigh in seasoned flour, then buttermilk, then back through the flour again. I dropped it carefully into the sizzling oil in the last open spot in the cast iron skillet, then clamped on the glass lid. I stirred a huge pot of collard greens and listened in on the boys in the battlefield. Despite their peace offering to my mother of a half-gallon of Rocky Road ice cream, they never stood a chance.

"How come yer a cop, Tom?" I heard Mom ask. "You got some kinda problem with aw-tharity?"

"No ma'am. I just like helping people."

"Hmmm."

I chuckled to myself. "Hmmm" was Mom's typical response to something she didn't believe. I guess it was more polite than screaming "bull hockey" or "liar," something I'd also seen her do plenty of times. Maybe she was mellowing in her old age. To my surprise, Winky stepped up and saved Tom from further interrogation.

"I shore do like your spare toilet roll holder, Mrs. Short. I ain't never seen a purtier crocheted poodle. You do that yourself, ma'am?"

"Why no, Winky. My sister Vera Jane done that. God rest her soul."

"Well that's a real keeper, fer shore. I seen me a pink one a'fore. And a yeller doll-type one, you know. But I never seen a yeller poodle. Yep, it's a real keeper."

"I 'preciate that, Winky. You and me got off on the wrong foot. But now I see you got good manners *and* good taste. Val could do a lot worse than to settle on you."

"Oh. Thanky, ma'am. But they's nothin' goin' on with me and Val. Strictly platonical, if you know what I mean. Besides, I think she's sweet on Tommy boy, here."

I was desperate to hear what came next, but the dang oil in the skillet boiled over and sent a plume of white-hot smoke billowing through the dingy kitchen. I ran around opening windows and fanning the air like an idiot, trying to keep from setting off the smoke alarm. By the time I got the air cleared and the chicken pieces turned, the battlefield topic had moved on.

"No I ain't much on flea markets," Mom said. "Growin' up, just about everything we had was give to us. We was poor. I mean *dirt* poor. I won't have nothin' now, 'less'n it's new and we can pay cash money for it, right Dale?"

"Yes'm, honey."

I grinned. Short and sweet. That was Dale.

"Vallie!" Mom's razor-sharp voice startled me so I nearly dropped the plate of chicken I was carrying. "You about burned up that chicken dinner yet?"

Short and not-so-sweet. That was my mom.

Chapter Thirty-One

I'd set the alarm on my cellphone for 6 a.m. to avoid another one of Mom's flyswatter wake-up calls. I heard it beep, switched it off, then lolled back to sleep on the wispy memory of a dream.

Glad and I were laughing together. I sat behind her, my arms wrapped around her as we rode on a giant blue-and-green dragonfly. Suddenly, she and I shrunk to the size of matchsticks, and the dragonfly we rode was of normal size. Together, we soared over Glad's Minnie Winnie, which was parked on the sugar-white sand between the shoreline and Caddy's beach bar. The sky was blue and warm, and Glad was leaning back, whispering something in my ear. It tickled. What was she saying? Be Glad? Glod. Glorf. Glorf. Grrof. Her breath smelled like kibbles and barf....

I shot awake. Mom's yappy little dog was licking my ear. I sat up on the couch and pushed the pooch away. My ear was sopping wet with slobber.

Gross!

I got up and scurried down the hallway to the bathroom, holding my ear and cursing under my breath. Preoccupied, I ran headlong into Tom.

"Wow, Val. You really *aren't* a morning person."

Someone kill me now.

"Told ya."

He wrapped his arms around me and squeezed. "How about a good morning kiss?" he teased.

"Not the time or place," I said, trying to squirm out of his grip as smelly dog saliva trickled down my ear.

"Come on," he insisted. "It's okay. We've already had our first kiss, remember?"

Unlike mine, Tom's breath smelled minty fresh. As a courtesy, I turned my face away before I spoke.

"Yeah. I remember. We kissed in a nuthouse."

Tom touched the side of my face and turned my head gently until we were eye to eye.

"I heard that's good luck," he joked in a deep, sexy, morning voice.

I snorted out a sarcastic laugh. "Come on, Tom. You're spoiling my bad mood."

His smile evaporated. He pulled his hand from the side of my face and examined it. "Is your ear *leaking?*"

Horrified, I pushed past Tom, ran into the bathroom, and locked the door behind me.

BY SOME REDNECK MIRACLE of ingenuity, Tiny got the 4Runner up and going by breakfast. Tom and Dale had taken the golf cart up to IGA at half-past six and scored two big boxes of donuts. I guess their chore had freed Tiny up so he could dive right in to fixing the oil line. It didn't take him long, either. In fact, he was done in time to join the five of us at the breakfast table.

I watched as Tiny washed up at the kitchen sink, then turned a dining chair around and straddled it. As he lowered his huge bulk precariously onto the unlucky chair, it protested with groans and squeaks. A few minutes later, we were fresh out of donuts.

"Well, Valiant Jolly, when are me and Dale gonna see you again?" Mom asked, cramming the last half of a cream-filled donut into her mouth. She shot me a "poor-me" look that would have made Mother Teresa feel like crap.

"It's Fremden now, Mom. My German name."

"Fremden? I never can remember it. What in tarnation is a Fremden?"

I'd wondered the same thing a few years back. Lots of names like Smith and Jones didn't really have any meaning. But Fremden did. I'd looked it up in my German-to-English dictionary.

"It means stranger, Mom."

"Well, you do keep gettin' stranger and stranger to me," Mom snorted, amusing herself so much she nearly choked on a slug of Maxwell House.

I nodded silently, and counted her intended insult as personal gain.

I sure hope so.

"Tiny, thanks again for fixing up the 4Runner," Tom said, coming to my rescue by changing the subject. I shot him a grateful smile. Tom actually *did* look a bit like a superhero—especially sitting amongst this lot.

"No problaymo, Tom," replied Tiny. "Only thing I like better'n donuts is gettin' under the hood of a vehicle. Even if it *is* a Ty-otee."

"It's been a real pleasure havin' you and these boys here," Dale, said in my direction. He took out a hanky and dabbed at his nearly useless eyes. He was a small, delicate man, and for some reason the thought of him and my mom together brought to my mind a pair of black widow spiders. After mating, the much larger female often annihilated her partner by eating him alive. The male had to be crafty to avoid such a fate. I suddenly hoped Dale was crafty.

A rogue wave of melancholy unexpectedly washed over me. I knew I had to either bust out crying or get busy doing something. I chose the latter.

"Thank you, Dale," I said, and stood up. "It's always a pleasure to see you...and Mom. I guess I better get started on the dishes if we're going to get out of here anytime soon."

"Leave 'em. I'll do 'em," my mother said. My knees nearly buckled in shock.

"Thanks, Mom." I reached over to hug her.

"You don't never get 'em clean enough anyway," she said without looking up, and took a huge bite from the last remaining cruller.

SOME THINGS SIMPLY look a lot better from the rearview mirror. As we drove away, I watched the reflection of Mom and Dale waving from their front yard until the image shrank and faded away. Despite the feeling of relief, my throat got tight and my nose grew hot. Longing to return to a fairytale that never really existed is, I guess, the ultimate irony of family.

Tom noticed me tearing up, and offered me a hanky that came with the welcome bonus of a tender squeeze of my hand. I blew my dripping nose into it and realized I had something else to be grateful for. My nose had been healed up enough for my mom not to notice. I never had to explain to her why I got punched in the face.

"Did I hear your mom call you Valiant?" Tom asked.

My gratitude dried up. I took a quick glance in the backseat. Winky was already passed out.

God bless you whoever invented Dramamine.

"Yeah. Val is short for Valiant. Valiant W. Jolly. That's the name my parents gave me."

"So...is there a story that goes with the name? I've never heard of anyone called Valiant before."

I glanced over at Tom. He appeared to be seriously interested. And handsome. His blond bangs gently moved with the cool gusts from the air conditioner. His mirrored shades lent a sort of movie-star cop mystique.

"Yeah. But it's a short story. My dad said he called me that because he thought I was brave."

"What did you do that was brave?"

I scrunched my eyebrows quizzically. "You know, I don't think I ever asked him. I guess I never thought about it. Maybe I was brave just to be born into a family run roughshod by my mother."

I laughed it off, but Tom didn't.

"I could see where that would count for something," he said. "So what's the W stand for? Who, what, where, when or why?"

Tom took his gaze from the road and shot me that grin I'd begun to enjoy so much. I liked it when he joked. It was easier to breathe. Serious Tom made me nervous...in more ways than one.

"Another mystery," I answered. "Mom said she thought adding a W to my name would make me sound more distinguished. Trouble was, the two of them couldn't decide on anything for the W to stand for."

"A distinguished redneck, huh?" Tom quipped.

"Right. Talk about being born into irony...."

"Well, you *are* pretty distinguished, if you think about it. You're college educated. You lived in Germany. You speak the language."

"Danke," I said sourly.

"And you're pretty *redneck*, too."

"What do you mean?"

Tom resurrected his horrible Southern accent. "You know how to cook vitals. You was born in Chattahoochee. And you speak the language."

I laughed. "It's vittles, not vitals."

"See? You speak fluent redneck."

"And *you* don't. So please, drop that horrible accent or I'm sending you back to Maryland."

Tom laughed. "Yes ma'am."

"Since you aren't from around here, I guess you've never had the pleasure of experiencing redneck foreplay," I joked.

"Redneck foreplay?" Tom said. "You've got my attention. What's that?"

I sidled up to Tom and poked him hard on the bicep with my index finger. "Hey. You awake?"

Tom stared at me for a second. "That's it?"

"Exactly."

Tom burst out laughing. "You're pretty funny, Valiant."

"Oh! *Please* don't ever call me that!"

"Why?"

"Just *don't.*"

"Okay, done. How about we change the subject?

"Yes, please."

"I think she likes me. Your mom, I mean. She said I was good looking, 'If you go for that sort of thing.' "

"I didn't hear her say that."

"Aha! So you *were* listening in."

I smirked. "Busted. But I didn't get to hear everything. I was busy cooking vittles, you know."

"And they was some gosh-darn good vittles, too. That chicken is somewhere up in heaven crowing about how good you fried him up. Deeeelicious."

I shook my head. "What did I tell you about that accent, officer?"

"Sorry ma'am." Tom winked. "What do you redneck girls do with naughty boys who won't listen?"

I grinned.

"Wouldn't *you* like to know."

I LET TOM CONCENTRATE on driving as we wound our way east on I-10 through the busy section of Tallahassee. As we came out the other side, we were facing over an hour of boring highway until we hit Lake City. Winky was still sawing logs in the back, but not too loudly. However, every now and again he would let go a bout of flatulence that sent us both scrambling to roll down the windows before we asphyxiated.

We'd just ventilated the 4Runner for the third or fourth time when a thought occurred to me.

"Tom, when was it you had your first case? The Buckaroo Bandit?"

"November a hundred years ago."

I slapped his arm playfully. "I'm *serious*."

"Twenty years ago...so...1989."

"Do you remember the month?"

"Fishing season. So, May or June."

"Tony and Glad got married in October that same year. Tom! If that *was* Bobby's skull in that Piggly Wiggly bag, that would mean *he was dead before Glad and Tony got married*. Their marriage would be legit. I wonder...do you think Glad *knew* Bobby was dead before she married Tony?"

"Huh. There's a thought. Or maybe Tony did. It's pretty convenient, timing-wise. That is, if the skull really *is* Bobby's."

"It's his. Who else's could it be?"

"Okay, let's assume it is. Jacob said he pulled Bobby's teeth out in like, 1987, right? That leaves two years of unaccounted time before the skull was found. Anything could have happened in between. If Jacob left Bobby alone in the woods, he could have bled to death. Or Bobby could have recovered and later had a fishing accident. Or Jacob could be lying and he actually finished Bobby off himself. That way Jacob would be able to tell Tony and Glad that the coast was clear, so to speak."

So to speak, not sore to speak! He's literate! Hurray!

I looked over at Tom. He seemed even more handsome somehow. I forced my mind back to the case at hand.

"Maybe Glad didn't know anything about what Jacob did," I speculated. "But if she didn't, why would she marry Tony if she knew she was still married to Bobby?"

"People do it all the time, Val. It's just a piece of paper until you mail it in. Even then, different states, different names. Cross-checking public records has its limitations."

"Hmmmm."

"You sound like your m...."

The stone-cold look on my face froze Tom's mouth mid-word. He fumbled for a recovery. "I mean...it sounds like you haven't been to your mom's in a while."

"Yeah. Like she said, I'm a stranger now. And I keep getting stranger."

"Jolly to Fremden. Think about it, Val. You went from being happy—Jolly—to being a stranger—Fremden. I hope along the way you didn't become a stranger to being jolly."

How poetic. And apropos.

I sat back in my chair and sighed. "Me too."

Chapter Thirty-Two

We got lucky and Winky slept all the way to Tampa, giving Tom and me a chance to get a little more personal with our conversation, and to sneak in that second kiss. The touch of his lips on mine was worth both the wait *and* the guilt I'd felt over drugging Winky with Dramamine—*again*. The poor guy was still a bit groggy when we arrived back at my apartment. Jorge was there, sitting in his old grey-and-bondo Buick, dutifully staking out the squirrels and other varmints loitering around my street.

He spied Tom's 4Runner and jumped out of his vehicle. As we emerged, he greeted us with handshakes and Old Spice-scented hugs.

"Hola, guys! Como estas?"

"No, she wat'n in no coma, mister," grumbled Winky as he climbed out of the backseat. He rubbed his head and stumbled over to Jorge's Buick. "She was just crazy. That's all." He shot us a bleary-eyed stare. "Y'all don't mind me. I'm gonna go take a nap." Winky crawled into the backseat of Jorge's car. His head disappeared behind the front seat.

Jorge looked quizzically at Tom and me. We both shrugged. Jorge smiled and shrugged too, then presented me with my apartment key as if he were handing over the crown jewels. What he said next was really good news. He and Goober had located the whereabouts of Bulldog Thelma's secret lair.

"So, where is it?" Tom asked Jorge.

"This woman, she's staying at the Landmark Motel over by Mirror Lake. She's not alone. There's some old gringo guy with her."

"Señor Blanco?"

"Jes. Everything blanco. White shirt, white belt, white shoes." Jorge touched his chest, then waist, then shins as he talked, as if doing some type of show-and-tell calisthenics routine.

"Did they come by *here* again?"

"No. But Goober called about a half an hour ago and said they were back at Tony's place again. They tried the front door and then walked around back. He said they were back there for a long time, and he was tired of waiting. He said he was going to sneak a peek behind the back corner of the house. I could hear the Bulldog giving old Blanco hell, and then Goober tried to tell me something, but he was whispering too low. I couldn't make out what he said. Then he hung up. You're gonna have to get the rest of the story from him."

"Where is he now?"

"Probably still in front of Tony's. He told me he ran out of gas."

"Okay. Good work, partner." Tom patted Jorge on the shoulder. "Thanks for taking Winky home, too. You did great."

Jorge beamed. Tom turned to face me.

"Val, I'm going to head over to Tony's. I've got a spare gas can in the back of the 4Runner."

"I'm going with you," I said.

Tom smiled.

"No argument here."

IT WAS ALMOST 3 P.M. when we turned onto Bimini Circle. Goober's car was parked about four houses down from Tony's. The Dodge was empty except for about four million mangled Marlboro cigarette butts. They spilled like a jumbled waterfall out of the ashtray and onto the floorboards. There was no sign of the white Prius.

We drove on to the house and pulled up in the driveway. Still no Goober. Tom tried him on his cellphone. No answer. But we *did* hear a faint ringing coming from the backyard. It was the theme from *Superman*.

It was Goober's ringtone, of course.

I snickered. But the look on Tom's face caused my mood to switch over to worry.

Before I could say a word, Tom raced around the side of the house. I followed, picking my way through the gravel as quickly as I could in silly sandals. As I rounded the corner, I saw Tom kneeling beside Goober. He was splayed out on the back landing, his phone a few feet from his right hand. I was about to laugh with relief when I spied a huge red knot in the middle of Goober's forehead.

"Goober, buddy, wake up," Tom said. He shook Goober gently by the shoulders.

"Hmmm?" Goober groaned and tried to sit up.

"You okay? What happened?"

Goober touched his forehead and winced. "I don't know." His eyes focused first on Tom, then on me. A grin crept over his pale face. "I guess I OD'ed on Screwitol."

I smiled and breathed a sigh of relief.

At least his sense of humor was still intact.

"Looks like the back door's been jimmied open," said Tom. "Val, stay with Goober."

"I'm going with you," I said.

"You keep saying that."

"I've been in the house before."

"I've been in, too, Val. DNA samples, remember?"

"Yeah. But I went through Glad's personal stuff. I think I'd notice if more than a few toenail clippings were missing."

Tom studied me for a moment. "Fair enough."

Tom propped Goober up against the outside wall. I got him a glass of water from the kitchen, then scrounged around in my purse for an aspirin. The best I could come up with was Extra-Strength Midol. I thought twice before handing the tablet to Goober.

Goober examined the pill and snorted. "Perfect. You know, Val —"

"Careful. I can make that knot a matching set."

Goober flinched, then acquiesced. "I was just going to say that you're a really sweet lady."

I looked at Goober and his swollen forehead and remembered he'd been injured in the line of duty...*for me*. "And you're a nice man. I'm just not in the mood for a joke right now."

"Maybe you need this more than me." Goober held out the Midol tablet.

I shook my fist at him and laughed despite myself.

THE HOUSE HAD BEEN ransacked. Drawers had been pulled out. Papers were strewn everywhere. The unknowledgeable might have not noticed the disarray, given the normal state of Tony's hoarder house. But I knew better. When I made it through the garbage-lined hallway to the bedroom, I saw Glad's three shoeboxes had been dumped out on the bed. The sight hit me hard in the gut. It was pretty obvious who the perpetrators were. But as far as I could tell, nothing was missing from them.

"What do you think they were looking for?" Tom asked.

"I was about to ask you the same question. Maybe the marriage certificate?"

"Maybe."

I sorted through the papers and mementos strewn all over the bed. Something *was* missing!

"The picture of Glad and Tony on the beach is gone, Tom. Tony's letter to Glad from boarding school, too. Crap! So is the picture of Glad with her baby!"

"How about cash? Jewelry?" Tom asked.

My mind flashed to the little green rhinestone oval. It was still in my travel bag. I pictured Glad on the beach, and thought of something else.

"Glad used to wear a lot of rings. I think she had them on when they took her to the morgue. Where would they be now?"

"Probably still there. When you signed for her, did they give you a bag with her personal effects?"

"No. I never thought to ask."

"Maybe you should go check it out."

I nodded. "I will tomorr –"

I was stopped short by the sound of Goober's voice from outside. He was yelling a stream of obscenities. Tom and I locked eyes, then dashed toward the hallway. Tom grabbed my hand and we pushed and pulled our bodies through the narrow passage clogged with newspapers and magazines. Finally, the garbage pile opened up. We'd made it to the kitchen. Tom flung open the back door. We practically tumbled over each other into the backyard.

"Gaul-dang pile of junk! Let me loose!"

I could hear Goober, but I couldn't see him. It was like trying to find a chirping cricket in a junkyard.

My eyes scanned across the sea of junked appliances and furniture heaped in the backyard. Finally, Goober flailed one of his long, baboon arms and I spotted him. He was twisted backward around a deep freezer, his belt loop hung up on the handle. Tom hurtled over a pile of rusty lawn furniture to reach him, and worked Goober loose from the Frigidaire's rusty grasp.

"They got in the RV, too," Goober said, exasperated.

Tom helped me climb over the deep freezer and we both peered inside Glad's old Minnie Winnie. It looked like a tornado had picked up a ton of garbage and flung it around inside. The sickly sweet smell of air freshener failed to mask the funk emanating from the abandoned RV. A greenish-brown film covered the upholstery, and there was ample evidence that when Glad moved out, mice and other unknown squatters had moved in.

"There's a new can of air freshener on the table. They must have sprayed it," Tom said.

"I can't blame them." I felt like retching.

Tom climbed inside the Minnie Winnie and scrounged around in an open kitchen drawer. He pulled out a set of tongs and picked up the aerosol can with them. "Fingerprint evidence."

Tom brushed by me with the can.

After he stepped out the door, I climbed in. That's when I finally noticed the overwhelmingly obvious. Every inch of wall space in the RV was covered in cut-out pictures and stickers and drawings of dragonflies. It was a never-ending, dizzying decoupage of fairy-like insects. I stood, open-mouthed, in awe of the mad, hypnotic splendor of Glad's artwork.

Goober stuck his head in the Minnie Winnie and sniffed.

"Who farted flowers?"

"He said this place was covered in *butterflies*," I muttered.

"Who?"

"Jacob."

"Who the heck is Jacob?"

"Señor Blanco."

"You *talked* to him?"

"Yes. He said Glad's RV was covered in *butterflies*."

"Butterflies, dragonflies. What's the difference?"

I shook my head at the indifference of the male species.

"Men!"

Goober returned my sneer with his own.

"Women!"

TOM DROPPED THE CAN of air freshener in an evidence bag and drove us down to where Goober's car sat on the side of the road like an abandoned cigarette coffin. Tom emptied the five-gallon gas can into the Dodge's tank and handed Goober some money for his efforts.

"Negatory," he said, and shoved Tom's hand away.

"Take it. You earned it," Tom insisted.

"I don't take money for helping friends."

"Then let me buy you dinner."

"*That* I'll do. As long as it includes a beer."

"Of course."

"Or *two*," Goober added quickly.

"Don't push your luck," Tom joked. "How about the Sea Hag?"

Goober looked over at me. "I guess she can come, too."

The guys burst out laughing.

"Very funny," I said, and punched Goober on the arm.

Sea Hags was the name of a popular restaurant in St. Pete Beach. If it were any more casual it wouldn't have had a roof. Nestled nearly under a causeway on Blind Pass Road, Sea Hags was a great place to kick back and have a few cold ones. Best of all, it was close by. In less than ten minutes, the three of us were sitting at a wooden table throwing back a beer.

"So, how'd you get the knot on your noggin, Goober?" Tom asked, then took a sip from his mug of beer.

Goober touched the red knot on his forehead and seemed surprised by its size.

"Actually, I don't remember. I was talking to Jorge on the phone, and all of a sudden I blacked out. I don't know if I fell over or got whacked."

"That's not unusual. To not remember, I mean," Tom said, switching to his cop voice. "People with concussions often forget the last few minutes before they sustained their injury. Those missing minutes will probably never come back. They get erased like an Etch-a-Sketch."

Goober touched the knot on his forehead again. It looked mean and angry, as if a horn was trying to break through.

"I've lived through worse. Thanks for the Midol, Val. It actually helped."

I nodded, relieved he was okay. "Anytime."

"Good thing you didn't give him aspirin," Tom interjected. "It's a blood thinner. Could have made any internal bleeding even worse."

A pang of guilt shot through me. "Oh. I didn't know."

"It's all good," Tom said reassuringly.

Under the table, I felt his hand give my knee a light squeeze. My feelings of inadequacy melted under the electric heat that shot through my body. Tom didn't appear to notice. Instead, he shifted his attention back to Goober.

"You remember what kind of car they were driving?" Tom asked.

"A white Toyota. One of those hybrids."

"A Prius," I said. "That's the same car Jacob drives."

"Jacob?" Goober growled. "You on a first-name basis with these jerks, Val?"

"Just one," I answered defensively. "The guy. He started talking to me in the Water Loo's parking lot the other day. He wanted to tell me what he knew about Tony and Glad."

A sudden streak of anger overwhelmed me. "Crap! Now that I *think* about it, Jacob *set me up*! Holy crap!" I turned to Tom. "I probably told him too much. About the letter, and the marriage license, I mean."

"Don't worry about it," Tom said, and squeezed my knee again. Ironically, his protective gesture felt both reassuring and scary at the same time. He shot me a sympathetic smile. "You don't need to contact him again, Val."

"Bulldog Woman, either," Goober said. "Unless, that is, you'd like your nose to contact her fist again." He moved his right arm, miming a boxing uppercut.

I instinctively touched my nose, then recycled Goober's line.

"I've lived through worse."

The waitress delivered our fish sandwiches and fries, and we ate and drank and swapped war stories like old pals. I noticed Tom only had one beer, then switched to water. Afterward, he drove Goober back to his car and me to my apartment. I lingered in the cab just long enough to give Tom a hug and a nice, but not-too-naughty kiss. I couldn't encourage him. I hadn't shaved my legs in two days.

"We're both tired and grimy," I said. "I just want to jump in the shower and go to bed."

Tom looked relieved. His reaction caused a tinge of insecurity to shoot through me.

"Yeah. It's been a long day," he said.

"Thank you for everything."

"Sure thing." Tom touched my face and smiled tenderly. "We're on our way, Val."

My heart skipped a beat. "What do you mean?"

Tom withdrew, embarrassed.

"I mean, the *case* is on its way. We've got the evidence at the lab. Just a few more odds and ends to do while we wait for the DNA results."

"Oh. Yeah. Sure!" I said too brightly. Embarrassed, I scrambled for a new topic. "Um, is the air freshener can from the RV part of the odds and ends?"

Tom looked relieved. "Maybe. It never hurts to gather ammunition, even if you never need it. If nothing else, we could use it to charge Jacob and Thelma with breaking and entering. It's still a crime in Florida, as far as I know."

My lips twisted to one side. "Unless the house ends up belonging to the perpetrator."

Tom sighed. "Point taken."

Chapter Thirty-Three

Wednesday morning I awoke with time on my hands. Given all the harried happenings lately, it seemed as if a month had passed since I was free to be a shiftless vagabond. In actuality, it had been less than a week.

I thought about going to Caddy's, but a peek out the window showed cloudy skies. Still, I got myself dressed, and before I knew it, I found myself riding along with Maggie as she tooled down First Avenue North in the direction of St. Pete Beach. I watched in dismay as my audacious little automobile pulled right into Water Loo's parking lot as if she owned the place.

Geez! I really am *getting to be pathetic.*

I sighed and put Maggie in park.

What the hell. I really don't *have anything better to do.*

IT KIND OF GRATED ON my nerves that none of them looked surprised to see me. I guess I was becoming an official member of the pack. A fourth stooge.

How apropos.

Goober scooted over for me as I walked up to the greasy booth. He was still sporting that nasty knot on his forehead.

"Morning, schnoz," he said after moving his spoon to the side of his mouth.

"Morning, cyclops," I said, and scooted into the booth beside him.

Winky chuckled at our exchange, and spilled coffee down the front of a faded Donald Duck t-shirt, the latest from Water Loo's donations for half-naked humans. He cursed under his breath. I shot a glance over at Jorge. The poor guy was face down, snoring, marinated in hair-of-the-Mad-Dog-20/20, no doubt.

Awesome.

I was in the company of a lumpy bum, a dumpy bum and a skunky bum. As for me, I'd just gotten a text from Jamie informing me that *Double Booty* was barely passable, and that I shouldn't hold my breath on winning the publishing contract.

Yep. The four stooges' race to the bottom was really heating up.

"So what's on the old agenda for today?" Goober asked me, temporarily halting the clicking of his spoon in his mouth.

"Good question," I sneered. I glanced over at Goober's now-familiar grin, and had mixed feelings over the realization that I was probably going to see a lot more of it in the future.

Winnie, the once-surly waitress, dropped off my cup of coffee with a cheery, "Good morning." Shocked, I looked over at Winky. He snorted and licked his lips. Jorge lifted his noggin from the table and wiped away a puddle of drool with his bare hand. My chest tightened.

Was this my new "normal?"

Diametrically opposed waves of comfortable ease and horrified unease crashed over my head and threatened to drown me in my own irony. Part of me was desperate to leap up and run the hell out of there. Part of me was planted firmly as a pig in mud. I closed my eyes and took a deep yoga breath. When I opened them again, all three stooges were staring at me. Their stubbly faces registered amused curiosity, as if they'd placed a bet on when I would abandon all hope.

I squirmed in my seat, uncomfortable at being the focus of their attention. I was just about to prompt them for Glad's memorial toast when my phone buzzed.

I wanted to kiss whoever was calling.

"Hello?"

"Ms. Fremden?" The deep, raspy voice on the other end of the line sent my memory racing.

"Yes...."

"Some lady's here asking about your aunt."

The clerk at the morgue!

"What's she look like?"

The rasp turned into a whisper. "A French bulldog."

Curiosity got the better of me. I had to ask. "Why French?"

"She's got a long French braid down her back," he whispered.

"Oh. So why are you calling me?"

"Something seems fishy. The lady's got your aunt's date of death right, but the name wrong. She showed me a picture of your aunt with some guy on a beach. It was her, all right. For some reason, that old leatherback stuck in my mind. Probably because of you. You know how to take a joke."

"Uh...thanks. What does she want?"

"Your aunt's effects. More specifically, her two-carat diamond ring. She asked about it specifically."

My jaw tightened so hard I thought my teeth might shatter. Before I could unclench my mouth, the clerk spoke again.

"Should I release your aunt's effects to her?"

I tried to calm the fury inside me. "Under no circumstances give that woman anything, please. I'll come by for my aunt's things tomorrow."

"Okay. I'll hold up a day for you. But you've got to bring the old lady's official ID with you. For the records."

"Sure thing."

I hung up. The stooges were all staring at me, slack-jawed. Goober tried to say something, but I shushed him with a curt wave of my hand and punched Tom's number on my cellphone.

"Tom, we have a problem."

"Not *another* one," Tom said sourly.

"What do you mean, not *another* one?"

"I just found out Tony's ex is seeking a petition from her lawyer to gain access to the inside of his house."

"You're kidding! That's a bit after-the-fact, isn't it?"

"Sure. But I guess they didn't find what they were looking for the first time."

"I know."

"What do you mean?"

"Bulldog Thelma showed up at the morgue today with Glad's picture, trying to get her rings. Apparently there's a two-carat diamond at stake. Jacob must have known about it."

"Incredible. But she's going to need more than an old picture to get Glad's effects released. She's going to need official documentation."

"Yeah, that's what the clerk told me. I'm sure that's why she and Jacob need to get back in the house. To find Glad's ID. That bulldog witch-woman is too fat to fit down the hallway. She must have sent Jacob in to do her dirty work. But it looks like he didn't get the job done to her liking. That's probably why they were arguing, like Jorge said he heard when he was on the phone with Goober."

"That makes sense."

"Tom, what can we do about the search petition?"

"Nothing. We have absolutely no grounds to be messing around with this, remember?"

"Crap. You're right. How long will it take for her to get the petition?"

"A day or two."

"Good. That means we've got a chance to sneak in the house one more time."

"What?! What for, Val?"

"For Glad's ID! I need to find it before they do. For the morgue. I've got to make Glad legit."

"Make her legit?"

"Uh, yeah."

"Why is Glad not legit, Val?"

"I...uh...kind of told them she was my aunt. Gladys Fremden."

"Your mom's right. You do keep getting stranger and stranger."

"Very funny. It's a long story. Will you help me?"

"Under one condition. You give the rings to Tony's estate attorney."

"That was my plan all along."

"Good. Meet you there after work. Six o'clock."

"Thanks, Tom."

WINKY WAS BECOMING a serious threat to my budding romance. When I told the guys I was going back to Tony's house with Tom, Winky threw a fit until I promised he could go along. He complained he'd gotten cheated by having to stay in the car the first time around. I didn't know how to stop him. Besides, I figured it was better to appease the savage redneck now than forever listen to his whining about it later.

I picked him up in Water Loo's parking lot at 5:45 p.m. When I drove up, he was half sitting, half lying under the shade of a palm tree in a median in the parking lot, as if that was a normal, acceptable thing to do. He was still wearing that coffee-stained Donald Duck rag of a t-shirt. I wondered if he'd spent all day at the coffee shop. Then I wondered why I was wondering about it.

At the sight of me pulling up in Maggie, Winky sprang to life like a Mexican jumping bean.

"Val Pal!" Winky hollered.

"Hey Winky. Hop in."

Winky's eyes lit up like a child at a pony ride.

"I always wanted to ride in your car. Sweeeet!"

As he climbed in, I realized that, for a man who had next to nothing, Winky possessed something of which I was downright envious. He had the ability to enjoy the simple things in life. Like food, shelter, and free coffee refills. The things my jaded eyes and heart had long ago learned to take for granted were still treasures to him. His childlike enthusiasm was contagious, and I rewarded it by punching the accelerator on Shabby Maggie, doing a three-sixty, and pealing out of the parking lot with her twin glass-packs roaring up to high heaven.

"Woooheeee!" Winky hollered, his face awash with bliss.

Not long later, I had my own blissful moment. Lieutenant Tom Foreman was standing in the driveway of Tony's house in his full police uniform.

I wanted to be arrested. Right then. Right there.

"Look at that shiny copper!" Winky said, his words clipping the wings on my fantasy. They fell to the wayside like a fly sprayed with Raid.

"Hey guys. Let's make this quick." Tom was in official cop mode. I guess he had to be.

I turned to Winky. He was wriggling in the seat like an antsy two-year-old.

"Okay, Winky, behave yourself. Like you promised."

"Yes ma'am," he replied.

But I could tell his squirrely dog brain was already drooling in anticipation of unearthing some maniacal milk-bone.

DESPITE THE CHAOS INSIDE the house, I managed to find Glad's ID by using my secret weapon: I knew how to think like a woman. Glad didn't have a driver's license. But thanks to a recent law, she'd been required to have a picture ID. I found her Florida identification card in a small, green, wallet-sized purse hanging on the doorknob behind the bedroom door.

"Got it!" I called out in victory.

"Good. Let's get out of here!" I heard Tom call from down the cluttered hallway.

I met him in the kitchen. The squirming banana blob on the counter had dried up to a thick, black stain. I guess all the maggots had turned to flies and found a way to escape. It seemed like vermin always did. Tom opened the back door and we stepped out into the humid air. The sky was just beginning to pink-up in preparation for sunset.

"Val, remind me again. Why are we doing all of this?" Tom asked.

I was beginning to wonder myself. But some primal urge compelled me to keep going, like a compulsive shopper with a fistful of coupons that were about to expire.

"I dunno. Just in case, I guess."

"In case of what?"

"In case there's a chance Glad's things belong to someone else. I just can't let that horrible bulldog of a woman get her paws on Glad's stuff. Not if Glad's got a daughter out there. I feel like I owe it to her. Can you understand that?"

Tom blew out a breath. "Yeah. I get it. But promise me. This is *it*. Okay? You pick up Glad's stuff at the morgue tomorrow and we'll let the lawyer sort it out from here. No more playing amateur detective. Let the chips fall where they may."

I sulked, but I knew he was right. "Okay."

Tom smiled and reached up to touch my face.

"This ain't nothin' but a gaul-dang garbage dump!" Winky bellowed.

Like Dr. Livingston emerging from an urban jungle, Winky crawled out from amongst the mangled maze of junked windows and rusty stoves and dishwashers that littered the back yard.

Tom's hand dropped to his side. "Let's get out of here."

"Best i-dear I heard in years," Winky said.

The three of us walked back to the front yard. Winky and I climbed back into Maggie and waved goodbye to Tom in the dimming light. With the help of a hot cop, I'd just committed my second B&E with a homeless redneck. As we drove away, I wondered if Tom thought I was a criminal. Or insane. Or both. I bit my lip and pulled onto Gulf Boulevard. At Winky's command, I headed north, in the direction of his place, wherever that might be.

"Pull over here," Winky instructed when we reached a familiar destination. We were back at Water Loo's.

"Do you actually *live* here now?" I asked.

Winky smiled. "Workin' on it. Thanky for the ride, Val Pal. Maggie's a sweetheart."

He patted Maggie's dashboard and climbed out of the car. As he did, I noticed a bulge in his right pants pocket.

"Winky!"

He whirled around. "Yes, ma'am?"

"What's in your pants pocket?"

"I didn't think you thought a me that way," Winky joked, wagging his eyebrows.

"Ha ha. Very funny. What have you got in there?"

"A souvenir."

Anger shot through me. "Did you *steal* something?"

Winky shrank back in horror. "No ma'am. I just took me a mo-mento."

"Let me see it."

Winky hung his head like a kid caught red-handed. He reached into his pocket and pulled out a yellow and green ball of yarn.

"What is that?"

Winky tugged on the ball until it took on a familiar shape. It was a crocheted poodle wrapped around a spare toilet roll.

"It's like the one at your mom's place," he said. "I found it in Glad's Minnie Winnie."

"You shouldn't have taken it," I said harshly.

Winky appeared genuinely wounded. "Oh. I see. It's okay for *you* to take something, but not *me*."

I was caught in a trap I'd set for myself.

My nose grew hot and painful. My vision blurred.

I was guilty. Busted.

"I'm sorry, Winky."

"She was *my friend*, too, you know."

I couldn't argue with that.

"You're right, Winky. I'm sure she would want you to have it."

Winky's face softened and his eyes brightened again.

"An' as they say, it always pays to have a spare roll!"

He held the yarn poodle over his head like a trophy, and waved it in the air as he danced a funny victory jig. I shot him a smile, and he turned and disappeared into the darkness, his woodpecker laugh trailing behind him.

I put Maggie in reverse and glanced over at Water Loo's. The plate glass windows gave off a dingy, yellowish glow against the slate-blue night. The place looked empty. Then I caught sight of a faint silhouette in the front window. Peering out through the glass was Winnie the waitress. She smiled at me and waved.

I waved back.

Chapter Thirty-Four

My stomach grumbled. I wanted Caddy's biscuits and gravy, and a walk on the beach. But both would have to wait until tomorrow. Today, I had things to do and people to annoy.

First on my list was a trip to the morgue to claim Glad's things. Then I needed to stop by Tony's lawyer's office to drop them off. I jumped in the shower. I was feeling good, belting out my rendition of Gloria Gaynor's *I Will Survive*, when a horrible thought occurred to me.

I might be aiding and abetting the enemy.

By delivering Glad's rings to Tony's attorney, I might be putting them right into the dirty, grasping paws of Bulldog Thelma!

I pondered the irony of the situation while I toweled off and fumbled around with Mr. Coffee.

If I didn't go straighten out Glad's name on public records, it could gunk up the works for Bulldog Thelma. Maybe for a long time. But it would also make it pretty near impossible for any of Glad's next-of-kin to ever find out what happened to her. Ditto if I didn't pick up Glad's rings.

I could only make it possible for Glad's true heirs to get them if I also made it possible for Tony's ex.

The conundrum soured my mood. I felt sad and confused and alone. I needed advice on what to do from the people who had known Glad even better than I did. For better or worse, that meant only one thing.

Water Loo's, here I come.

WHEN I WALKED IN, THE stooges were reverently passing around an old, wrinkled-up piece of paper as if it were the deed to the Taj Mahal.

"Val Pal!" Winky hollered. "You're not gonna believe this!"

I scooted into the booth next to Goober. He slid the ragged, yellowed paper across the sticky table to within my reach. Six somber eyes followed my every move as I peeled the paper from the table and read it in disbelief.

It was the birth certificate for Thelma G. Goldrich, dated December 22, 1965.

I nearly fell out of the booth.

"Where did you guys *find* this?" I nearly screeched.

"Ready to eat some crow?" Goober asked. "You have *Winky* to thank for it."

Goober pointed his spoon at the grinning, freckle-faced sleuth. He was beaming as if he'd just won a NASCAR trophy.

"Yep," Winky said proudly. "That there toilet-roll poodle had a big surprise waitin' inside it. Nature called this mornin' and I answered. I was about to wipe my butt with this here piece a paper when I noticed it had writing on it."

"Good ting you can read," Jorge sneered.

"I might be ignorant, Jorge, but I ain't illigiterate," he shot back.

"I tink you mean illiterate, Pincho."

Winky scowled. "I'm gonna pinch yore –"

"Guys! Enough!" I yelled.

To my surprise, everyone shut up and stared at me. Once I had their attention, I stated the obvious.

"Don't you realize? This is *absolute proof* that Glad and Tony had a baby together." I pointed at the paper. "Glad names Tony as the father right here!"

"Yeah, we know, Val," Goober said dryly. "As has been pointed out by someone just recently, we *all* can read."

My face reddened.

Goober laughed and poked me in the ribs with his elbow. "Good news, eh?"

I smiled. "Absolutely!"

Goober knitted his bushy eyebrows together. "Val, why in the world would Glad put something as important as her baby's birth certificate in a spare toilet-roll holder?"

"It makes perfect sense to me," I said.

"What do you mean?"

I blew out a breath. The three stooges leaned in to hear what I had to say.

"Okay. Look at it this way. We all know how much Glad liked to hide things, right?"

The stooges nodded.

"Well, it's simple women's logic. Men never change the empty toilet roll. It's the last place a man would ever think of looking."

The men exchanged glances, then shrugs, then more nods amongst themselves.

"When you're right, you're right," Goober said finally. "Let's raise a toast to our clever girl Glad!"

"Jes! A toast!" Jorge echoed.

I raised my mug with them, put my left hand over my heart, and waited on Jorge's double-click.

ON THE WAY TO THE COUNTY morgue I felt close to Glad again. It was as if she was in the seat right next to me, beaming that crooked, smeary-red-lipstick, clown-denture smile of hers. Tucked away safely in my purse, I carried Glad's ID, her daughter's birth certificate, and that little gem-encrusted oval piece of jewelry I'd found in one of her shoeboxes. In a way, Glad really *was* along for the ride—what was left of her, at least. After I collected Glad's personal effects, I planned to keep my promise to Tom and hand all the stuff over to Tony's attorney and "let the chips fall where they may."

I pulled into a parking space at the morgue and rehearsed a scenario in my mind. I could lie and say Glad's name wasn't Fremden because she got married and I didn't know it.

Yes. That could work.

I climbed out of Shabby Maggie and a thought hit me.

Duh! You don't have to lie, Val. That part is actually true!

I shook my head, climbed out of the car, and headed for my date with the devilish clerk. When I walked in, he recognized me right away.

"Ms. Fremden! You showed! Whew! I was beginning to feel the heat."

"What do you mean?" I stared into his piercing blue eyes that were so much like Glad's.

"Frenchy's called here twice today, trying to find out how she can 'bend the rules' and get her hands on your aunt's stuff."

"You're kidding!"

"No, I'm not. See it all the time. Dead bodies attract relatives like hungry sharks." He looked around and lowered his voice. "People don't understand. It's like a personal-effects feeding frenzy around here."

"Oh. That's awful."

The dimpled devil of a clerk shrugged. "Hazard of the biz. So, what have you got to show me, Ms. Fremden?"

"Her Florida ID. Will that work?"

"Sure will."

"Great! But I'm curious. How do you remember my name?"

The goateed clerk winked a blue eye at me. "I guess because I thought it was funny. You were obviously scrounging around for your aunt's ID last time. I knew you didn't have one. As I said, I've seen it *all* here at the morgue. When you handed me your driver's license, I saw your name was Fremden. My parents are German. I recognized that your last name means stranger. So that made you Valiant Stranger."

"I don't get it," I said.

"Valiant Stranger? Come on! Doesn't that sound like the coolest superhero name? And then your birthdate. April Fools' Day? That was pure gold!"

I was gobsmacked. This guy obviously had *way* too much time on his hands.

"Wow. That's...uh...*interesting*. So, tell me. If you were so suspicious of me, why did you let me claim Glad's body?"

The cute clerk glanced around the room quickly, then shot me a devilish grin that could make an angel think twice about busting through the pearly gates.

"Easy. I make it a point not to mess with superheroes. Especially *hot* ones."

The clerk laughed, revealing a perfect set of gleaming white teeth. His slightly elongated incisors added to his devilish magnetism.

How had I missed that before?

I couldn't help but grin.

"Thanks. But my aunt isn't a Fremden anymore. She's a Goldrich. She got married. I didn't know." I handed him Glad's ID.

He gave it a quick glance. "Okay. That'll work. Let me just make the corrections in the computer here and I'll get the envelope with her effects. You want to examine them?"

"No! Leave the envelope sealed. I'm dropping them off at her lawyer's. I don't want to give anyone any ammunition to say I stole something."

"Good idea. People can get really hinky when it comes to cash and prizes."

He punched the computer keys a few times and disappeared behind a door. A nearby printer jerked to life and started zapping out something. A minute or so later he came back and snatched the document off the printer. He handed it to me, along with a manila envelope. He'd placed a seal over the flap and scrawled his signature over it.

"Okay, Ms. Fremden. Here's your updated death cert and your aunt's effects. I made sure no one could argue that the envelope had been opened. Gave it the official Darren Dudley seal of approval."

"Thanks. What's your name?"

"Uh...Darren Dudley?"

I cringed. "Oh. Yeah. Darren Dudley. Of the official seal. Duh!"

Darren flashed me another sexy smile. My gut churned with a strange mixture of attraction and repulsion. Darren was cute. Dead bodies weren't. But I didn't have time for contemplation. I needed to be on my way.

"Uh, thanks again, Darren. Just for the record, you're pretty cool."

Darren brightened like a megawatt bulb.

"You too! Wanna go out sometime?"

The directness of his question caught me totally off guard.

"Uh...let me think about it. I've got a few things on my mind right now."

"Sure thing. Hey, Valiant. Don't be a stranger!"

I groaned. "That was awful. I might have to avenge that one."

Darren grinned. "I'm hoping so."

After vanquishing Bulldog Thelma and flirting with devilish Darren, I left the morgue feeling like Wonder Woman—the beautiful and powerful *Valiant Stranger*! I smiled and laid Glad's envelope in the seat next to me, then shifted into reverse and headed for my next stop.

Along the way, I thought about Darren's offer of a date. Maybe I should have accepted. After all, Tom hadn't actually asked me out. So far, he'd just been helping me with this crazy mission of mine. And he'd met my mother....

Gawd! He probably thinks I'm nothing but a crazy hillbilly bent on revenge!

I slammed on the brakes and felt my superhero powers tumble over the windshield and evaporate in the hot breeze.

Chapter Thirty-Five

When I stopped to drop off Glad's things at the law offices of J.D. Fellows & Associates, I felt my super powers return a little. The birth certificate Winky had found was definitely going to put a kink in Bulldog Thelma's chain. I looked down at the envelope bearing Darren Dudley's seal and wondered what it contained.

Canine kryptonite, I hope!

I couldn't help but smirk as I stepped into the posh lobby of Tony's estate attorney. It reminded me of one I'd seen in a movie once. My sandals clicked on the gleaming, grey-granite floors. The navy-blue walls were accented by huge canvases of modern art that perfectly matched the sleek European furniture. This guy was certainly doing well for himself.

I fingered baby Thelma's birth certificate for the hundredth time. Hopefully, it was the key to solving this whole bloody mystery. I heard a noise and looked up. A tiny little man approached. He looked like one of Santa's elves, only in a grey Armani suit. He stopped in front of me and spoke.

"Ms. Fremden?"

"Yes, that's me."

I figured the diminutive man was a clerk or something. But I should have known better. Underlings couldn't afford Armani. Not in this economy.

"I'm J.D. Fellows. Nice to meet you."

I stood up and shook his hand. "Nice to meet you, too, sir."

I followed him back to his office. The furniture was expensive, but something seemed off about it. Then it hit me. Everything was *smaller* than normal scale. Mr. Fellows must have had every stick of furniture in the room custom-made to suit his smaller stature. I took a seat in a burgundy-colored leather chair in front of his desk. Being five-foot-four, my feet usually dangled from such chairs. But it was a perfect fit.

I settled into the comfortable cushions. They lured me into a false sense of security, as I had no idea I was about to be attacked.

"So tell me, Ms. Fremden," said the tiny Mr. Fellows, Esq. from his towering position across his mahogany desk, "what exactly is your involvement with this case?"

His words sounded more like an accusation than a question.

"I...uh...I just came to drop off Glad's...I mean Mrs. Goldrich's personal effects."

"And how did you come to be in possession of them?"

The tone of his voice was one I'd only heard before on TV—during a heated courtroom interrogation.

"Are you a relative of Ms. Goldrich's?"

"Uh...no sir."

"Then, I ask again, how did you come to be in possession of her personal effects?"

"Excuse me, sir. Am I on trial here?"

The question caused a tiny fracture in the man's serious expression. He eyed me carefully and let the fracture grow into a smile.

"No. Forgive me, Ms. Fremden. It just seems...*highly unusual.*"

"I understand. I'm a friend of Glad's. I mean, I *was* a friend of Glad's."

"I see. I was, too. *And* of Anthony's." Mr. Fellows let out a puff of laughter. "She was an original, that woman."

I relaxed a little bit and smiled. "She sure was."

Mr. Fellows looked at the envelope in my hand and spoke with a softer tone, stating the obvious. "So, do you have the effects with you?"

"Oh. Yes. Here."

I handed him the envelope.

"Still sealed, I see."

"Yes sir. I just want whatever's in there to end up in the right hands."

"And whose hands would those be?"

"I'm not sure. *You're* the lawyer. But if you'll indulge me, Mr. Fellows, I have a theory."

The small man burst into a surprisingly large laugh.

"A theory. Okay. I'm game."

"Tony's will states that everything is to go to Thelma G. Goldrich, right?"

"Yes. Don't remind me. She's been calling me every day with her demands."

My gut flopped. "I didn't know that. What does she want?"

"I'm sorry. I'm not at liberty to say."

"Of course. Right. But isn't her name actually G. Thelma Goldrich?"

"Yes. That's the only reason I haven't released the will yet. That, plus a favor for a mutual friend of ours. I believe you know Mr. Thomas Foreman?"

My face felt as if I'd just stuck it inside a pizza oven.

"Yes. So...you already know the whole story?"

"No. Mr. Foreman only asked me to delay distribution of the will for a few weeks. He said he had good cause. I figured there was no harm in it."

"Pardon me for being up front, but I think G. Thelma Goldrich is not the person Tony had in mind as his heir."

Mr. Fellows leaned forward. "Go on."

I handed him the piece of paper that yesterday nearly met its fate in the crack of Winky's butt.

"That's the birth certificate for Glad and Tony's daughter, Thelma G. Goldrich. I believe *she's* the true heir named in the will."

Mr. Fellows' eyes grew wide. "Where did you get this?"

I borrowed a line from him. "I'm not at liberty to say."

Mr. Fellows smiled wryly. He laughed again and spoke in a more casual tone.

"Please, Ms. Fremden, go on."

"There's more, Mr. Fellows. I think we've found her, too. The only thing is –"

"She's insane," interrupted Mr. Fellows.

I was stunned speechless. My mouth hung open like a dead trout. Tony's attorney sighed and leaned back in his chair.

"Let's just say that I've been down this road before, Ms. Fremden. She's not a match, my dear."

"The woman in Chattahoochee? You already tested her DNA?"

"Yes, and it was inconclusive."

"Crap!" I yelled, then caught myself. "Sorry. How long ago did you do the test?"

"I can't recall offhand, but it's been a long, long time."

"Maybe the tests were wrong. Lab tests get screwed up, you know. And with today's technology, maybe they can do a better job now."

Mr. Fellows sighed and studied me for a moment.

"You are an interesting woman, Ms. Fremden. I admire your tenacity. And your hopefulness. Maybe you're right. What would it hurt to have the woman's DNA tested again? DNA technology has come a long way in the past few years."

"I was hoping you'd say that. It shouldn't be long now. The DNA samples are already at a lab in Tallahassee."

Mr. Fellows' right eyebrow shot to his hairline.

"I see. You certainly *are* the resourceful one, I'll give you that."

He looked to the left for a moment and absently tapped his right index finger on his mahogany desk. "I tell you what, Ms. Fremden. I am at liberty to delay distribution of the will until Friday of next week. Will that buy you the time you need?"

"The time *I* need? I'm sorry, but I'm officially done with the case. Tom...uh...Mr. Foreman is having the lab forward its DNA findings to you. It's all in your hands now."

"Very well. But tell me the truth, Ms. Fremden. Why are you *really* involved in this case?"

"If you knew Glad like you say you did, sir, then you already know."

Mr. Fellows looked at some distant point and smiled.

"Yes. And *you*...as I said before, are an interesting woman, Ms. Fremden. I hope you're right."

Chapter Thirty-Six

Two days had passed since I'd heard from Tom. I flopped onto my ugly couch and checked my phone again. No voice messages. No texts. No nothing. I presumed, like the rest of the world, Tom just wasn't interested in someone as screwed up as me. I tossed my phone on the couch and bit my lip.

Another potential relationship down the crapper.

I vowed to myself not to call Tom, then tromped to my bedroom to change into my bathing suit. A trip to Sunset Beach might cheer me up—or at least keep me from going more nuts than I already was.

I was yanking my shirt off over my head when I heard a loud banging sound. I pulled my shirt back on and went into the living room. Someone was beating on my front door!

I peeked out between the slats in the blinds covering the window pane that made up the top half of the door. To my horror, Bulldog Thelma's angry, red eyes stared back at me! I dropped the blinds like they were molten lava. The doorknob rattled as if it were being throttled. Then the banging started again, even harder and louder than before.

"Who the hell do you think you are?" Bulldog Thelma screamed through the door. "Keep your busybody nose out of my business!"

She was silent for a moment. Maybe she was waiting on a response from me. I didn't give her the satisfaction. Besides, I was at a total loss as to what to say.

"Tony was *my* husband!" she screamed again. "It's *my* money. I'm warning you! Keep your trashy behind out of my affairs!"

Oh my lord! She must have gotten wind of my visit to J.D. Fellows!

Adrenaline pumped through me, blanking my mind and making me itch to flee. I screamed out the only response I could think of, inspired by a whispered voice in my ear.

"Screw you, kiddo!"

For a moment, Bulldog Thelma stopped banging the door with her fists. Then she began kicking it instead.

"I'll teach you to curse at me, you meddling tramp!"

"The police are already on their way!" I lied.

The banging stopped again. I peeked through the blinds. Bulldog's sausage-link ponytail swung wildly to and fro as she waddled a hasty retreat. I flopped knee-first onto the couch and looked through the living room blinds, which had a view of the staircase. When Thelma's wide-load butt reached the bottom of the rickety stairs, I decided to run out the door to give her a piece of my mind.

I flung my front door open and raced to the staircase landing. She must have heard me coming. The sausage-haired witch turned around at the base of the stairs and sneered up at me like a rabid bulldog.

My stomach turned to ice. My mind went blank.

Bulldog put a fat foot on the bottom step.

Panic shot through me like a hot-mustard enema. I fled back into my apartment and bolted the door behind me.

I flung myself on the couch, wrapped my arms around a lumpy brown pillow, and stared at the door like a frightened child. Would the monster come back and finish me off?

I sat still as a stone, my heart thumping in my ears, for what seemed like an eternity. Nothing happened. Somehow, that only served to make me even more scared. Not knowing what else to do, I decided to break my promise to myself.

I called Tom.

"WELL, TECHNICALLY, Val, it's not a crime unless she hit you or threatened bodily harm," Tom explained.

"She threatened me! She threatened to...to...she said she would *teach* me not to curse at her!"

"That sounds brutal. Sorry, Val. Close, but no legal cigar."

I felt foolish. "Okay. Thanks, Tom. Sorry to have bothered you. Goodbye."

"Hold up!"

My heart fluttered. "What?"

"Are you okay? By yourself, I mean?"

"I guess. I don't know. Should I be worried, Tom?"

"I'm not sure. I'll check on some things and get back with you."

"Okay."

"Goodbye, Val."

"Goodbye, Tom."

Our goodbyes sounded like final ones to me. Yes. It was as official as the tone in Tom's voice. Our budding romance was never going to bloom.

Crap!

I was already unhappy about giving up my role in helping to find Glad's daughter. This "back-to-business" attitude from Tom was just another low blow. I felt purposeless again. My life was officially void of meaning. A clean slate. Nada. Zilch. Zero.

What am I going to do now?

Like a mission bell, my phone rang.

"Hello?"

"Hello. Is this Valiant Stranger? I'm in desperate need of being rescued from certain death from prolonged boredom."

I perked up and laughed. It was Darren.

"How did you find my secret lair?" I teased.

"A beautiful woman came by my office with a clue."

"What kind of clue?"

"Her phone number and address on a release form."

I shook my head. "Clever. You must be a prodigal genius."

"Some say I have a few good brain cells left knocking around the old noodle. Speaking of noodles, want to have dinner with me tonight at the new Vietnamese place on Central? I hear they make a mean pho."

"A mean foe. Sounds like a job for Valiant Stranger."

"Ha ha! You're funny. Meet you there at six? Say yes. *Please!*"

"Yes."

And just like that, I had something to do.

I WAS IN A WRESTLING match with a pair of black leggings, getting ready for my first official date since the Bush administration, when Tom called.

"Hi, Val. I want to drop by tonight to discuss what's going on with that Jacob fellow and Bulldog Thelma."

"Hi, Tom. I'm sorry. I can't tonight. I'm busy."

"You're *busy*? Doing what?"

"I have a *life*, you know."

"Oh, sure. Hot date?" he joked.

My silence said it all.

"Oh. I see." Tom's tone went back to strictly business. "Well, how about tomorrow. I really do need to speak with you. I have some news. But it can wait."

"Sure, Tom."

"Hooker Tea at ten o'clock?"

"Okay."

He clicked off before I had a chance to say goodbye. As my squirrely mind analyzed Tom's every word, it latched onto the name of his suggested meeting place. Hooker Tea.

Was he suggesting something else as well?

Sparks of hurt and guilt and anger ignited a bonfire of conflicting emotions within me.

Why should I care? I don't owe Tom anything.

I put away the jean skirt and button-down shirt I was planning to wear on my date with Darren, and picked out a sexy little sundress instead.

IT DIDN'T TAKE LONG for my date with Darren to hit an iceberg. He was handsome. And nice enough. I gave him that. But all he wanted to talk about was work. Call me squeamish, but cadavers just didn't make for good dinner conversation. Neither did morbid humor.

As the date dragged on, I felt a wall of insulation thicken between me and Darren. My initial excitement and anticipation tarnished into dull, familiar disappointment. When Darren reached over the table and touched my hand, the thought of what that hand had been doing all day proved the Achilles' heel for Valiant Stranger. His appeal vanished like a cartoon villain, leaving a trail of palpable awkwardness in its wake.

"Thanks for a nice evening, Darren," I said as we left the restaurant.

"You're welcome. I guess I blew it."

I winced. "Why do you say that?"

"The look on your face at dinner. I was a train wreck. I know I shouldn't talk about dead bodies at the dinner table. But you make me nervous. I didn't know what else to say."

"Next time, why don't you just ask some questions? Let the girl do some talking."

"Next time? Does that mean you want to go out again?"

"I guess I should have said, 'With the next girl.' "

"Got it." Darren looked away, then back at me. "Thanks for being straight up with me, Valiant Stranger. I guess from now on, you'll just be Stranger."

I smiled and hugged Darren.

"No. I think *you'll* be stranger."

We laughed together for a moment, thawing the awkward chill a bit. We said goodbyes that seemed more like farewells, and I walked alone down Central to Beach Drive. I took a left and watched the lights twinkle in the oak trees as I passed Vinoy Park. I sighed and shuffled my sad-sack little self back to my sad-sack little life in my sad-sack little hovel of an apartment above somebody else's garage.

Chapter Thirty-Seven

I faced the new day determined to quit sulking about my love life and to get out more. I started with a trip to Sunset Beach. After all, it was the perfect July day. When I pulled into the lot at 7 a.m., the morning sun had felt nice and toasty as I strolled the shoreline and searched for shells. But within an hour, the air was hot enough to melt wax. As I cruised on back home, the heat coming off Maggie's red vinyl seats approached nuclear meltdown. I needed a cold shower and an even colder drink. Then I thought about my meeting with Tom at ten and wasn't sure even an iceberg could cool down my mood.

Hooker Tea my rear-end. Screw you, Tom!

I CRACKED THE TAB ON a tallboy Fosters, headed for the bathroom, and set my superhero dial to self-destruct mode. In keeping with the theme, I decided to wear the same dress that sank last night's love boat. It seemed like a good idea at the time. I'd had no breakfast, and the pint of Fosters in my empty stomach was making the world all glassy and far away and untouchable.

I stumbled down the stairs of my apartment and picked my way carefully down the sidewalk on Beach Drive. Hooker Tea was just a few blocks past the oak hammocks of Vinoy Park. It was blazing hot.

So hot! Maybe I could stop and take a nap on a bench under the trees....

I flopped down on a bench, right on top of one of those stupid new armrests. My temper soared to match the pain emanating from my tailbone.

"Nobody cares about the downtrodden," I said out loud to no one in particular.

That was when I knew I was in real trouble.

I was too tipsy to tango. I turned my butt around, took two steps toward home and ran right into Tom's stupid, manly-man chest.

"Hey! You all right?" he asked.

"Yeah, suurre," I said, and blinked in an attempt to sharpen my focus.

"How was your date?"

His dang cop voice sounded like an interrogation again.

I thought about coming clean for a second and confessing it had been a disaster. But a painful streak of humiliated Southern pride wouldn't let me admit defeat. Trouble was, I was an exceptionally bad liar. Especially when I was drunk. I decided the best strategy was to keep my answers short and simple.

"Fine."

Tom took me by the arm and we walked to Hooker Tea. I was desperate for a coffee, but they didn't serve java. Just tea.

"Chai tea," I sputtered, then leaned against a wall while Tom picked up his order and paid the tab. I trailed behind like a sad puppy as he walked over to a table in the corner by a window.

"Have you talked to Jacob?" he asked, handing me my tea.

I stuck with my monosyllable plan. "No."

"I tried to reach Jacob but his phone number's been disconnected."

I studied Tom.

Why did he have to be so handsome? Why?

"Why?" I grunted.

"I just wanted to see if it was still working, actually. In case I needed to reach him."

"Oh."

"Just so you know, Thelma Goldrich was granted access to the house, Val. This whole will thing might get sticky before it's all over. I want to gather up any information you have on Jacob Timms and Bulldog Goldrich while it's still clear in your mind."

Clear in my mind. That's a hoot!

"Kay."

"Are you trying to use up all your little words today?" Tom asked. He looked kind of pissed.

"No."

"Then what's up?"

"Nothing!"

Tom scowled. "In other words, *everything.*"

"Right. Mr. Cop know-it-all. You know *everything.*"

"Val, are you...have you been *drinking?*"

"No!"

Tom studied me with his sea-green eyes. I didn't want him to add hopeless drunk to my already impressive list of crazy-ass-loser-woman attributes. I tried hard to focus. Concentrating made something click in my head.

"Wait a minute. You said Jacob *Timms.*"

"Yes."

"How did you find out his last name?"

"Like you said. I'm a cop. I know everything," Tom sneered.

I looked down at my cup. "I'm sorry."

Tom sighed and his voice softened. "I'm sorry, too, Val."

I looked up and we exchanged sad smiles.

"You know how I found out?" Tom spoke as if confessing. I shook my head.

"Jorge. He got a meter maid to tell him. She'd given Jacob a ticket for parking illegally on your street. Turns out, he'd been a real jerk about it and she'd remembered his name. Anyway, I ran his priors. If Jacob Timms *did* kill Bobby Munch, he got away with it. Not even so much as an assault charge was filed. He's clean."

The caffeine in the tea was doing its job. Everything was coming back into focus—even the things I didn't *want* to see.

"I've been thinking about it, Tom. That night I met Jacob at the park, then saw Bulldog Thelma on my way home.... She must have been waiting for Jacob."

"Most likely."

"But why would Jacob tell me all that horrific stuff about Glad? Why would he tell me about yanking Bobby's teeth out? Was he setting me up for something?"

"More than likely he was trying to gain your trust. It's a classic criminal tactic. I tell you something in confidence, you tell me something. I'm sure he wanted you to tell him what you knew about Glad and Tony's daughter. Especially if you had any hard evidence of her existence. In other words, he was fishing around to see if there was anyone else in the running for Tony's inheritance."

"Yeah. That makes sense. And they got away with it. They took the letter from Tony and the picture of Glad with the baby. That was the only evidence that Glad and Tony had a child together...until Winky found the actual birth certificate." I snorted out a sad laugh. "I was such a sucker, Tom. I actually started to trust Jacob. Then he creeped me out with that story about Bobby, among other things."

Tom straightened up in his chair. "What other things, Val?"

"Oh, I don't know. It's nothing, probably."

"Any detail could be important."

"Well, he asked how my lunch date with you had gone. At Ming Ming's, remember?"

"Yeah. Crappy day, as I recall." Tom grinned.

I smiled back at him sheepishly.

"I'm being serious. Thing is, I don't remember telling him about having lunch with you."

Tom's face went serious again. "That's interesting."

"Also, Jacob said he'd been pretty close friends with both Tony and Glad. But he didn't know Glad was dead. If they really had been so close, wouldn't Tony have called him and told him his wife died? Anyway, Jacob could have been lying about everything. I only wonder if maybe *he* was the reason Tony and Glad had kept a low profile here in St. Pete. Jacob said Bobby had abused Glad. But Jacob knew where Glad was for six years before he told Tony. Instead of rescuing her, could he have taken his own turn treating her just as badly?"

"Wow. That's dark, Val. And highly possible. Do you remember anything else?"

"Yes. Jacob told me about Bulldog Thelma's sham marriage to Tony. That she got a BMW and lifetime alimony out of the deal. How would he know that?"

"That's good, Val. In case we need to prove conspiracy to defraud. Or build a case for a restraining order."

"A restraining order?"

"Yes. We've got to keep you safe, Val."

"From what?"

"You've already seen what these two will do for money. They don't seem to have any qualms about squashing anyone who stands in their way, friend or foe. Right now, you and your theory about loony-bin Thelma are standing in their way."

I gulped down a knot of rising fear. "What can I do about it?"

"I suggest house arrest until the DNA results come back."

"House arrest?"

"Stay home. Lock your doors. I'll put Jorge back on your street. He did a good job last time. If you need someone quick, he'll be a minute away. It'd be good for you *and* for him. It might help him re-build his confidence."

"So I get to be Jorge's target practice."

"Something like that."

"Gee, Tom. You sure know how to make a girl feel special."

Chapter Thirty-Eight

The next week under house arrest dragged on endlessly like a washed-up old tranny. I couldn't afford cable, so I never bothered to buy a TV. On day five I'd watched every show known to Netflix and played 10,000 games of solitaire on my computer. On day six I even got desperate enough to start writing a first draft of *Double Booty*, just in case. Thankfully, Bulldog Woman and her tooth-pulling sidekick hadn't come banging at my door again. Sadly, neither had Tom.

I was down to naming the tiny red ants crawling in a line up my kitchen wall and wearing a face mask I'd concocted from a half-rotten avocado when the phone finally rang.

It was Tom. My heart skipped a beat.

"Val?"

"Yes. Hi, Tom."

"It's a match."

"What?"

"I just got off the phone with my friend at the lab. It's a match. We've found her, Val! Looney-bin Thelma is Glad's missing daughter!"

My knees buckled. "That's great!"

"Yeah. It really is. You know, I couldn't believe it. I really thought all of this was going to turn out to be a wild goose chase."

"Thanks for the vote of confidence."

"Don't be a sore winner, Val. Anyway, that's the good news. The bad news is we don't have much time left to deliver the evidence. I called Mr. Fellows to let him know about the match. He told me he's postponed the distribution of the will as long as he can. Bulldog Thelma has her attorneys breathing down his neck. They're busting his chops, saying there's no reason to wait. They know about the old DNA test. They're arguing that the woman in Chattahoochee isn't related to Tony. Fellows did what he could, but with no evidence he had to agree with the other attorneys on a date for distribution. It's official, Val. At 5 p.m. tomorrow, the estate goes to that bulldog witch."

"No! That's horrible!"

"Don't give up just yet. We're not totally sunk. Unless, that is, we don't get the DNA proof to Fellows on time. Fellows says irrefutable proof would trump any other claims Bulldog Thelma might have. He also said that the original report of the new DNA results and that birth certificate Winky found should be all he needs to get that money-hungry she-wolf out of the loop for good."

"That's wonderful!"

"Yes, but like I said, the clock's ticking. I don't want to leave this to chance. I'm going to make a quick run up to the lab in Tallahassee, then over to the state hospital to tell Thelma in person. I thought you might want to come along."

"I...uh...when?"

"Right now. I'm on my way over. We can be back late tonight, if we get a move on."

"Uh...okay."

"I'll be by in ten minutes to pick you up."

I clicked off the phone and made a mad scramble to the bathroom. A slimy green corpse stared back at me from the mirror. I scrubbed the avocado mask from my face and pinned back my scraggly wet hair. I dove into a denim sundress and was trying to slap on some blush when the clock ran out. Tom texted me. He was waiting downstairs in the 4Runner.

I flung on some sandals, grabbed my purse and sunglasses, and dashed out the door.

BITTERSWEET RELIEF washed over me as I flew down the rickety steps of my apartment.

We'd found Glad's girl!

I tried to read Tom's face as I climbed in the 4Runner, but it was undecipherable. I stole a glance in the backseat. It was empty.

No Winky. This time Tom and I were on our own.

Part of me was thrilled. The other part was scared spit-less. I sat close to the passenger door and held onto the armrest. Tom seemed all business. The awkward gulf between us seemed ten miles wide.

We traveled in tense silence for about ten minutes. It wasn't until Tom pulled onto I-275 that he finally spoke.

"So tell me, how does it feel to have solved your first case, Detective Fremden?"

I breathed a sigh of relief. Tom had tried to tell a joke.

"It feels great. Not so much for my sake, but for Glad's."

I smiled over at Tom, thinking the ice was broken between us. But it was only cracked. The silence returned and filled the 4Runner like a million Styrofoam peanuts. I stared at the sparkling blue water of Tampa Bay as we crossed the Howard Frankland Bridge and wracked my brain for something to say. But for once in my life, I was completely stumped.

Tom came to the rescue with another attempt at humor.

"Off in Lady Lala Land?" he asked.

Geez. That man could not *tell a proper joke.*

I shrugged. "I guess."

"Seriously, Val. What are you thinking about? Are you nervous?"

His question caused me to bristle unexpectedly.

"Nervous? What should I be nervous about?"

"About seeing loony-bin Thelma again."

"Oh. Until you mentioned it, I hadn't thought that far ahead."

"Sorry. My bad. If we stop for a cold drink along the way, you're not going to drug me, are you?"

I smirked. "We'll see."

Tom laughed, then spoke in a soft, serious tone. "Why so quiet?"

Why? Because it's torture to sit here, knowing you don't want me, Tom! Knowing that you think I'm a lunatic. A drunkard. A hooker! A drug pusher!

"I dunno. I guess I just don't know what to say."

"Fair enough. How about telling me about your time in Germany."

I watched the big green sign for Bearss Avenue flit by, the last exit for Tampa. Nothing but two hours of boring highway ahead.

"What do you want to know?"

Tom reached in a little cooler by his feet. He handed me a can of Dr. Pepper.

"How about starting with why you went."

"Thanks," I said. I took the soda and cracked the tab on it. "Honestly, I guess I just wanted to see if I was in the wrong country. The US, I mean. For some reason, I've always felt like I didn't belong. That's why I went to Europe."

"Didn't belong?"

I shot him a knowing glance. "You've met my mom."

"Oh. Yeah. But what about before that, when you made your big escape from Two Egg?"

I looked over at Tom. A ping of sadness flitted across my heart. He was wearing a white button-down shirt with the sleeves rolled up to his elbows, and the same jeans I'd picked French fries from just a century-long couple of weeks ago. My heart began to ache.

"You really *do* remember everything people say."

"The interesting things, yes."

"You thought *Two Egg* was interesting?"

Tom looked over and cocked his head. "Sure. Why wouldn't it be?"

"I dunno. You've seen so much of my life. Correction. My *crazy, screwed-up life*. Why would that be interesting to *you?*"

Tom laughed and crinkles formed beside his sea-green eyes.

"The crazy parts are the best parts of life, Val. Don't you know that by now?"

"What are you talking about?"

"I'm talking about our imperfections. Our quirks. They're what make us *real*. They make us who we are. They're like...the *best* part of us, Val. Without them, we'd be like...I dunno. Like *generic zombies*. Everybody the same."

Something loosened up inside me, allowing me to breathe for the first time since I got in Tom's vehicle.

"Oh," I said, and blew out a sarcastic laugh. "When you look at it that way, I must be the Queen of Quirkiness."

Tom laughed.

"The secret to quirks is to *own* them, Val. Don't fight them. Celebrate them! If you don't, it's kind of like...*disowning* part of yourself. And you know what they say about a house divided...."

"It cannot stand. I get it, Tom. But I *can't* stand...I mean, I can't stand *myself*, sometimes."

"Oh. That's normal. That's when you need a friend to lean on."

I looked over at Tom. He was grinning at me from ear to ear. I was powerless to keep myself from grinning back.

"Are you my friend, Tom?"

"Of course I am, Val."

I sat back and grinned some more.

"That's very nice to know."

Chapter Thirty-Nine

We made good time, stopping to refuel in Lake City and grabbing a quick bite at the Krystal Burger drive-thru. I was too embarrassed to order fries. By the time I got over my indigestion, we were driving by the capitol building in downtown Tallahassee. The odd, red-and-white awnings on the façade always made the place look like a peppermint-candy-striped house of ill repute.

Tom made a few more turns and maneuvered the 4Runner into the parking lot of Phelps Labs, a shiny glass building that looked like a three-story block of blue-grey mirrors. He cut the ignition and looked over at me.

"Well, here we go."

We entered the lobby and Tom asked to see his buddy, Darryl Gonzales Foreman. The receptionist punched some numbers in a switchboard and motioned for us to take a seat. "Is your buddy a relative?" I asked Tom.

Before he could answer a woman appeared from behind a glass door. She was a knockout. A luscious Latina in a lab coat. She could have made J-Lo scratch her own eyes out in envy.

"Hello, Tom!" she said, raising her arms to embrace him.

"Hello, Darryl."

The two exchanged hugs and kisses on the cheek. Then the woman turned and looked at me.

"You must be the budding detective Tom told me about."

I felt like a total schlep. I shook her hand and bemoaned my sorry state. No makeup. Greasy hair in a ponytail. I couldn't have felt any frumpier if I'd been wearing curlers and a ratty bathrobe.

"Yes, I'm Val Fremden. Nice to meet you."

"Nice to meet you, too. I'm Darryl, Tom's ex-wife."

I TRIED NOT TO COLLAPSE from the surprise punch to my gut. I bit my tongue, raised my chin an inch and slapped on my best fake smile.

"Well, then, Tom's ex. Should we get down to business?"

Darryl led us to a small conference room. She closed the door behind her and opened a green file. She showed us some papers with dots and charts, but all I could see were disillusion-filled stars. I half-listened as she droned on with her perfect, beautiful, pouty-lipped mouth.

"Tests confirm the mitochondrial DNA from the woman's hair and the..."

This should be a great moment for me. Why do I feel like I want to die?

"...man's toenail clippings prove patriarchal bonds. The McGoldrick-Gesson test..."

Suck it up, Val. This isn't about you.

"...just one generation away. Chances are around 2 billion to one..."

Focus! Focus! Focus!

I snapped out of my pity party just in time to hear Ms. Foreman's final words.

"It's definitely a match. You've found your missing daughter."

I burst into tears.

"Are you okay, Val?" Tom asked.

"Sure. I just need a moment. Great news. Is there a lady's room around here?"

"Yes. Let me show you the way," offered Darryl. "This place is like a maze. You'll never find your way there and back."

Darryl led me down some corridors to the women's restroom. She stood and watched as I dabbed at my runny eyes in the mirror.

"So you're Tom's ex-wife?" I croaked, trying to sound nonchalant.

"He didn't tell you? Typical Tom." Darryl blew out a breath and a short laugh. "Just like him to not mention the five-hundred-pound gorilla in the room. Yes. I'm Tom's ex."

Something inside me shifted. I stared at the brilliant beauty queen for a moment.

"What happened with you two?" Suddenly, I remembered my manners. "Ooops! Sorry. It's none of my business!"

Darryl laughed.

"It's okay. No big secret here. We were together for ten years. He's a good guy. It's just that...well, sometimes you just know it's time to say goodbye. It's nobody's fault. Why do you ask?"

"Well, we've...I've been...."

"Say no more, I get it."

"Geez. I'm sorry, Darryl. I have no claim on him."

Darryl laughed again.

"Not to worry, Val. If you want him, he's all yours. He's a good guy. Just remember, relationships don't come with lifetime guarantees. You just have to enjoy the moments as they come. Accept what is. Be responsible for your own happiness. That way you always know where you stand."

"You sound like a friend of mine. Glad."

"Sure. I'd be glad to be your friend."

I didn't try to correct Darryl. Instead, I just accepted her offer.

"Thanks, Darryl." I looked at her, then back at my bedraggled reflection. "You wouldn't happen to have some makeup on you...I had to run out the door...."

"Makeup? You don't need it, Val. But if you want, just give me a sec."

Darryl disappeared, then reappeared with her makeup bag. In five minutes, she had me looking like a Caucasian version of herself. Well, almost. When we reappeared together in the conference room, Tom stood up.

"Wow! You two look gorgeous! I'd take you both out for drinks, but Val and I have got to get a move on."

I hugged Darryl and whispered, "Thank you."

She whispered back, "You're welcome, anytime."

Tom and I turned to leave, but Darryl held out a hand to stop us.

"Before you two leave, I was curious about something."

Tom and I looked at each other, then back at Darryl.

"What?" Tom asked.

"The samples. How did you collect so much blood from the daughter?"

"What do you mean?" Tom asked.

"The saliva on the cup wasn't a match. But that bloody handkerchief was. It was like you punched her in the nose or something."

"Oh my God!" Tom said, and turned to me.

"Val...that blood...it belongs to *you!*"

Chapter Forty

I awoke to find Tom reenacting his original heroic role from Caddy's. He was sitting on the floor of the lab's conference room with his back against the wall, holding my head up, staunching my bloody nose with his handkerchief. Apparently I'd fainted dead away and fallen face-first to the floor.

"Wad happened?" I asked.

"You just became Glad's daughter," Tom reminded me.

"What? How?" I asked, struggling against his grip. I wriggled around to face him.

"That day at Caddy's...the one freakishly similar to this one?" Tom said.

"Yeah."

"I put your bloody hanky in an evidence bag. We're trained to treat blood like hazardous waste, nowadays, you know. Plus, I didn't want to stain up my car. So I put the bag in a manila envelope. I forgot about it. I must have put Thelma's cup in the same envelope and sent it off to the lab by mistake."

"Oh, it was no mistake," said Darryl, laughing. "The world works in mysterious ways."

"But...wait. How can I not be my own mother's daughter?"

"That's a very good question," said Tom. "Why don't we take a little trip and find out."

THE HOUR-LONG DRIVE to Mom's house took two weeks. My head throbbed from the fall. My ears were full of whooshing sounds timed to the beat of my thumping heart. My mind whirled back and forth between Glad and Mom...or the woman I thought was my mom. When we finally pulled up in the yard, I was so nervous I could barely walk. Tom took my hand and helped me to the door. He knocked on it gently.

"Who's thar?" Mom called out.

"Mrs. Short! It's Tom. I've got your dau...I've got Valiant with me."

I frowned and stuck an elbow in Tom's ribs.

"Ow!" Tom grinned at me. "So feisty!"

"Always has been," Mom said through the screen door. "You're back sooner'n I thought, Valiant. Y'all come on in."

Mom unlatched the screen door and we stepped inside her liar's lair of fakery. She plopped her butt in her recliner. Tom and I took positions on the couch, below the gallery of false family photos. I felt like I was trapped inside a cheap time-travel movie, experiencing déjà vu from another lifetime. I was sad, confused, angry and somehow elated all at the same time.

But mostly, I just wanted to cry.

"Am I your real daughter?" I asked, my voice cracking.

Mom leaned back in her recliner and studied us. Her eyes shifted back and forth between Tom and me. Finally, she said, "So's you done gone and found out, have you?"

My inner child threw a fit.

"What? It's true? Why didn't you tell me?"

"Well, now, Val, before you go gettin' up on that high horse a yours, I *did* tell you. One time when you was about six. You just went to squallin', so I told you I made the whole story up."

"What *is* the whole story? I'm ready to hear it now."

"You sure?"

"Yes."

"All right then. Not much to tell, really. It was a warm spell in April, 1965. I remember 'cause your dad...well...Justas...your dad.... Anyway, Justas had decided he'd go fishin' for bream. Them fish get hungry as the dickens when the water starts warming up in spring."

Mom looked off in the distance for a moment.

"Okay. The fish get hungry," I said.

Mom's attention returned to the room. "I remember I was getting all the fixin's together for a fish fry when Justas come in saying he'd caught a whopper. I figured it was one a them big old catfish or a lunker, and my mouth started to waterin'. I love me some catfish, don't you know. Then he handed me a bundle wrapped up in *The Jackson Times*. I laid it on the counter and it started to squallin' like a baby. I opened it up and there you was. A dad-burned baby."

Mom laughed. "Justas said he found you along the road by the culberts. That's his favorite fishin' spot. You wat'n old enough to sit up yet, so you was just laying there, all quiet-like in the grass off the side of the road. He said if he'd a drove another two feet, you would a been squashed under his tire. But he didn't. And you wasn't. You was just layin' there, like I said, all quiet-like."

Mom adjusted herself in the recliner and leaned toward us. "Justas thought you might be dead, but when he poked you with a stick, you opened your eyes and giggled. Well, he thought that took a lot of courage. He brought you home and we kept you for a week without tellin' no one. We checked the papers, but nobody claimed you. We was gonna turn you in, but by then Justas was heartsick in love with you. We decided best thing to do was just keep you for good. Figured it was better than you ending up in a orphanage. Besides, you was cute and had spunk. We went to the Chattahoochee health clinic and told em you was borned at home."

"Nobody ever came to claim me?"

"Nope. Justas wanted to call you Courage, but I thought that sounded too mannish. We settled on Valiant, 'cause at least you could have a good nickname—Val. See? What'n that smart a me?"

Mom looked at me for praise and approval. I smiled politely and nodded.

"I mean, what could you do with Courage? Coo? Curr? That ain't no good. On the certificate, I wrote down your birthday as April Fools' Day, 'cause I thought it was funny. And I still wat'n sure what we were doing wat'n a pile of foolishness. Get it?"

Mom grinned at her own cleverness. I smiled and nodded again.

"Anyhoo, them folks at the clinic didn't ask no questions, Val. They just typed up the certificate. And that's how you came to be our other daughter, Valiant W. Jolly."

I shook my head in disbelief. "Why didn't you tell me later, when I was grown?"

"Tell you what? That you was throwed out like trash? That nobody wanted you? What good would a come a that?"

Her words stung, but they made sense in hindsight. "You did the right thing, Mom."

Mom looked defiant. "I know that. You ain't got to tell me."

"Okay. Sorry. Mom, I know it sounds weird, but did you find anything in my diaper?"

"Besides a mess a turds? Woo, child you stunk to high heaven!"

"Something besides that," I said as my face grew hot.

"Now that you mention it, yep. There *was* something. I plum near forgot about it." Mom laughed to herself. "Darndest thing. It was a little jewelry bug. A moth or a June bug or somethin'. I remember it woulda been purty if it wat'n busted."

"Do you still have it?"

"I used to catch you playin' with it all the time. I had to hide it away. 'Fraid you might swaller it. Last time I seen it, it was in the bottom drawer of my jewelry box. Why don't you go fetch it, Valiant."

I raced to Mom's bedroom. Buried amongst piles of lotions and perfume bottles, I found her jewelry box. I opened the bottom drawer. At the back underneath a tangled heap of cheap costume jewelry, I found what I was looking for. A little blue-bodied dragonfly with one green wing. I held it to my chest, closed my eyes and took a deep breath.

Apparently, my sentimentality was taking too long for Mrs. Short. Her voice bellowed from the living room.

"Valiant! You die in there or somethin'?"

I opened my eyes and smiled. When I walked back into the living room, Tom was standing. He rushed over and put his hands on my shoulders.

"Did you find it?"

"Yes." I opened my palm and showed him the dragonfly.

"Amazing," he said, shaking his head.

"Let me have a look!" Mom grunted.

I held the jewelry out for her to see.

"Yep, that's it. I was gonna trade that thang to your Aunt Vera-Jane for a set of Harlequin Romance novels. But when she saw it was busted the deal was off."

My mom. Ms. Lucille Jolly Short. An ironic blend of incredible generosity and unbelievable thoughtlessness.

I stared at the woman I'd called my mother for forty-five years. She'd always been a stranger to me. Now that I knew she actually *was*, I'd never felt so close to her.

How ironic can life get? The woman I thought had ruined my life had actually saved it. Literally.

Tom interrupted my thoughts. "Sorry to say it ladies, but we've got to go. Val, the clock's ticking."

I hugged the woman who had raised me, and thought about the one who, long ago, had been forced to let me go. Whether Glad left me behind, Bobby had tossed me out a car window, or Tony's father had paid Jacob to snatch me away and leave me for dead, none of it mattered any longer. I suddenly felt whole and happy and loved.

And that was all the answer I'd ever been looking for.

IT WAS ALMOST 5 P.M. when we drove away. Mom didn't see us off at the door. It was time for *The Price is Right*. Dale drove up in the golf cart as we were leaving. I got out and gave him a hug and promised to see him again soon.

"We love you, Val," he said as I climbed back into Tom's 4Runner.

"I love you, too, Dale."

Tom hit the gas, raising a cloud of orange dust on the clay road. Once we were on I-10, I realized I was absolutely famished.

"Have we got time for a Chattaburger?" I asked.

"Does it come with fries?" Tom teased and shot me a lurid look.

I blushed. Tom noticed and switched gears. "Big day for you. How you holding up?"

"Okay, actually. I feel pretty good. I don't know how to describe it. I feel lighter, I guess."

"Too bad you gave back the other piece of the dragonfly pin. It would have been nice to see if it fit. It would have been the final *piece du résistance*."

"Yeah. I uh...."

"You *kept* it. I knew it!" Tom grinned. "You are a *thief*, Val Fremden!"

"I am *not!*" I shot back.

"Then why did you keep it?"

"Let's just say I had a gut feeling it belonged to me."

"Huh. You are a funny girl."

I fished around in my purse and found the little silver oval encrusted with green stones. I touched it to the broken part of the dragonfly pendant. It fit perfectly. My last doubts evaporated.

"I guess it's official. I really *am* Glad's daughter."

Tom turned and gave me a loving smile.

"So then, Glad's daughter. Do you really want to celebrate the news with a Chattaburger? The exit's coming up."

"Sure."

Tom hooked a right on the Chattahoochee exit and in a couple of minutes we were at a picnic table, munching on Chattaburgers and fries. Maybe I was also savoring a different kind of satisfaction, but the burgers really *were* world-famously delicious.

"I'm curious," said Tom, after washing down a mouthful of burger with a swig of root beer. "Your name is Valiant. Your dad's was Justice. Those are some pretty heavy-duty names for simple country folk."

"Simple country folk? Really?" I laughed. "You already know how I got *my* name. My dad's name wasn't Justice as in J-U-S-T-I-C-E. It was Justas. J-U-S-T-A-S. As in, 'Just as Jolly.' He told me once that his family wanted him to be just as jolly as he could be. It was a play on words with his last name. Get it?"

"Yeah. So your weird sense of humor runs in the family."

"I guess. Wait a minute. They're not my real family. Are you trying to be ironic, Mr. Foreman?"

"Maybe." Tom affecting his bad Southern accent again. "I heard you do *love* you some irony, Miss Val."

I shook my head.

"I *do* love irony. But apparently, irony doesn't love me back. Why else would I be so unlucky at love? It's either irony, or I just know too much about human nature."

Tom leaned across the picnic table until his face was just inches from my own. He touched the side of my face tenderly.

"Maybe you just don't know *enough*."

He kissed me hard on the mouth, and I nearly fainted all over again.

I WAS AT THE BEACH in front of Caddy's. I spied an old woman on a pink lounger. I walked over and sat next to her. She smiled at me with crooked red lips and poked me on the shoulder. She didn't say a word. She just kept poking me gently on the shoulder. Finally, she whispered something in my ear.

"Hey. You awake?"

The voice was too deep to be Glad's. My lids flew open and I stared into a pair of sea-green eyes.

Tom!

It all came flooding back. We hadn't made it to St. Petersburg last night. Instead, we'd stopped and shared a room, and more, at the Sandman Inn. I won't go into details, but I will say this: I've definitely changed my mind about the cops in Quincy.

"Redneck foreplay," I croaked in a voice still raspy from sleep. "Do you remember every joke someone tells you, too?"

"Afraid so. Part of cop training."

Tom's blond hair was still damp from the shower. He knelt beside the bed wearing nothing but a towel and a sexy, crooked smile. He kissed me lightly on the forehead, then crawled under the covers and wrapped me in his strong arms. He brushed my hair back from my face and gave me another one of his fabulous, knee-melting kisses.

"You're beautiful when you're all messed up in the morning," he teased.

"Just in the morning?"

"Oh, that's right. You're messed up all the time."

"That's not what I meant!" I bit him on the ear.

He laughed and kissed me again, making my toes curl.

"I hate to say it, Val, but we've got to be on our way. Ticking clock and all that. Are you ready to roll?"

"Yes."

I was ready to roll. And I was ready to be on my way.

Epilogue

I could hardly believe it. In less than a month I went from hapless hobo to happy heiress. I wish you could've seen the look on Bulldog Thelma's face when she found out Glad's daughter turned out to be *me!* I honestly thought she might poop a puppy! And as much as I love irony, I think it must actually love me more. If Bulldog Woman hadn't punched me in the nose, none of this would have happened, and she'd have gotten away with Tony's fortune.

And yes, it turns out that it *was* a fortune. Tony's hovel of a house was in a truly sorry state. But while Tom and I and the stooges were cleaning out the mountains of garbage, we came across a trash bag full of uncashed pension checks and stock certificates worth nearly half a million dollars! Garbage wasn't the only thing my real father hoarded. And now his trash had become my treasure—yet another irony that made me smile.

For helping me, I gave Jorge, Goober and Winky each a $5,000 finder's fee. I didn't tell them it was for helping me find myself.

My *Double Booty* synopsis didn't win me a contract. But the book is still a work in progress. So are Tom and I. With his help, I'm learning more and more every day that it's not the destination, but the laughs along the journey that count.

Life feels good.

I thought about calling Tamella and a few of my other fair-weather friends to let them know of my good fortune. Then I realized I really didn't give a crap anymore what they thought.

Sweet!

I'm holding onto my amateur detective hat, too. Right now I'm helping Tom gather information in hopes of one day solving his old cold case, The Buckaroo Bandit. Jacob Timms better watch his back. It turns out that Tom is a pretty persistent guy when he finds something that really interests him.

As for Glad, I guess I'll never know the true story of my real mother, or how we came to be separated. But I have my own precious memories of her. I cherish those six beautiful weeks on Sunset Beach when she taught me how to smile at life again. I got to know her right before her own sunset, and for that I will always be grateful.

Part of me likes to believe Glad knew somehow, deep inside, that I was her daughter. But either way, she was a true blessing to many of us. It's weird, but thinking back on it now, I found my real mother on Mother's Day. I guess my life really *was* built on irony!

By the way, I got Glad's dragonfly pendant repaired. It never leaves the silver chain around my neck. I still spend a lot of time on Sunset Beach, too. I like watching the tourists and snowbirds from my mom's pink lounger. Every once in a while, someone comes up to say hello, then realizes it's me.

"Oh. I thought you were Glad," they invariably say.

I always tell them the same thing.

"Thank you. I am."

DEAR READER,

Thanks so much for giving Glad One a try. I hope you enjoyed the story. I wrote it because I wanted to explore the idea of a middle-aged woman who returns to the US to find her entire life erased.

With no family for support, where could she turn? Like anybody who's been around awhile, we know life can be painful. But as I've learned along my own twisting journey, humor can soothe a lot of wounds.

But humor is subjective. That's why my stories draw laughs using a wide net—from Pat Conroy's twisted, dark family humor to Bridget Jones's slap-stick situational gaffs. Things don't always turn out like Val planned. But hey, that's life—when it's *truly* lived.

Val's journey doesn't end here. In fact, it's just beginning! Check out her next adventure, Two Crazy. If you thought Val's life was crazy, you haven't seen anything yet! Just for fun, I included a snippet of the story in the back of this book. Enjoy!

More Val Fremden Midlife Mysteries

by Margaret Lashley

Absolute Zero
Glad One
Two Crazy
Three Dumb
What Four
Five Oh
Six Tricks
Seven Daze
Figure Eight
Cloud Nine

"Life is a comic mystery. Might as well get busy turning some pages."

Val Fremden

KEEP THE LAUGHS COMING—JOIN my Newsletter!

If you'd like to know about special book offers, crazy happening in my life, giveaways, and when my future novels come out, please subscribe to my newsletter. I promise not to sell your name, or to send too many notices to your inbox. As a special welcome gift, I'll send you a link to download a **free copy of Absolute Zero**, the prequel novel that tells the story of how Val went from top-shelf business woman to bottom-rung social outcast. (Or, if you prefer, you can buy it on Amazon for $3.99.) To join my newsletter, just click the link below. I look forward to having you on board!

Newsletter Link: https://dl.bookfunnel.com/nt7dwuwlpg

Thanks again for reading Glad One. It's true, isn't it? Crazy really *is* a relative term. ;)

All my best,

Margaret Lashley

P.S. If you'd like to check out the next book in the series, Two Crazy, I've included a sample for you in the back of this book. Or click here and read the "Look Inside:"

https://www.amazon.com/dp/B071KYVB8X

P.S.S. I love reviews! The link to leave yours is on the next page.

P.S.S.S. (Sounds like I sprung a leak, lol!) If you'd like to contact me, you can reach me here:

Website: https://www.margaretlashley.com

Email: contact@margaretlashley.com

Facebook: https://www.facebook.com/valandpalspage/

What's Next for Val?

I hope you enjoyed *Glad One: Crazy is a Relative Term.* *Click the link below now and leave a review. I read every single one!*
https://www.amazon.com/dp/B06XTKBMWT#customerReviews
Thank you so much! You rock!
Don't miss another new release! Follow me on Amazon and BookBub and you'll be notified of every new crazy Val adventure.
Follow me on Amazon:
https://www.amazon.com/-/e/B06XKJ3YD8
Follow me on BookBub:
https://www.bookbub.com/search/authors?search=Margaret%20Lashley
Ready for more Val?
Enjoy the following excerpt from the next Val Fremden Mystery:
Two Crazy!

A Sneak Peek inside Two Crazy—Val's Next Adventure!

<u>Chapter One:</u>

The tread-worn, whitewall tires squealed on the hot asphalt. I shifted into park and climbed out of Shabby Maggie, my 1963 Ford Falcon Sprint convertible. Like me, Maggie was creamy-white and a bit girlie on the outside, but underneath her hood beat a V8 engine that could kick butt with the big boys. I'd been cruising along Gulf Boulevard, a block from the beach, when a thought latched on-to me like a starving mosquito. I pulled a one-eighty in the middle of the road and made a beeline for the drugstore at the corner of 107th in St. Pete Beach.

It was my birthday, and I was going to celebrate it in style with a king-sized Mounds candy bar. I knew for a lot of folks, that wouldn't have sounded like much of a present. But for me it was. I *never* kept chocolate at my place. It was the only thing I couldn't be trusted with.

I high-tailed it inside the store and grabbed a candy bar from a rack by the register. A minute later, I strolled outside with both chunks of delicious, gooey heaven crammed into my mouth like Lu-cille Ball at that chocolate factory. Distracted by the commingling of chewy coconut and rich, dark chocolate, I didn't notice someone was in Maggie's passenger seat until my butt was already wedged halfway in on the driver's side. When I caught site of her, just inches from me, I totally freaked.

I jerked back and let out a high-pitched scream that could only be heard by dogs and dolphins. Before my brain could put two-and-two together, I swung my purse at her and busted her square in the face. As my pocketbook hit pay-dirt, I had what I called an *idioment;* an idiotic moment of doomed recognition—like seeing the car keys hanging in the ignition just as you slam the locked door shut. There was no turning back. I'd have to live with the consequences. I sucked in a surprised breath and nearly choked to death on chewed-up coconut.

"Aaarrrgh! Oh crap!"

I cringed. My eyes doubled as she flew backwards off the seat and tumbled onto the floorboard. Dressed as she was, no one in the whole world would've recognized her except for me. It was Glad—still wearing that plastic Mr. Peanut piggybank she'd been shaking around in the very last time I'd seen her, less than an hour before her botched burial at sea last year. That day, someone had taken Glad from my car in this very same parking lot. Today, they'd returned her. And on my birthday, no less. I wasn't sure if that qualified as ironic or not, but the timing was definitely weird.

Whoever Glad's kidnapper had been, he'd left a hand-written note on the seat. I picked it up. The torn scrap of yellow paper read, "*Sorry. Mr. P.*" I glanced around the parking lot. None of the tourists milling around the place looked like perverts or body snatchers. (Well, maybe one.) I picked Glad up, hugged her to my chest, and set her back on the passenger seat beside me. I turned the ignition and smiled. It might sound crazy, but over the rumbling of Maggie's twin glass-pack muffler, I'd swear I heard Glad say:

"Screw you, kiddo."

I turned and gave her a wink.

"Nice to see you again, too, Mom."

Keep on reading. Get your copy of Two Crazy with the link below:
https://www.amazon.com/dp/B071KYVB8X

About the Author

Like the characters in my novels, I haven't lead a life of wealth or luxury. In fact, as it stands now, I'm set to inherit a half-eaten jar of Cheez Whiz...if my siblings don't beat me to it.

During my illustrious career, I've been a roller-skating waitress, an actuarial assistant, an advertising copywriter, a real estate agent, a house flipper, an organic farmer, and a traveling vagabond/truth seeker. But no matter where I've gone or what I've done, I've always felt like a weirdo.

I've learned a heck of a lot in my life. But getting to know myself has been my greatest journey. Today, I know I'm smart. I'm direct. I'm jaded. I'm hopeful. I'm funny. I'm fierce. I'm a pushover. And I have a laugh that makes strangers come up and want to join in the fun. In other words, I'm a jumble of opposing talents and flaws and emotions. And it's all good.

In some ways, I'm a lot like Val Fremden. My books featuring Val are not autobiographical, but what comes out of her mouth was first formed in my mind, and sometimes the parallels are undeniable. I drink TNTs. I had a car like Shabby Maggie. And I've started my life over four times, driving away with whatever earthly possessions fit in my car. And, perhaps most importantly, I've learned that friends come from unexpected places.

Made in the USA
Monee, IL
12 December 2023

48872093R10178